ALSO BY
KAREN E. QUINONES MILLER

I'm Telling
Satin Doll

USING
WHAT
YOU
GOT

A NOVEL

KAREN E.
QUINONES MILLER

SIMON & SCHUSTER
New York London Toronto Sydney Singapore

SIMON & SCHUSTER
Rockefeller Center
1230 Avenue of the Americas
New York, NY 10020

This book is a work of fiction. Names, characters,
places, and incidents either are products of the
author's imagination or are used fictitiously. Any
resemblance to actual events or locales or persons,
living or dead, is entirely coincidental.

Manufactured in the United States of America

ISBN 0-7432-4614-4

ACKNOWLEDGMENTS

I want to start by thanking my brother, Joseph T. Quinones, who has always been in my corner. I don't know what my life would be without you.

I would also like to thank my agent, Liza Dawson, who has taken countless telephone calls from me during the writing of this book, and never once acted as if I were bugging her. <smile>

The same goes for Denise Roy, my editor at Simon & Schuster. You are a wonderfully patient, understanding, and loving human being.

I also want to thank Hilary Beard, Jenice Armstrong, Kamal Rav, Sheila Simmons, and Leslie Esdaile—the members of The Evening Star Writing Group in Philadelphia. I'm so proud to be a member—you guys are simply the best. And a special shout-out to Evening Star member Daranice Miguel, who read everything almost as soon as I typed it.

A big thank you to Martina "Tee C." Royal, Gayle Jackson Sloan, Dorothy Pettis, Cheryl Ferguson, and Adeea R. Rogers, who were all kind enough to give me critiques on my opening chapters to make sure I was headed in the right direction.

Thanks to my daughter's friends at Central High School, Hillary and Sharae, for also reading through the manuscript and making sure I was staying on point.

There are so many people who have supported me, and I'm sure I'm going to blank out on a couple of names, but let me at least mention Gloria Truss, Bahiya Cabral, Fiona Maughn, Al Hunter, Jr., Sandy Bullock, Fran Taylor, Vonda Paige, Tee C., Hannah and Hassan Sabree, Butch Cottman, Sherlane Freeman, Daaimah S. Poole, Yasmin Coleman, Helen Blue, Bobbi Booker, Belinda Cunningham, Estelle Cunningham, Aunt Bernice, Deanna Corbett, Harold King, Makeela Thomas, Cheryl Wadlington, Adrian Thomas, Renee Thomas, Lorraine Ballard-Morrill, Tremain Smith. I want to thank you all for believing in me.

I have to give a huge shout-out to the young princesses of the family, Charnell, Camille, Davina, Takia, Toni, Taiece, Manimah, Chloe—all of you are so very precious to me. And another huge shout-out to my wonderful nephew Zegory "Tunde" Grimes.

A special mention to my dear, dear, twin—Kitty. I love you!

And a remembrance to those who transitioned over the past year—Eddie James, Renard Simmons, and Alfred Davis.

Big thanks to the book clubs that have supported me and other African American authors. United Sisters, Sisters Uptown Book Club, Circle of Sisters, RAWSISTAZ Journey's End, Eye of Ra, Diva's Den, No More Drama, 4 The Love of Books, Escape Book Club, African Jewels, Sistahs On The Reading Edge, Pure Essence, Shades of Color, Sistah Time Book Club, Black Novel Book Club, EDM Book Club, Circle of Friends Book Club, Sistas Are Reading Book Club, APOOO, Me and My Sister Book Club, Just Sisters, Beta Ka Awqoute Book Club, Black American Princesses, Darjeeling's Book Club, VA Luncheon Book Club, Page Turners Book Club, Spirited Sisters African American Book Club, Between The Lines

Book Club, Women of Color Book Club, Sistahs Book Club—you are all so wonderful, and so appreciated by me.

I have to thank the book store owners who have been so sweet, encouraging, and supportive. Betty Liguorious of Liguorius Book Store, Lecia Warner of Basic Black Books, Larry Robin of Robin's Book Store, Andre and Kim Kelton of Our Story, Sherry McGee of Apple Book Center, Emma Rodgers of Black Images Bazaar, Stacy Foster of Kujichagulia, Janifa Wilson of Sisters Uptown, Lloyd Hart of The Black Library, Trust Graham of Nubian Heritage, Larry Cunningham of Culture Plus, Frances Utsey of Cultural Connections, Malita McPherson of Heritage Books, Adline Clark of Black Classics Books and Gifts, Haneef and Haneefa of Haneef's Book Store, Felicia Winton of Books For Thought, Nia Damali of Medu Bookstore, Michele Lewis of the Afro-American Book Stop, Brother Simba of Karibu, Robin Green-Carey of Simbanye Book Store, and Scott Wyth of Reprint Books.

I've met so many other authors who have been very supportive and loving; I'm glad to call you colleagues and friends. Especially Gloria Mallette, Mary Morrison, Eric Pete, Kieja Shapodee, Daaimah, Nancy Flowers, Darlene Johnson, Marlene Taylor, Brenda Thomas, ReShonda Tate Billingsley, Edwardo Jackson, Timmothy McCann, A'Lelia Bundles, Trevy McDonald, Tracy Price-Thompson, Kimberly Lawson-Roby, and Zane. Thanks guys!

And last, but certainly not least, I want to thank my daughter, Camille, who badgered me every day for a new chapter of *Using What You Got*, and took the time to critique it for me. Actually my editors at Simon & Schuster should probably thank her, too, because without her harassment, I may have never finished. <smile> I'm so fortunate to have such a wonderful and dedicated child.

USING
WHAT
YOU
GOT

PROLOGUE

He looked around, furtively, as they approached the checkout at Daitch Shopwell. He had begged his fifteen-year-old sister to go to the supermarket on 135th Street and Fifth Avenue, but she complained about dragging their old rickety shopping cart on and off the bus. Not that she had to do any heavy lifting; that was his job. She picked out the food, and he hauled it home. It was the least they could do to help out while their mother slaved at a bracelet factory downtown. And besides, Charlene had added, she didn't have bus fare to go all the way to 135th Street, and she knew he didn't. Charlene usually liked to take long walks. She loved the attention she got from the boys hanging out in the streets, and with her long legs, tiny but perfect shape, green eyes, and long auburn curls, she got a lot of attention. But on this hot summer day it was easier to go to their usual market on 116th Street and Seventh Avenue, only two blocks from the apartment they shared with their mother in the Foster Projects.

A teenage girl got on the checkout line next to theirs, and he tried to take a good look at her out of the corner of his eye. No, she wasn't in his eighth grade class. In fact, he didn't think he'd ever seen her at Wadleigh Junior High School. Good, he didn't know her. But she was kinda cute. A white halter top and green hot pants. Her two 'fro puffs were kinda lopsided, though, making her look a little like a black Pippi Longstocking. Naw, she was way too pretty to compare to Pippi

Longstocking, he decided, as he took a sidelong glance at her long cinnamon-colored legs. He resisted the urge to take the Afro pick out of his back pocket to give his curly 'fro a quick work-over to make sure it was perfectly rounded. No, he didn't want to seem vain, just in case the girl was peeping over at him through her peripheral vision. Still, he was glad that he was wearing his new bell-bottom jeans and bur-gundy muscle tee-shirt, just in case she was scoping him out, too. Just as long as she wasn't watching when they paid for the groceries.

"Reggie, you'd better not be standing there looking stupid. Help me put this food on the belt!"

He grimaced, but started unloading the overflowing cart, while bobbing to the lyrics of The Jackson Five's "ABC," which he sang in his head, in an effort to appear outwardly cool.

"Wait a minute. You've got to separate the stuff, Reggie. Put the soap powder and deodorant and stuff on last, 'cause we can't pay for those with food stamps. Act like you got good sense."

"Why you gotta talk so loud, Charlene? You need the whole store to hear you talking that jive?" Reggie grumbled, his head bowed low into the cart as he continued to unload the groceries.

"Oh, boy, please." Charlene rolled her eyes as she dipped her hand into her windbreaker pocket and pulled out an unsealed white enve-lope.

"Cash or food stamps?" the cashier asked before blowing a large pink bubble of gum. Reggie's cheeks slowly crimsoned, and he buried his head lower into the cart.

"You see we're separating the groceries, so what does that tell you?" Charlene snapped.

The girl blew another bubble in response, and started ringing up the food.

"Sixty-eight dollars and forty-eight cents," the cashier pronounced finally. Charlene pulled out three books of food stamps from the enve-lope, and handed them to the girl.

"We ain't allowed to take them outta the book. You gotta do it."
The girl blew and popped another bubble.

Charlene sucked her teeth and started yanking stamps from the
books.

"Will you hurry up?" Reggie whispered. He didn't even want to
glance in the cute girl's direction to see if she could hear what was going on. Charlene ignored him, handing the cashier a bunch of multi-
colored paper currency.

"You're supposed to count them out to me." The cashier rolled her
eyes.

Charlene's lips turned up in a sneer. "You mean your lazy ass can't
even— "

"Look, I'll count them out. Go on outside the store and wait for
me," Reggie snatched the food stamps from his sister, and started quietly counting the stamps into the cashier's hand. Everyone on the line
was looking at them, he was sure. Maybe even everyone in the whole
store. And he just knew the lopsided Afro-puff girl in the other line
was probably laughing her cute little butt off.

"Hey." The cashier smacked her gum and cocked her head as she
took a good look at Reggie. "With this air conditioner blowing, why
you sweating like that?"

"No reason." Reggie wiped the beads of perspiration that had be-
gun to trickle down from his hairline.

"You okay?" she asked.

"I'm fine. Here you go. Sixty-nine dollars." Reggie placed the last
stamp in the girl's hand. She glanced down at the stamps, then closed
her fingers over the money. She pursed her lips and nodded to Reggie,
signaling she understood his embarrassment.

"Fifty-two cents change." She gave his hand a sympathetic squeeze
as she gave him the two quarters and two pennies.

Reggie mumbled a quick thanks, then busied himself packing the
groceries in brown paper bags and placing them in his shopping cart.

He approached the automatic door so fast it didn't have time to fully open, and he gave it a violent push, then stormed out.

It was bad enough when he and Charlene had to take the shopping cart and go to the food distribution center to pick up the welfare food—the large cans of peanut butter and potted meat, the huge blocks of cheese and butter, and the big brown bags of flour and cornmeal—but this was a lot worse. Pulling out food stamps in the middle of a supermarket and letting everyone know they were on public assistance. This was all his father's fault. No doubt about it. The old bastard had left his mother to raise him and Charlene four years before, and they'd barely heard a word from his since. And the unbelievable thing was that he'd left his mom—whom everyone agreed was the prettiest woman in the projects—for an ugly old bat with rotting teeth and a big old wart on the left side of her nose. Reggie would never do anything like that to his family. He was going to get married one time, to one woman, and he would never leave her. And he would never ever abandon his children, and make them have to get welfare food and go to the supermarket and pay for groceries with food stamps so they could be teased by the other kids. His mother had told him that "Reginald" meant "king," and he was going to treat his family like royalty. Not like trash the way his father treated them.

"Damn it, Reggie. You ain't heard me yelling to you?"

The light punch on his shoulder snapped him out of his daze. "Huh? Oh shoot, Charlene. I forgot all about you."

"You was walking so fast I had to run to keep up," Charlene gave a few dramatic gasps to illustrate her words. "What's got into you, anyway?"

"Nothing." He began walking again.

"Well, I didn't give you the money to pay for our other stuff. Our soap powder and things."

Reggie stopped and smacked his forehead. "Oh man, I completely forgot."

"Well, we gotta go back, then." Charlene started tugging on his arm, but he pulled free.

"No way. I ain't going back there right now," he said gruffly. "It's too hot to be going back all the way over there now. I'll go back later."

"Ooh, Reggie. You ain't fooling no one at all. You don't want to go back there because you think that old slutty looking girl in the hot pants saw you paying with food stamps." Charlene sucked her teeth. "Looky here, that girl weren't even thinking about you, boy. And if she don't want you just because your momma got you using food stamps at the store, she's too stupid for you anyway. You're too good for someone like that."

"Naw, sis. Ain't nothing wrong with that girl, and I wasn't thinking about her no way."

"Oh, good, 'cause she sure wasn't thinking about you!"

Reggie bit his lips to stop tears from forming in his eyes. A girl who looked that good is supposed to want a guy with a little something going for himself, he thought. There'd be something wrong with her if she wanted some guy on welfare. I wouldn't even respect her.

I

D addy, tell Tiara to get out the bathroom! I gotta pee!"

"Oh, shut up, Jo-Jo! You always gotta pee! You're such a little pain in the ass." Tiara carefully twirled the black eyebrow pencil just below the corner of her lips, making sure her new beauty mark was perfectly placed. Deciding it was barely noticeable against her smooth chocolate complexion, she gave it another twirl, pressing harder. She used the same pencil to outline her startling hazel eyes, then started moving her shoulders to the new Usher song. *I look damn good,* she thought. *Better than them light, bright, and damn near white video ho's they're always having up BET. If they ever shoot a video over here at the Foster Projects, I know they'd spot me in the crowd and make me a star. 'Cause I got it like that.* She snapped her finger at her image in the mirror, then ran her fingers through her long ebony weave, striking a couple of quick poses. How did the old song go? Five-five with brown eyes—smile like the sunshine. *Yeah, that's me. I'm the shit.*

"Tiara!"

"Jo-Jo, shut the hell up, and wait until I get out," Tiara snapped.

"Daddy, Tiara's cursing in the house again!"

Ignoring her little sister, Tiara picked up the tweezers to pluck an errant hair on one of her otherwise perfectly arched eyebrows. She grimaced as the tweezers pinched her skin.

"Quit the noise, you big baby. You're making me mess my face up!" she shouted as she leaned over the sink to get closer to the mirror.

"Daddy, Tiara's calling me a baby again. Tell her to stop!" Jo-Jo started banging on the door again. "Let me in!"

Tiara rolled her eyes. God, she wished Daddy would hurry and buy a brownstone like he'd been talking about for years so she could have her own bathroom and her own room instead of having to share her space with Jo-Jo. Here she was, almost nineteen, and she had to put up with a twelve-year-old brat. Maybe she could even have her own floor in the new brownstone, maybe the basement level, so she could have her own entrance and everything. She'd miss all her friends here at the Foster, but after all, they could visit. And maybe she could talk her father into buying her a car for her next birthday, so she could cruise down to the projects whenever she got the urge. Yeah, she'd be real fly, cruising down Malcolm X Boulevard with the top down on her red convertible. *A two-seater so a buncha people won't be trying to push up on my ride and shit.*

"Daddy!" Jo-Jo hollered at the top of her lungs, while still banging and kicking at the door. "Daddy, make her let me in!"

Damn that girl, Tiara thought. Tiara snatched open the door, causing Jo-Jo to tumble in and onto the bathroom floor, and the heavy scent of Victoria's Secret Pear Glace Body Splash to rush out into the hall. "Okay, satisfied now? You're in. Now shut up."

"Creep." Josephine scowled at her sister then sat down on the edge of the bathtub. "That's why I can't stand you. Why do you have to put your makeup on in the bathroom, anyway?"

"'Cause the light's better in here, stupid." Tiara started stuffing makeup into her already bulging cosmetic bag. She took another quick look in the mirror, turning her head from side to side to make sure she looked good from all angles. Then she grabbed her CD player and headed down the hall to her bedroom. Just as she figured, Jo-Jo was right on her heels. The girl was taller than her by almost four inches, but she still wanted to follow Tiara like a puppy. A noisy—and nosey—puppy at that.

"I thought you had to pee." Tiara sat down in front of the gold-trimmed ivory-colored vanity and started brushing her European Straight weave with a wooden hairbrush.

"You made me wait so long I don't have to go anymore."

"Jo-Jo, why don't you admit you wanted to get in because you wanted to watch me make myself up?" Tiara teased. She reached over and straightened the snapshot of herself that she had stuck in the upper right-hand corner of the vanity mirror. She glanced at the collage of pictures of herself she had pasted on the wall, and made a mental note to add the snapshot. She also had to hang her new poster of Michelle from Destiny's Child to go along with the ones she already had posted of Aliyah, Ashanti, and Jay-Z. Another, slightly tattered wallet-sized photograph of a smiling, petite dark-skinned woman with dark hair flowing onto her shoulders fell from the mirror onto the dresser. Tiara looked at it with near disinterest. She might as well throw the picture out. It wasn't like she was ever going to see her mother again after all this time, anyway.

"Don't nobody wanna look at you." Jo-Jo plopped down on a twin bed covered with a blue quilted bedspread printed with images of basketball stars. Above her, on the wall, were posters of Mark Jackson, Michael Jordan, Shaquille O'Neal, and Allen Iverson, along with pennant flags from the New York Knicks and the New Jersey Nets. She balled up a piece of paper lying on the pillow, and made a perfect shot into the tin wastepaper basket five feet away. She clasped her hands over her head and jiggled her shoulders. "She shoots. She scores. And the crowd goes wild!"

"Whatever." Tiara rolled her eyes. "Just don't be shooting your air balls on my side of the room. You still owe me for the perfume you knocked over last week."

"You shoulda had the top on tight." Jo-Jo plopped down on her stomach and started flipping through the pages of a *Sports Illustrated*.

"Yeah, uh huh. That's why you owe me twenty bucks for the perfume."

"Oh yeah, and you really think you're going to get it, huh? And it's not like you bought it outta your money anyway. Just get Daddy to give you the twenty bucks like you always do. You going out with Keith tonight?"

"Nope." Tiara walked over to the full-length mirror that hung on the back of the closet door and did a slow twirl, checking over her shoulder to make sure her butt looked nice and full in her size two Pepe jeans. Her black see-through shirt was unbuttoned down to her midriff, so that the purple camisole she wore underneath was framed almost in the shape of a valentine.

"Michael?"

"That doofus? Puleeze."

"Why's he a doofus? I think he's cute."

"He's broke."

"Hmmph." Jo-Jo propped herself up on one elbow and looked at Tiara curiously. "So who are you going out with then?"

"Me and Shakira are going to Club New York, downtown. They're having a private party for some new rapper." She popped in Jay-Z's CD and started dancing in front of the mirror, making sure she could execute the Harlem Shake in her black stiletto heels. Yeah, she was on. "Ain't you gonna go to Shakira's little sister's party at the rec center tonight? I thought it was supposed to start at six. Ain't you late?"

"I ain't wanna go to Asia's dumb old party," Jo-Jo said sullenly.

Tiara stopped dancing and turned to look with disbelief at Jo-Jo, who was rapidly flipping through the magazine pages. "I know that little nut invited you, right? Y'all in the same class and everything, and me letting her old stuck-up sister hang out with me and shit, I just know she invited you."

"Yeah, I got invited. I just don't wanna go. The Knicks are playing tonight." Jo-Jo pushed aside the *Sports Illustrated* and eyed her older sister. "You look nice. But how you gonna get in? I thought they took your fake ID last week when you tried to get in that club in Brooklyn."

"I got another one, if you gotta know, Miss Nosey." Tiara moved back in front of the mirror. "You need to stop worrying about me and start taking your little butt outta this house sometime instead of always being holed up in front of the television watching some stupid basketball game."

Both girls turned as they heard two short taps on the door. "Are you two dressed?"

"Yeah. Come in, Daddy." Tiara straightened the spaghetti straps of her camisole under her blouse.

At six-foot-six, Reggie Bynum had to bow his head slightly to clear the doorway. He rubbed his neatly trimmed salt-and-pepper beard. "Mmm, you're looking good, Princess. I can see you're planning on breaking some hearts tonight. Where are you heading all dolled up?" Not waiting for an answer, he strode over to Jo-Jo's bed and lightly swatted her on the head with the rolled-up newspaper he held in his hand. "Why you always gotta make such a racket, girl? People probably heard you all the way down the street, talking about you gotta go pee."

Jo-Jo scooted away from her father and folded her hands over her chest with a pout. "See that?" she said. "You heard me and you ain't even tell her to get out or anything? Man, you let Tiara do anything she wants."

"Oh, you going to go say she's my favorite again, huh, Little Girl?" He reached over and ruffled her shoulder-length braids, being careful not to get his thick gold-link bracelet caught in her hair.

"You know she is. She's a spoiled brat." Jo-Jo poked her lips out further.

"Oh, shut up," Tiara snapped.

"You shut up," Jo-Jo retorted.

Reggie grinned. "Oh, I guess since she's my favorite I'm going to ask *her* if she wants to go to the game tonight."

"What game?" Jo-Jo quickly sat up on the bed. "You got tickets to the Knicks game?"

"On the floor, Sport. We'll be so close you'll be able to smell their funky underarms." Reggie smiled. "Or we would be if I were taking you to the game."

"Ooh, Daddy, you're the best father in the world!" Jo-Jo grabbed him around the neck and kissed him loudly on the cheek.

"So, now, who do you think is my favorite?" Reggie said teasingly.

"Me!" Jo-Jo jumped up from the bed, ran over to the brown bureau on her side of the room, and started pulling out sweatshirts, athletic socks, and boxer shorts, and throwing them on the floor. "I've gotta find my Mark Jackson jersey."

"Hey, hey, Sport, you're making a mess!" Reggie said, kicking at the growing pile of clothes forming near the bed.

"Daddy, she's always making a mess. That's why I can't stand sharing a room with her." Tiara sat down on the bed next to her father and leaned her head on his shoulder, breathing in the subtle masculine scent of his Aramis aftershave. Reggie Bynum's job as a trash collector meant he was around garbage all day, but he was so meticulous in his hygiene—showering three times a day—you'd think he was a manager in the front office. There was a time when Tiara was ashamed to tell people that her father worked for the New York City Department of Sanitation, and she still didn't broadcast it, but she certainly wasn't too embarrassed. At least her daddy had a job, which was a lot more than many of her friends could say. *Shoot,* she used to comfort herself, *Most of my friends barely even see their fathers, and then they gotta take a number 'cause of all the other kids he got all around the city.* She and Jo-Jo were Reggie Bynum's only children, and he showered them with love and affection. A lot of other fathers would have tried to stick them on one of their grandmothers after their mother abandoned the family right after Jo-Jo was born. But not Reggie. He became superdad and supermom, even learning how to braid and cornrow to make sure his daughters looked good every time they stepped out of the house. Of course they looked even better when Tiara was old enough to take over hair duty, but Reggie had certainly done his best. He used to get old loudmouthed Aunt Charlie to come over and watch them while he worked, but as soon as Tiara was old enough, she put a stop to that too. All that scar-faced witch wanted to do was make everybody as miserable as she was. She acted like she wanted to punish the world because the left side of her face was all messed up from some car accident when she was a teenager. She had her good points—number one that she could cook her butt off—but it wasn't worth having to hear her mouth, day in and day out, about how Reggie spoiled the girls.

Tiara nuzzled her head further into Reggie's shoulder. And he was so handsome, too. With his dark-brown curly hair, light skin, and hazel eyes he had all the women vying for his attention. He had his little flings from time to time, but he never brought any of these dalliances home.

"Get off my bed, Tiara, since you don't want to share a room with me." Jo-Jo sucked her teeth as she continued to rummage through the bureau drawers.

"Why can't you two get along?" Reggie shook his head in exasperation.

"Because she's so immature, Daddy. That's why I need my own room. She's driving me crazy," Tiara said plaintively.

"I know you do, Princess. Soon as we move you both can have your own rooms." Reggie kissed Tiara on the top of her head. "Now where are you going looking all fine and stuff, and on a Wednesday, at that?"

"You think I look nice, Daddy? Me and Shakira got tickets to

Showtime at the Apollo, so you know I gotta look nice, 'cause you know they gonna put the camera on me." Tiara jumped up and twirled around in front of her father, who whistled appreciatively. "Can't you just see me profiling up on TV? That's why I had to look real sharp. I just got these jeans today."

"Oh yeah?" Jo-Jo turned to face her. "So how much did they cost?"

Tiara turned around to threaten her sister, but remembered their father was in the room, so instead she went back and sat on the bed next to him. "Daddy, you see how she's always butting in my business?"

"Oh, please, you ain't fooling nobody. You just don't want Daddy to know your jeans cost a hundred dollars." Jo-Jo rolled her eyes.

"So what if they did?" Tiara snapped at her. "It ain't your hundred dollars, now is it?"

"Jo-Jo, leave your sister alone and get ready so we can leave." Reggie pushed Tiara away from him, then planted a kiss on her forehead before rising from the bed. "Did you get your African-American history test back from your teacher yet?"

"Yeah. That old skank gave me an eighty-five, but when I went over it I saw she marked one of my essay questions wrong."

"What was the question?"

"Who was Cassius Marcellus Clay, and what was his contribution to African-American history?"

"Muhammad Ali? That's an easy question," Reggie scooted a short distance away from his daughter and looked at her suspiciously. "What did you put down?"

"That he was a rich white man from Kentucky who freed his slaves and became an abolitionist."

"What?"

"He was, Daddy," Tiara giggled. "Maybe if the teacher had asked who was Cassius Marcellus Clay, Jr., I would have said that he was the man who later changed his name to Muhammad Ali and was a three-time boxing heavyweight champion of the world, but she didn't put down junior."

"So you telling me Muhammad Ali was originally named after some white man?" Reggie chuckled as he rubbed his beard.

"No, he was named after his father. I guess his father was named after the white man," Tiara grinned. "He was one tough white man, though. One time he was giving an anti-slavery speech and some dude pulled out a gun and shot him in the chest. He jumped down from the stage, pulled out his Bowie knife, and cut off the guy's nose and one of his ears."

"Damn!" Reggie threw his head back and gave a hearty laugh.

"So, anyway, I challenged her on it, and I wound up with a ninety-five on the test." Tiara tossed her head. "So I'm pulling a solid 'A' in the class. I should make it to the president's list again this semester."

"Good for you, Princess. But don't be going around calling your teachers skanks. They gotta be pretty smart to be teaching up in college. Show some respect."

"Daddy, can I have some money to go downtown to the movies after the show is over?" Tiara said in a little girl voice. She glanced out of the corner of her eye to make sure Jo-Jo wasn't going to open her mouth about Club New York, but Jo-Jo had slipped behind the closet door to change into a sweat suit.

"Sure, Princess." Reggie reached inside his pants pocket and took out his wallet. "Will thirty dollars be enough?"

"Well," Tiara hesitated. "I guess I can make do with that."

"Oh, you can only make do on thirty dollars, huh?" Reggie laughed. "And just how much would it take for you to have a really good time?"

"Um, could I get fifty dollars?" Tiara said hopefully.

"Yeah, but don't be trying to hit me up for any more money this weekend, hear?" Reggie slipped two twenties and two five dollar bills from his wallet. "Now, remember what I've always told you. You can go out there looking like that, and all the men are going to be looking. And they should, because you're looking damn good. You can make them look, but you better not let them touch, okay?"

"Okay, Daddy," Tiara gave her automatic response to her father's habitual lecture.

"Okay, because you're too damn good for most of these knuckleheads out here," Reggie said in a more gentle tone. "I raised me a thoroughbred, baby. You don't wanna be messing with none of these broke Negroes out here. You want someone who can do something for you, right?"

"Right, Daddy." Tiara resisted the urge to glance at her watch.

"And don't forget, you're a Bynum girl, and that means these knuckleheads better act like they know when they get around you—"

"I won't forget, Daddy. I promise." Tiara kissed him on the cheek, slipping the money from his grasp. She then jumped up and ran to the closet, pulling the door open and exposing Jo-Jo just as she was pulling her sweat pants on over her basketball shorts.

"Dang, Tiara, I'm trying to get dressed!" Jo-Jo hit Tiara on the shoulder.

"Oh, please. You ain't got nothing nobody wants to see." Tiara pulled a waist-length black suede jacket off a hanger and quickly slipped it on. "Okay, I'm outta here, folks." She already had twenty dollars, but now that she had another fifty, she was going to stop and get some Alize and pick up a bag of weed so she and Shakira could be feeling nice by the time they got to the club.

"So early?" Reggie looked at his watch. "It's not even seven o'clock."

"The show starts at eight, Daddy." She kissed him on the cheek, and turned to head out the door, but her father grabbed her hand.

"How late you going to be out? I don't want you late for classes or anything."

"Daddy, my classes don't start until eleven-thirty on Tuesdays and Thursdays. You know that." Tiara turned to go.

"Well, just hold up for a minute, Hon. Jo-Jo and I are going to grab a cab down to Madison Square Garden. We'll drop you off," Reggie stood up, still holding on to her hand.

"No, that's okay, Daddy. I gotta pick up Shakira." Tiara was trying to think fast. Shakira had a big mouth, and she didn't want her to slip up and let Reggie know that they were going to try to get into Club New York. Her father was pretty lenient, but he did draw the line at letting his eighteen-year-old sneak into downtown clubs with a fake ID.

"Not a problem. I don't mind stopping for Shakira." Reggie pulled Tiara to him and put his arm around her shoulders, planting a kiss on the top of her head.

"Aw, Daddy, the Apollo's not on our way to the Garden," Jo-Jo whined. "And you know how slow Shakira is. We're going to miss tip-off if we gotta wait on her."

"Yeah, Daddy," Tiara said soothingly. "You know how Shakira is. You guys go ahead, don't let us mess up your evening waiting on that slow child."

"You sure? I really don't mind . ."

"Daddy, I mind!" Jo-Jo stamped her foot. "I want to get to the Garden early enough to get some of the good souvenirs."

"All right, all right!" Reggie grinned and shrugged his shoulders. "Just be careful out there, okay?"

"Don't worry, Daddy." Tiara kissed her father's cheek again and headed out the door, but not before mouthing "Thanks" to Jo-Jo, who simply winked back and rubbed her fingers together signaling that she expected payment for her assistance. She was going to have to slip Jo-Jo a couple of bucks for her help, but it was well worth it.

"Okay," Tiara said as she stepped out the front door. "Time to get my party on."

2

It was chilly out, a little too chilly for the light suede jacket, and Tiara briefly considered running back upstairs to change into her leather, but decided against it. Better to brave the cold than risk Reggie once again insisting that he give her ride to the Apollo.

She dug her hands as deep as she could into the shallow jacket pockets as she walked across the housing projects playground and into building number 5, where Shakira stayed with her mother, father, three sisters, and an uncle. Shakira wasn't a real friend, but she was a good hang-out partner because she was always game for whatever Tiara wanted to do. Plus, Shakira was pretty—in a sleazy kind of way—so she wasn't jealous of Tiara's looks like so many other girls in the projects. Or at least she wasn't *as* jealous.

Both of the elevators were out of order, so Tiara wound up walking up the three flights of stairs. The dueling smells of fried chicken, crab legs, and curried goat from the various apartments greeted her as she walked through the fourth floor hallway to apartment 4G and pounded on the steel door.

"Who is it?" A bloodshot eye appeared at the peephole and

looked Tiara up and down. "Who is it?" the man demanded again.

Tiara rolled her eyes. It was Shakira's uncle, Mr. Jacob. Three months ago he had moved into the three-bedroom apartment that already housed six people. He had seen her umpteen times since then, so why was he looking her up and down and yelling "who is it?" She wanted to yell back at him, "Who the fuck do you think it is, you stupid asshole?" But she didn't need the lecture she'd get when her father found out she was cursing out grown men. And in the projects, everyone finds out about everything. "It's me, Tiara," she said instead.

"Who?" Mr. Jacob demanded again.

"She done told you who it is, Uncle Jake," a young woman's voice shrilled in the apartment background. "Why don't you just let her in?"

"Shut the hell up, Shakira. You ain't got no damn respect," Mr. Jacob stepped back from the door and started unlocking the three locks. "You better act like you know I was doing you a favor in the first place. I ain't even had to answer the goddamned door."

Tiara followed him inside the living room where three men sat around a small folding table playing poker. Shakira's mother, Tiara guessed, was downstairs at her youngest daughter's birthday party at the recreation center.

"Yo, man, didn't I tell you to watch your goddamn mouth when you talking to my kids!" Shakira's father growled but didn't look up from the cards he was arranging in his hand.

"You oughtta teach your kids to show some respect," Mr. Jacob grumbled as he plopped down on a beat-up brown couch. A rusty floor lamp next to the couch shook slightly. Shakira's and Tiara's apartments were laid out the same, but that was the only thing they had in common. Shakira's apartment stunk with the smell of beer, cheap brandy, and cigarettes. Empty potato chip bags and candy bar wrappers littered the hard tile floor, and an overflowing ashtray was perched precariously on the edge of the card table. The room was a mess. Nothing unusual for Shakira's house, though. Thank God,

Aunt Charlie's a neat freak and is always coming over and cleaning up, Tiara thought. She couldn't imagine living in a pigsty like that. She complained about Jo-Jo being a little sloppy, but at least she wasn't nasty.

"Shut up, you old drunk bastard," the man answered.

"Tiara! Hold up. I'll be right out," came the shrill voice. "I'm in the bathroom."

"How you doing, Mr. Richard?" Tiara addressed the man who had admonished Jacob.

"Hmph. I'm all right. How you doing?" Mr. Richard answered. He took a cigarette he had stuck behind his left ear, tapped it on the table three times, then stuck it in his mouth, unlit.

"I'm fine," Tiara answered politely.

"Damn right, you fine," Jacob leered. "You wearing them jeans, ain't you, little mama?"

Fucking dirty old man, Tiara thought, as she pushed her hands further into her waist-length jacket. She wasn't even going to dignify his comment with a smart remark.

"Now, see, I thought I told you to shut the fuck up." Mr. Richard put his cards face down on the table and turned around to his brother-in-law.

"Aw, man. I ain't said shit. I'm just complimenting the girl," Jacob said in drunken indignation.

"Don't tell him nuttin'," Mr. Jimmy, a burly dark-skinned man with a gold tooth and a jeri curl, said. "He don't know that's Reggie Bynum's girl, do he? Shit, just let Reggie kick his stupid ass for talking to the girl like that."

The men around the table all started laughing. Tiara shifted from one foot to another, wishing Shakira would hurry up.

"I ain't a-scared of that motherfucker," Jacob half-roared from the couch. "Who the fuck is he that I gotta be scared'a him?"

"Yeah, play dumb, motherfucker, you ain't been down South that long. You know damn well you ain't planning on messing with Reggie. That man will beat you so bad your mama won't know you. Remember when we used to go watch him fight down at Gleason's Gym? I remember when he had that big bout with that Jewish kid from Jersey." Mr. Richard picked up his cards and studied his hand as he talked. "He knocked that motherfucker out in the second round. Bam! Caught him right square on the jaw and that was all she wrote. That bitch still probably ain't woke up."

"Yeah, man, I remember. I made me three large ones on that fight. I don't know why that boy ain't go pro. I coulda got rich," the third and oldest man at the table, pocked-faced with graying red hair and thick black-rimmed glasses, answered with a laugh. "This is his young'un, huh?" He gave her a respectful up and down glance. "You'se good looking, just like your mama."

"Thanks," Tiara said in a disinterested tone.

"Your daddy sure was something, though. We used to call him Sugar Reg," the man grunted and went back to studying his cards. "I'm telling you the boy shoulda turned pro."

Tiara, her arms crossed around her chest, stood off to the side of the room and silently cursed Shakira. They had planned this night for more than a week. Why couldn't she have been ready on time? Now she had to stand there, in a room that was so hot her upper lip was beginning to perspire, and listen to a bunch of drunk men talk about her father's glory days. Shit.

"Nah, there weren't no way Reggie was going to turn pro. He was too pretty. Prettier than Muhammad Ali. And he had more coochie running after him than Billy Dee Williams," Mr. Richard grunted as he threw a card down on the table. "And he was luckier than a motherfucker. That man could play the shit outta some cards. He was the fucking poker king."

"Yeah, he was on the big circuit. Motherfucker used to travel to cities all over the country gambling," Mr. Jimmy said. "He used to make so much money people thought he was dealing drugs or something." He turned and looked at Tiara. "Your daddy ain't never was no drug dealer, girl. He was just that good. Had all the girls, too."

Tiara nodded politely, then strode down the hall to the bathroom and knocked on the door. "Shakira, will you come on?"

"I'ma be right out."

Tiara decided to stand outside the door rather than go back and join the men.

"Oh yeah, I remember that pretty motherfucker now. The yaller punk with them light eyes and good hair." Tiara could hear Mr. Jacob talking in the living room. "That's the only reason why the womens was after him. 'Cause he had them light eyes and good hair."

"You just mad 'cause ain't no woman ever want your funky ass," Mr. Richard laughed.

"Fuck you man," Mr. Jacob answered. "At least I had better taste than that motherfucker. I remember with all them women he had chasing him he was pussy-whipped by that girl from over 138th Street. Or was it 137th Street? You know that coal-black stuck-up bitch that used to fuck all the big-time drug dealers. What was her name? Sandra or Sharon or some shit. The biggest ho in Harlem, man."

Tiara's eyes widened. Oh no he didn't, she thought. She tried to control her breathing as she slowly walked back into the living room.

"Man, didn't I tell you a little while ago to shut the fuck up?" Mr. Richard was standing over the couch, fists clenched, bellowing at his brother-in-law.

"Aw man, what the fuck . . ." Mr. Jacob stuttered as he tried to scramble up from the couch. "What I say? What you was fucking her, too? I was just saying . . ."

"No, he wasn't fucking my mother, you drunk ass." Tiara said in a controlled voice that belied her rage. "And don't you be talking about my family, hear? You're just jealous because you don't have shit, never had shit, and never will have shit. You're not good enough to mention my daddy's name or my mother's."

"Tiara, don't you worry about this stupid dude. I got him handled." Mr. Richard tried to take her by the arm, but she shook him off.

"I'm not worried about him. And you don't even have to handle him. I just called my daddy on my cell phone. He's on his way over here right now to kick his drunk ass," Tiara said with a wave of her hand.

"Aw yeah. There's about to be some shit going down tonight," the red-haired man said, slowly pushing away from the card table. He took off his thick glasses, wiped them with a tissue he pulled from his pocket, and put them back on and stood up. "I'm going to see y'all later." He pulled a jacket off the back of his chair, then addressed Tiara.

"Girl, you tell your daddy that Red Oscar James said hello. And make sure you tell him I ain't saying nothing out of the way to you or about your family."

"Ain't this some shit? And I was winning for a change," Mr. Jimmy slowly got up from the table. "Wait up, Red, I'm getting up outta here, too."

"Oh man," Mr. Richard said plaintively. "Why you had to go and call him? I had everything under control. Shakira, get out here right now!" he yelled.

"Hold on, Dad. I'm doing my hair," Shakira called from a back bedroom.

"Girl, get out here now!"

Tiara, her arms crossed, continued to glare at Mr. Jacobs who was sitting on the couch opening and closing his mouth and shaking his head, as if to clear it. "Yeah, I see you ain't talking shit now that my daddy's coming over here," she spat at him.

"Tiara, call your daddy back and tell him you and Shakira are leaving and everything's all right." Mr. Richard was pulling Shakira by one arm while she was trying to put on her jacket with the other.

"Dad," Shakira whined as she was being pushed out the door, "I need some money."

"Girl, I'm your father, not your man. I ain't got no money," Mr. Richard snapped.

"Well, we're going to need some money for the cab." No reason not to take advantage of the situation, Tiara grinned to herself. "Daddy would get mad if he knew we were coming back from the Apollo on the subway so late at night, and Shakira had promised that she was going to get the money from you."

"Yeah, okay. Right. No problem." Mr. Richard reached into his front pocket and pulled out some wrinkled bills, then handed five singles to Shakira. "Now, y'all get outta here now. And call your daddy, Tiara. I mean it. Don't forget," he said as he closed the door behind them.

"Damn, what was that all about?" Shakira said as they walked to the stairwell. "I'm not finished with my hair. I can't go out like this."

Tiara looked Shakira up and down. Shiny black pants that were obviously pleather, not leather, and a red camisole. She looked trashy, Tiara decided, but then she usually did. Her makeup was okay, but Shakira was right about her hair: Her weave was on crooked.

"Girl, you look nice," Shakira said to her, obviously having done her own appraisal.

"Don't I always?"

"You don't have to be so conceited about it, girl. You're that, but not all that," Shakira answered as she reached up and tried to arrange her weave ponytail. "Come on, Tiara. Help me with this."

"Come on," Tiara answered as she trotted down the stairs. "We'll stop at Alice's house and you can fix it over there."

"Shit. Then that funky Dumbo the Elephant girl is going to want to go out with us," Shakira grumbled as she followed.

"So what?" said Tiara. "We'll just say no."

Shakira sucked her teeth. "Yeah, well, don't you go feeling sorry for her or any shit. You know how you get sometime."

"I just get sick of everyone picking on her all the time." Tiara shrugged her shoulders. She'd known Alice since second grade, and she did kind of feel sorry for the girl. But at the same time, it was her own fault. She should just go on a diet or something. "Plus, you know her moms is never home. We can send Alice for some weed so we can get our high on before we go out."

"Oh, well, you know I'm down for that." Shakira grinned. Tiara smirked. Shakira was always down for getting high on someone else's money. The broke witch.

"Hey! Why does my pop want you to call your dad?"

"He thinks I called daddy to come over and kick his and his stupid friend's ass, but I really didn't. I was just scaring them."

"Huh?"

"They were talking about my family, so I told them I was calling my father," Tiara said impatiently. "But since I didn't call him, I don't have to call him back. Got it?"

"What did they say about your family?"

"Some stupid shit. You know what an idiot your father and his homeboys are when they get drunk. They're some stupid motherfuckers."

"What the fuck?" Shakira stopped in her tracks, and put her hands on her hips. "So you get mad when someone talks about your family, but you can call my father a motherfucker?"

"Yeah, I can. 'Cause your father's fucked up, and mine's not." Tiara looked at Shakira as if she were an idiot for not agreeing.

Shakira looked as if she were going to retort, then just rolled her eyes and snapped. "You got a lotta shit with you, Tiara."

"Yeah, whatever," Tiara said as she banged on Alice's door. "Get over it."

3

It was past 11:00 P.M., but the streets were packed with theatergoers just getting out of Broadway plays and tourists gawking at the bright lights of Times Square and peeking around corners hoping to glimpse the legendary hordes of prostitutes that had all been run out of the area a few years back. Tiara was so pissed she didn't notice any of them.

"Now what we gonna do?" Shakira said, slightly out of breath as she tried to keep up with Tiara. "I told you we shouldn'ta brought Dumbo along. She's the reason you couldn't get in."

"Oh, Shakira, shut up. I couldn't get in because you forgot to bring your fucking ID," Tiara snapped. Shakira was right, she shouldn't have let Alice go with them to Club New York, but she figured she'd be useful. Ugly as she was no one was going to ask her to dance, so she could watch the jackets while she and Shakira were on the dance floor. When Shakira realized she didn't have her ID, she was willing to leave the girl behind, since she and Alice had been cleared. But then old stupid Alice got caught trying to slip Shakira her ID on the sly. The bouncers threw all three of them out, even though Tiara protested she didn't know either of them. And she wished she didn't.

"I want you to know I heard you," Alice said from three paces behind.

"Like I give a fuck," Shakira said over her shoulder.

"If I was her I'd punch you in the mouth. She wouldn'ta been caught if she wasn't trying to help you," Tiara snapped at Shakira. "None of us woulda been caught."

"Yeah, well, like you said earlier, get over it." Shakira snapped back.

Tiara rolled her eyes as she slid the strap of her pocketbook higher on her shoulder. They continued walking across Forty-third Street toward Seventh Avenue. Her buzz had worn off, and she was still upset about the stupidity that had gone down in Shakira's house, and in an all-around bad mood. And Shakira was getting on her nerves, obviously still mad that Tiara had busted on her stupid family. She almost wished Alice would haul off and give the girl a beat-down. She might even jump in and get a couple of kicks in herself, the way she was feeling at the moment. She glanced at her watch. 11:30 P.M. Too early to go in. She still wanted to salvage part of this evening. Maybe she could hook up with that cute guy from her journalism class that was always trying to talk to her. He wasn't really her type. All he ever talked about was getting high and making it big as a rap star. No motivation, just talk, was her assessment, but at least he'd be better company than Shakira and Alice. He had mentioned that he was deejaying Ladies Night at a club in the Huntington Park section of the Bronx. But first she had to get rid of her excess baggage. She might have wanted company going into a club where she didn't know anyone, but since they hadn't been able to get into Club New York, they had worn out their usefulness. She whirled around to face them.

"Look, y'all can go on back uptown, I'm going to grab a cab to go to this party I heard about in Brooklyn."

Alice simply nodded, but Shakira put her hands on her narrow hips with a look of disbelief. "Oh, you're just going to dump me now?"

"Well, you got money to split the ride to Brooklyn? It's going to cost about twenty dollars because it's all way out near Coney Island, so that's forty dollars round trip. You gonna pony up twelve bucks?" Tiara put her hand out, knowing that Shakira only had the five dollars her father had given her.

"Well, you obviously got it covered if you're going to go by yourself." Shakira retorted.

"I have enough money to pay my share," Alice said hopefully. Tiara ignored her and concentrated on Shakira.

"Girl, if you're going, you got to pay your share. How did your pops put it? I ain't your man. Don't be expecting me to pay your bills."

Shakira waved her hand in Tiara's face, her head bobbing. "You know what? Just forget you. Ain't nobody gonna beg you for a hand-out or a hang-out. Come on, Alice." She started stalking off toward the Seventh Avenue subway.

"I can split the cab fare," Alice said again, ignoring Shakira's command.

"Naw, you better go with Shakira. She's all high and stuff and she shouldn't be going on the subway by herself," Tiara said in the most earnest tone she could muster. "Me and you can go hang out by ourselves this weekend, okay?"

Alice sighed. Tiara didn't know if she could see through her excuse or not, but she didn't really care. She just needed to shake the girl so she could go about her business. She'd go grab something to eat so she could wait long enough to make sure Shakira and Alice caught their train, then she'd double back and grab the subway to the Bronx. No use in wasting cab money when it would only take about twenty-five minutes to get there on the train.

Alice must have bought it, though. She grabbed Tiara in a hug, almost knocking the girl off balance. Damn, now she's thinking we're best friends or something, Tiara thought as she pulled away.

"Alice, will you come on?" she heard Shakira call out to the reluctant girl.

"Okay, see you later. I'll give you a call tomorrow." Tiara started across the street. Damn, I got the munchies again, she thought. A green Ford Expedition slowly cruising down Forty-third Street suddenly slowed down even more, and the driver—who looked to be Puerto Rican—stuck his head out the window and started making kissing faces at her, not seeming to care that he was holding up traffic. Nor did he seem to care that he was blasting his car stereo so loud that people in the street were cursing in his direction. How ghetto, she thought. She looked straight ahead as she crossed the street. Like he really thought I was going to respond to someone actually beckoning to me like I was a dog.

Suddenly a hard blow struck her in the middle of her back. Her arms flung out, almost in reflex, as she tried to maintain her balance, and she felt someone jerk her purse off her shoulder.

"Hey!" Cars honked at her as she tried to chase the hooded figure that expertly dodged in and out of traffic and on to Seventh Avenue. He was wearing all black, and it was hard to keep him in focus as he weaved and bobbed through the crowd. She had started chasing him almost on reflex, but now as she ran she tried also to look around for a police officer. Damn it, she was going to get her fucking bag back. "Somebody stop him! He stole my purse!" But instead of someone reaching out and grabbing him, or even sticking a leg out to trip him, the crowd immediately parted in the middle as if to give him safe passage. They didn't want him bumping into them. The heel on Tiara's left shoe snapped, but she barely noticed as she kept up her pursuit. She saw him finally run into a multiplex movie theater, but when she tried to follow she was stopped by an attendant.

"You need a ticket," the red uniformed young man said as he grabbed her.

"But that guy . . ." She was breathing hard and struggling to talk. "That guy . . . that just ran in here . . . he stole my pocketbook."

"I can't let you in here without a ticket."

"Boy, are you insane? I'm getting in here right now." She pushed past him into the lobby and past the concession stand. When she turned the corner she saw to her dismay there were six theaters. Which one did he go in? She leaned against the wall and tried to fight back tears.

"Tiara!"

She turned to find a panting Alice rushing toward her, with Shakira close behind.

"Where did he go?"

"I don't know," Tiara said dismally, waving her hand at the six different doors. "Take your pick."

"Are you okay?" Shakira asked.

"No, I'm not okay!" Tiara snapped. "I just got my pocketbook snatched. How am I supposed to be okay?"

"Girl, don't snap at me. I'm just trying to be nice," Shakira snapped back. "How much did he get?"

"I don't know," Tiara said dismally. "I guess only something like forty bucks. But that's not the point."

"You want me to go look for him?" Alice asked.

"Just forget it. He probably already took my money and ditched my bag under one of the seats by now." Tiara wiped her eyes with the back of her hand. "Come on, let's get outta here."

The girls trailed out into the street, Tiara flipping the attendant the bird as they walked.

"What are we going to do now?" Alice asked.

Tiara shook her head and let out a sigh. "Let's catch a cab home. I just wanna go to bed at this point."

"How you going to pay your share of the cab when you got your purse snatched?" Shakira asked.

"I got her covered," Alice said before Tiara could respond.

"Taxi," Shakira stepped out in the street and waved her hand for a cab. A yellow cab pulled up immediately, and the three girls climbed in the back seat.

"One hundred and fifteenth and Malcolm X Boulevard," Tiara said as the taxi pulled off. The car suddenly stopped.

"Sorry, I can't take you that far uptown," the Arabic-looking driver said.

"Look. You have to," Tiara said angrily. "It's the law, remember? You have to take a fare anywhere they want to go in the city as long as they have the money to pay. And we have money."

"Miss, I'm sorry. But I'm getting ready to knock off for the night, and I don't want to go that far uptown," the driver said in a soothing tone.

"Don't give me that shit," Tiara banged on the Plexiglas partition that separated the back and front seats. "You just don't want to go to Harlem."

"I'm sorry, Miss, but you'll have to get out. I'm not going that far uptown." The driver turned the ignition key, shutting the car off.

"Well, we're not getting out." Shakira said.

"Fuck this!" Tiara opened the door and climbed out into the street. Shakira and Alice climbed out behind her. Shakira was about to slam the door, but Tiara stopped her. "No, leave it open. If he wants to knock off so bad let him come out and close the door himself!" She kicked the passenger front door of the cab, then the trio walked to the next corner, not bothering to see if the cab driver got out or not.

"Taxi!" Shakira waved down another cab. This time, however, Tiara walked over and knocked on the driver's window before getting in.

"Yes?" the surprised driver said after he rolled down the window.

"You got a problem with taking us to Harlem?" Tiara demanded.

The driver, an African-American man with a short Afro and a faint mustache, cocked his head to the side and looked at her with an amused half-smile.

"No. No problem, young sister," he said finally as he stroked his clean-shaven chin. "Why don't you get in, take a deep breath, and relax. You need to try and get in touch with some positive energy."

"I don't need a lecture, just a ride." Tiara snatched open the cab door and climbed in. Alice and Shakira climbed in after her. "One hundred and fifteenth and Malcolm X Boulevard, and hurry it up," she snapped.

The driver frowned at her through the rearview mirror. "Any particular reason why you can't talk to me like I'm a human being?"

"She's just having a bad night," Alice tried to rub Tiara's shoulders, but the girl knocked her hand away.

"Would you stop feeling on me, Alice? Dang!" She crossed her arms over her chest, leaned back in her seat and closed her eyes. She just needed this night to be over. She really wanted this night to be over. Her bag was gone. Her brand new shoes were ruined. And her makeup and hair probably looked a holy mess. Oh, yeah, this night had to be over. It would be so nice if she could do like Barbara Eden on *I Dream of Jeannie* reruns that she saw on Nick at Nite. She'd love to just cross her arms in front of her chest and blink her eyes and suddenly be in her bed, leaving the other people in the cab just wondering what the hell had happened to her.

"Don't pay her any damn mind," Shakira said haughtily. "Driver, just please drive."

"You know, Shakira? You've got some shit with you," Tiara, her eyes still closed, said as the cab pulled off. "You've got the nerve to have an attitude, and all of this shit is your fault in the first place. If you had brought your damn ID I wouldn't have been kicked out of the club in the first place, and I wouldn't have gotten my pocketbook snatched."

Shakira sucked her teeth. "Whatever."

The car was silent for fifteen minutes. Suddenly the driver looked in the rearview mirror and said, "Shakira, huh? That's a nice name. Do you know what your name means?"

"It doesn't mean anything. My mother made it up," the girl answered with a shrug.

The driver chuckled. "How do you spell it?"

"S, H, A, K, I, R, A."

"Uh huh, that's what I thought. It means 'grateful' in Arabic."

"Get out of here? It does?"

"Yep."

"Do you know what my name means?" Alice asked shyly.

"Your name is Alice, right?"

"Yes."

"It means 'noble.'"

"Really? I never knew that. That's neat."

"And Tiara, I guess I don't have to tell you what your name means?"

Tiara kept her eyes closed and said nothing.

"I think she's asleep," Alice offered.

"I ain't asleep. I'm just not going to answer such a stupid question."

"Don't pay her any mind, she's just ignorant," Shakira snapped. "What does her name mean?"

Tiara opened her eyes and leaned over Alice to take a good look at Shakira.

"Are you serious? You mean to say you don't know what Tiara means?"

"You're so damn conceited you think that everyone is supposed to know what your name means?"

"You know what? You are really stupid," Tiara started giggling. "Shakira, what's that jeweled thing that princesses wear on their heads?"

Shakira looked puzzled. "A crown."

"Oh, God, she's stupid." Tiara laughed and leaned back in her seat again.

"It's a tiara," Alice said, not bothering to hide her grin.

"Well, so? Whatever," Shakira's face reddened. "You don't have to be laughing."

"Anyway," Tiara said now that she had been drawn out of her funk. "How do you know the meanings of all these names? You keep a name book there in the front seat to use to impress your fares or something?"

"No." The cab was stopped at a red light, so the driver took the opportunity to fully turn around in his seat and look at Tiara. She noticed for the first time that he was kind of cute—and not much older than her. "I knew Alice because my sister's pregnant with a little girl and I was helping her choose a name from one of those books. And I knew Shakira because that's my old girlfriend's name."

"Your old girlfriend?" Tiara said, smiling flirtatiously.

"Yeah, old girlfriend," the driver smiled back. "Okay, we're here. Which corner?"

"Right there." Shakira pointed to her building.

"Why your building? My building's closer," Tiara demanded.

"Because Alice lives in my building so since there's two of us in one building, the cab should pull up there," Shakira said. She pointed to her building again. "Just get out with us and walk the five feet or stay in the cab and have him drive you five feet for all I care."

"May I make a suggestion?" the soft-spoken driver spoke up.

"What's that?" Tiara asked.

"Shakira, why don't you and Alice walk Tiara to her apartment, and then walk back to your building so no one is actually out by themselves."

"Or you can park the car and walk me yourself." Tiara batted her eyes at the driver's reflection in the rearview mirror.

"Or I can park the car and walk all of you to your buildings," the driver said with a shrug of his shoulders. He ignored Tiara's pout and took a wad of bills from his pocket and removed the rubber band that was wrapped around the middle. "That'll be seven fifty."

"Pay the man, Alice!" Shakira said.

"You don't have to talk to her like that!" Tiara rolled her eyes at Shakira then patted Alice on the shoulder. "Look, thanks for helping me out this evening. I'll pay you back my share tomorrow when I get some money from my dad."

"That's okay," Alice smiled appreciatively. "I just feel bad you got your pocketbook snatched. And it was such a nice bag, too!" She handed the driver a ten-dollar bill. "Keep the change," she told him.

"You don't need to tip him!" Tiara suddenly—and loudly— protested.

"Why not?" Alice and the driver asked at the same time.

"Well," Tiara tossed her head and then slid her fingers through her hair, "he's getting to walk us up to our apartments, that's tip enough."

"Oh, I got it," Shakira snapped her fingers. "We shouldn't have to pay him at all, right? In fact, he should be paying us." She rolled her eyes. "Yeah, Tiara's back to normal. Tripping as usual."

"You know, Shakira, you're showing your true colors again." Tiara snapped her fingers in front of Shakira's nose. "Jealous as all shit."

"Jealous of what?" Shakira pushed the girl's hand away.

"Hey, hey, before you guys start really tripping in my backseat, let's get a couple of things straight," the driver said with a chuckle. "First of all, I didn't say I was walking anyone to their apartments. I said I would walk to you all to your buildings." He looked pointedly at Tiara. "And I intended it as a favor, not an opportunity to get any kind of rap on."

Tiara crossed her arms in front of her chest. "I didn't say you were trying to—"

"And second of all, I would appreciate it if you didn't tell Alice to forget the tip. I'm out here trying to make a living, and tips go a long way towards doing just that," the driver continued. "So, Alice here's your change." He reached over to give the girl $2.50. "If you still want to give me a tip, it would be appreciated. If you don't, no problem. It has no bearing at all," he looked at Tiara again, "on whether I walk you young ladies to your buildings."

"No, you please keep it," Alice said sheepishly, but avoiding Tiara's eyes.

"I mean, damn, can't nobody in this cab tell when a girl is joking," Tiara grumbled as she opened the door and stepped out onto the sidewalk, followed by Alice and Shakira. The driver turned off the ignition and joined them, giving Tiara her first good look at him. He was about six-foot-one, with a slender build and cinnamon complexion. He was wearing a black turtleneck sweater, jeans, and brown combat boots. He reached onto the front passenger seat of the cab, pulled out a green army jacket and slipped it on.

"Hey, you know all of our names, but you never told us yours," Alice said.

"Rashad." He gave a short bow in their direction, then extended his arms. Alice took one, and Shakira the other before Tiara could step up.

"Come on, don't hang behind, Tiara," Rashad said jovially as they began walking into the projects. "Walk up in front so I can see you."

Tiara smiled to herself and sashayed forward. So he was interested in her after all. He was just playing hard to get. After all, how could he possibly prefer Shakira and Alice to her? He was just being nice to them to make her jealous. But now he was letting her know he liked her best by all but saying he wanted to watch her butt as she walked.

"I just don't want anyone grabbing you from behind, young sis," Rashad said as if he was reading her mind.

Oh yeah, say what you want. You just wanted to look at my butt,

Tiara thought smugly. A look of uncertainty suddenly crossed her face. That was the real reason he told her to walk up, wasn't it?

"Right here," Alice looked at Rashad adoringly as they stopped in front of the building. "Thanks for being such a gentleman."

"No problem, fair ladies." Rashad gave another short bow.

"Now, where do you live?" Rashad asked Tiara when Shakira and Alice disappeared into their building.

"Just a few buildings down." Tiara ignored Rashad's outstretched arm, but walked closely by his side. She waited for him to start a conversation as they walked, but he seemed happy humming some stupid song she didn't recognize.

"What does your name mean?" She had to think of something to say or ask since they were almost at her building and he still hadn't said anything.

"'Righteous One' or 'One with Integrity.'" Rashad answered.

"That's a nice name."

"Thank you."

Oh, shoot. They were almost at her door, and he still hadn't hit on her. What the hell was wrong with him? As fine as she was, she was sure he was interested. And he was good looking, but he wasn't that fine that he could think he could diss someone as cute as her. Damn, it would be humiliating if he just walked her to her building, jumped in his cab, and then drove off without making a play for her. The heel of her left shoe suddenly caught in a crack in the sidewalk, and in its already weakened condition, it snapped off. "God damn it!" she yelled in frustration.

"You okay, sis?" Rashad quickly moved forward and grabbed her arm.

"My ankle!" Tiara said quickly. "I think it's broken. I don't think I can walk." She bit down hard on her lower lip, a trick she had learned could quickly force tears to her eyes.

"It's okay," Rashad said soothingly. "Just put your weight on me."

He wrapped his arm around her waist and pulled her toward his body. She had hoped he would sweep her into his arms and carry her into the building, but she settled for the support, which gave her a chance to inhale his body scent. Some kind of musk, like they sell on the vendor stands on 125th Street. She usually preferred Polo on her men, but the fragrance suited him.

"Is this your building here?"

"Yeah, but I don't think I can make it to my apartment alone," she said plaintively.

"I know, I know. I'll take you to your door."

Was that irritation she detected in his voice? She felt another tug of uncertainty. He should be ecstatic that he had an excuse to escort her all the way to her apartment. He was interested, wasn't he? He pulled the front door of the building with his free hand and asked, "Do you know if anyone's home?"

"Yeah, my father and my sister." Damn it. The look of relief on his face was unmistakable. To hell with him. She was almost tempted to straighten up and strut down the hall and tell him she didn't need his help. Almost. She held tightly onto him as he knocked on the apartment door. She could hear the strains of the Gap Band's "Burn Rubber."

> *I never ever had a lover*
> *Put to the pedal to the metal and*
> *Burn rubber on me, Charlie*

Hell, that probably meant Aunt Charlie was there. It was her favorite song, and even though Daddy hated it, he let Aunt Charlie play it every time she came over.

"Oh my God, Tiara, what the hell happened to you?" Aunt Charlie almost shrieked as she opened the door. Tiara glanced up at Rashad to see his reaction to her aunt's face, but he was expressionless.

38

"I'm okay. I twisted my ankle."

"Something's wrong with Tiara? What happened?" Reggie flew out of the bathroom just as Rashad helped Tiara to the mauve sofa.

"It's okay, Daddy. I just twisted my ankle, and Rashad helped me upstairs."

"Let me take a look at it." Reggie brushed Rashad aside without looking at him and knelt down beside the sofa, gently taking Tiara's foot in his hand. "Does it hurt?" he asked as he unstrapped the shoe.

"A little." Tiara gave a little whimper to accentuate her words.

"It doesn't look swollen." Charlene had picked up a glass of Johnny Walker Black and was looking over her brother's shoulder. "Shit, it doesn't even look red."

"That doesn't mean it doesn't hurt," Tiara snapped. Leave it to Aunt Charlie to mess up her game. She was about to bite her lip again, but thought the better of it. If Aunt Charlie noticed she'd call her out on that too. Miserable witch.

"It looks like it might be a little swollen," Reggie said soothingly. "Charlene, do me a favor and get me some ice from the kitchen."

"For what?" Charlene sucked her teeth, but didn't move. "There ain't nothing wrong with that girl. She just wants some attention."

"Excuse me, I'm just going to go and pull the door behind me, okay?" Rashad was backing out toward the door as he spoke. "You folks have a good night."

"No, you don't have to leave!" Tiara cried out. She started to jump off the couch and physically put herself between him and the door, but remembered the fake injury just in time. "Let me at least introduce you to my family. Daddy," she said nudging her father's shoulder so he would turn around and face the young man, "this is Rashad. He's a cab driver who drove us home after my pocketbook got snatched over in Times Square. Rashad, this is my father—"

"Your purse was snatched?" Reggie's mouth dropped. "Baby, are you okay?"

"Yeah, daddy. I just had a horrible night." Tiara whined. "Some dude grabbed my pocketbook, and I chased him into the movie theater and everything, but he got away. And I didn't have any money. If Alice and Shakira wasn't around I wouldn't have been able to even get back uptown."

"Why were you in Times Square anyway? I thought your father told me you were going to be at the Apollo with your friend." Aunt Charlie rattled the ice in her glass as she squinted down at Tiara.

"We tried, but we couldn't get in, so Shakira wanted to go to Times Square to catch up with her cousin who works in a coffee shop down there, and me and Alice just went along to keep her company," Tiara said quickly. "And Rashad, this is my father Reggie Byrum, and my Aunt Charlene. Y'all this is Rashad."

"How you doing?" Reggie said in a gruff voice. He shook Rashad's hand, then reached in his pocket and took out his wallet. "How much was the fare?"

"Daddy, we already paid him!"

"Well, let me give you a little something extra for all your trouble, and helping my daughter to the apartment and all." Reggie started pulling bills out of his wallet.

"Daddy, please!" Oh this was too embarrassing.

"Mr. Bynum, it's not a problem. It was nice meeting you, and nice meeting you too, Miss Bynum. I hope you all have a very good evening." Rashad was smiling as he backed his way toward the door. "And I hope you recover soon, Tiara."

"Well, um, thanks," Reggie said, but Rashad was already out the door and walking down the hallway.

"Oh man!" Tiara jumped up from the couch and stomped over to the door and twisted the steel bolt lock.

"Uh huh, I thought your ankle was twisted?" Aunt Charlie smirked.

"It's feeling better," Tiara grumbled. "And what are y'all up so late

40

for anyway? Playing music and everything this time of night. Don't you have to work tomorrow, Daddy?"

"No, I'm taking a personal day so I can go shopping with your Aunt Charlene for a new car."

"You getting a new car?" Tiara eyed her aunt with interest.

"Yeah. You got a problem with that? Or do you have a problem with me borrowing Reggie for a few hours?" Aunt Charlie stood with one hand holding her drink and the other on her hip as she looked her niece up and down. "After all, he was my brother before he was your father."

"Yeah, but if you went out and bought yourself a man like you be buying everything else you wouldn't have to be using Daddy every time you need a man around."

Reggie caught Charlene just as she flew at Tiara. "What the hell is wrong with you, girl?" he demanded as he struggled to hold his sister back. "Apologize to your aunt!"

"I apologize," Tiara flippantly said over her shoulder as she walked to her room.

"Tiara, get your ass back in here and apologize for real!" The tone of Reggie's voice started the warning bells ringing in Tiara's head. It wasn't often that she crossed the line with her father, but she had managed to cross it now. He was almost as protective of Aunt Charlie as he was of his daughters. Usually she was careful not to get into it with her aunt in front of her father, but she was just so pissed off she'd forgotten he was even in the room.

"I said get in here!" he demanded.

She meekly trailed back into the living room.

"That girl doesn't have any respect, Reggie." Aunt Charlie was hollering while swishing her drink around. "She thinks she can talk to me like that because you let her get away with everything. But she ain't gonna talk to me like that, you hear? That little chickee is going to have to—"

"I'm sorry, Aunt Charlie. I really am." Tiara stepped close to the woman, hoping her aunt would take a swing at her so her father could switch back over to her side. But Aunt Charlie was too smart. She stepped back from Tiara, put her hand back on her hip and started bobbing her head and waving her finger in the girl's face.

"I don't know why you think you're so grown that you can come out your mouth to me like that. You ain't that damn grown, you hear? If you was some woman in the street I woulda just knocked your ass to the floor and commenced to stomping you. But I ain't gonna do that because you ain't a grown-ass woman. You're a young girl, and you'd better start acting like it."

"Aunt Charlie, I said I was sorry. I'm just tired, and I know I shouldn't have said that, and I didn't even mean it."

"Oh, don't even try to pull that innocent act out on me. I ain't your damn daddy!"

"Daddy, see?" Tiara turned to her father. "I'm trying to apologize and all she's doing is hollering."

"Daddy see, my ass! Just 'cause you got my brother wrapped around your little finger and shit doesn't mean you're going to get away with talking to me like that." Aunt Charlie stepped between Tiara and Reggie and started poking Tiara in the chest with each word. "I'll whip your ass and whip his ass if he tries to stop me. I changed your dirty diapers and wiped your shitty ass, and you gonna come out your mouth like that to me?"

"Aunt Charlie, I said I'm sorry . . ."

"Okay, Charlene, that's enough . . ." Reggie gently tugged at this sister's shoulder but she shrugged him off.

"You ain't sorry," she said as she advanced on the retreating Tiara. "But you're gonna be sorry."

"Charlene, I said that's enough!" Reggie forcefully pulled Charlene away from Tiara. "The girl said she was sorry. What else do you want her to do?"

"She always says she's sorry!" Charlene hollered at him. "You let her do whatever she wants to do, then whenever you finally get mad all she has to do is say she's sorry and you act like everything is hunky-dory. Just like with her goddamned mother!"

"I knew you were going to say it. You always say it." Reggie threw his hands up in the air. "Tiara, go to bed. I'll talk to you about what you said to your aunt in the morning. Charlene, get your coat. I'm taking you home. Your ass done had too much to drink."

Tiara slipped into the dark bedroom and undressed without turning on the lights. It was amazing that Jo-Jo could sleep through all the racket in the other room, but the deep heavy breathing coming from her bed attested to the fact that she was indeed oblivious to the drama of the evening. She heard Aunt Charlie still cursing as Reggie pulled her out the door, but she could care less that her aunt was on a tear. It was nothing too unusual when Aunt Charlie started drinking, and anyway she knew her father wouldn't even bother mentioning her rudeness in the morning. What she was worried about was why Rashad had left without even asking for her telephone number.

4

And can anyone explain for me, please, why American journalism is considered the fourth estate in American government?" The teacher tapped the chalk impatiently on the blackboard, waiting for one of the yawning students in the 8:00 A.M. mass media class to answer. After a few seconds, he put the chalk on the desk and rubbed his scraggly auburn beard, then picked an imaginary piece of lint off of his faded jean jacket, and started strolling toward the back of the room.

Tiara slumped down in her chair, hoping to escape what she knew was coming next. Sure enough, the professor stopped a few inches away from her seat.

"Let's see, Miss Bynum, we haven't heard from you all day. Care to venture a guess?"

Tiara let out a loud groan.

"Is that your answer, Miss Bynum? Or are you just letting us know how much you care about your college experience?"

"No, just letting you know what I think of your teaching style," Tiara answered. A couple of the students around her snickered.

"Well, I'm sorry if my class isn't as exciting as you'd like, Miss

Bynum. And I'm also sorry that you've come to class unprepared. If you had deigned to do the required reading you'd know the answer to what is really a simple question." He tapped the back of her chair and moved off toward the front of the classroom. "Is there anyone, at all, in this class who can answer the question?"

"Journalism is called the fourth estate—the first three being the judiciary, the legislative, and the executive branches of government—because the media is considered as important as these three bodies, as it is the watchdog for the citizenry," Tiara monotoned.

The professor slowly turned and looked at her. "Why, thank you, Miss Bynum. Nice to know you've actually learned something in this class."

"The phrase was actually coined by an Englishman in the beginning of the twentieth century who believed that the media was as powerful as the aristocracy, the church, and the commons." Tiara half-covered her mouth as she let out a huge yawn, then looked the professor up and down. "All of which I was taught in my high school journalism course. I'm still waiting to actually learn something in this class."

The professor's face reddened, but before he could respond, Tiara looked at her watch, stood up, and started gathering her books.

"Okay, I guess that's it for today. Remember, the midterm will be given next Friday, so I want you to go over the handouts I gave you last week, and I'll see you all bright and early Wednesday morning." Tiara, along with more than half of the class, was out of the door before he was finished speaking.

What a jerk, Tiara thought as she stomped down the hall. One minute he wanted to act he like he was so down, and the next minute he was talking down to the class like they were a bunch of idiots. Jerk. He thought he was so smart because he went to Harvard and used to work at *The New York Times*. If he was really so smart he'd still be working there instead of pissing off students at City College.

"I should drop this stupid class," she said out loud to no one. "Fucking asshole."

"Yeah, he sure is an asshole, but you sure know how to handle him."

She didn't even bother to look around, since she recognized the voice. Jimmy, the part-time deejay who was always trying to push up on her. She quickened her pace, hoping he'd take the hint. He was a cutie pie with his Allen Iverson cornrows and his Sean John outfits, and he was all right to talk to sometimes—especially since she knew there were two girls in the journalism class who were jealous as shit because they dug him—but she didn't want to be bothered at the moment. She had too many things on her mind.

"Damn, girl. Why you always in such a hurry? You enough to make a brother think he got bad breath or something." Jimmy rushed in front of her to open the exit door.

"I don't wanna be late for class," she said between clenched teeth. Damn, why was it that guys you didn't want anything to do with were the ones that were sweating you, and guys who you're interested in don't even bother to ask for your telephone number? You'd think after five days that guy, Rashad, would have found some excuse to contact her, especially since he knew she didn't have any way to contact him. Not that she would anyway, she assured herself. It wasn't like he was such a great catch, but damn, she had to admit there was something about him that intrigued her. She just wished she knew what that something was. He was cute in an Afrocentric kind of way, but he wasn't all that fine. And it wasn't like he had all that much money. Shit, he was driving a cab. He seemed pretty intelligent, but it wasn't like she wasn't used to talking to smart guys. It was something else. She just couldn't figure out what.

"Tiara. Come on, girl! You acting like you ain't heard a word I said." Jimmy was tugging at her elbow.

"Boy, what's wrong with you!" She turned and snarled at him, snatching her arm away. "I don't remember giving you permission to touch me."

He grinned sheepishly, and looked side to side as he backed away to see if anyone had noticed the diss.

"Now see you're buggin', Tiara. I was just asking if you were okay. You ain't gotta go acting like I'm trying to attack you or some shit."

"Whatever," she tossed her head and rolled her eyes.

"Why you gotta do me like that, girl?"

"Why you gotta keep putting yourself out there like that?" she answered, ignoring the hurt and puzzlement in his voice. She turned to walk toward the bus stop on Amsterdam Avenue. She didn't even feel like being bothered with any more classes for the day. She would just go home and then spend the day watching soaps. And try to get that damn Rashad off of her mind. Damn him! Why the hell wasn't he trying to get with her?

"Excuse me, Miss? You got the time?" A tall muscular man—at least six-six—who looked about twenty, wearing a brown athletic shirt under an open black leather jacket, smiled as he walked next to her.

"I don't have a watch," Tiara grumbled as she continued to walk.

"Well, can I buy you one, with your pretty self," the man grinned. "Damn, you got some pretty-ass eyes. I ain't never seen a chick as dark as you with hazel eyes like that. You wearing contacts?"

"No." Like she would tell him if she were. Jerk. Tiara rolled her eyes and quickened her pace.

"Yo, babe, I didn't catch your name."

"Yo, creep, I ain't throw it," Tiara retorted.

"Creep? Shit, girl, why you gotta come out your face like that?"

"Shit, boy, why you gotta be all up in my face?" First Jimmy, now this asshole. She was at the bus stop now, and she turned to face the guy. "I'm walking down the street minding my own business, and you think you can just walk up and drop a line, and I'm supposed to drop my panties or something? What? You on dope or something?"

"Bitch, you ain't all that fucking fine to be thinking you can talk to a brother like that . . ." the man balled his fists as he stepped closer to her, forcing her to back into the corner of the bus shelter.

"Whoa, whoa. Man, you got a problem or something?" Seemingly out of nowhere, a dark-skinned man wearing a quarter-length brown leather jacket stepped in front of the threatening man.

"I ain't got no problem that's any business of yours," the man snarled.

"Miss, you know this man?" the newcomer asked Tiara, though his eyes never left the man.

"Mister, I've never seen him before, and I'd appreciate it if you could get him outta my face," Tiara said in a defiant tone which belied her fear.

"You heard the lady, man. Why don't you just roll on outta here?"

"Why don't you just mind your business?" The man drew his right shoulder back, as if readying to swing a punch.

"I'm making this my business, man." The newcomer quickly drew his unbuttoned jacket open further and his hand moved to his waistband.

The man froze for a moment, then slowly backed away. "Man, I ain't got time for this shit. You want the bitch, you got her." He turned and stomped into a nearby restaurant.

"You okay?" The newcomer turned and faced the breathless Tiara.

"I don't even know that dude. He just walked up on me acting like some kinda nut," she said in a rush. "Then when I wouldn't talk to him he acted like he was going to hit me or something. I ain't even do nothing to him."

"Yeah, I know. I was scoping out the situation when I was at the stop light, and then when I saw him cornering you I just parked and jumped out my car to make sure you were all right." The man waved toward a black 2003 Porsche turbo convertible with a rear spoiler parked haphazardly near the curb. Damn, Tiara thought. *Nice car.* She patted her hair to make sure it was in place, and took a good look at her savior. He was kind of short, but not too short. Sorta like Wesley Snipes. He was the same complexion as Wesley Snipes, too, and had a nice build. His clothes—he wore a cream-colored turtleneck and brown slacks, and tan Versace loafers—were understated, but obviously expensive. It was evident the dude had some bucks.

"Are you sure you're going to be okay?"

"Yeah, yeah, I'm fine."

"Okay then, I'm going to take off." And with that, he walked over to his car and got in without even a backward glance, peeling off so fast his tires screeched.

Damn! The rude-ass could have at least offered me a ride. Tiara leaned back on the bus shelter, fuming. This was turning out to be a really messed-up day. To hell with the soaps, she wanted even more to climb in her bed and pull the blanket over her head. If the bus didn't come in the next five minutes she was just going to hail a cab.

"Excuse me, Miss?" The rude-ass hero must have circled around the block, because there he was sticking his head out of that fine-ass black Porsche.

"Yes?" Tiara said as nonchalantly as she could.

"I'm thinking I should probably give you a ride. I don't want that guy to double back and start hassling you again."

"Thanks." Tiara climbed into the car quickly. "I was wondering why you didn't offer in the first place."

"Sorry, I just wasn't thinking." The man screeched off again, just barely beating the red light. "My name's Lionel Evans, by the way."

"I'm Tiara." The soft black leather seats with gray stitching were divine, and the new car scent was intoxicating. The lower part of the instrument panel was also leather, and the windows and even the sunroof were tinted dark gray. She'd been in expensive cars before, but nothing like this. She pulled the passenger seat visor down to check her makeup. Lighted vanity mirror. Nice.

"Nice name. Where's home, Tiara?" Lionel kept his eyes on the road as he talked.

"Foster Projects." Tiara leaned back in the leather seat enjoying the new car smell.

"Where's that?"

"You know, the Martin Luther King Towers. I still call it Foster, though. Almost everyone does."

"Okay, but I still don't know where it is." ˙

"One hundred and fourteenth and Malcolm X Boulevard. You're not from Harlem?"

"No. I'm originally from D.C. I'm living in the Village now while I go to school."

"What school do you go to?"

"NYU. I'm a business major."

"Oh, cool." Tiara was silent for a minute, wondering if she should ask the next question, then decided what the hell. "So, if you're a student, how can you afford a car like this?"

Lionel grinned. "How do you think?"

Tiara chuckled. "Well, my guess is you're dealing."

"And does that bother you?"

"It ain't none of my business," Tiara shrugged.

Lionel leaned his head back and laughed. "Girl, I'm not a dope pusher."

"Well, why did you say you were?" Tiara said irritably.

"I didn't."

"So, why do you carry a gun, then?" Tiara challenged, remembering the way Lionel's hand had moved toward his waistband during the confrontation with the guy who had been harassing her.

"Girl, please. I don't carry a gun. I was just bluffing to back that guy off." Lionel laughed.

"Well, then where do you get your money?"

"Mostly from my parents, to be honest. My father was a software developer in California back in the day, and he came up with a program that Microsoft bought for two million big ones."

"Two million? Cool!" Tiara's eyes widened.

"Yeah, well, what's really cool is my mother's a stockbroker, so she turned that initial two million into a whole helluva lot more millions. And since I'm an only child, I reap the benefits," Lionel grinned. "Sounds like I'm boasting, huh? I'm sorry. I just get a kick out my life. If I wasn't me, I'd sure as hell want to be me."

"I don't blame you." Tiara's brain was racing. Man, to have that much money!

"So anyway, I've told you my life history. What about you? What's your story?"

Tiara shrugged. "Well, I'm studying pre-law at City College. I'm planning on going to Columbia Law after I graduate and study commerical law. Right now I live with my father and my younger sister. And . . ." she faltered, "and . . . um, I guess that's it." Her life suddenly seemed pretty dull.

"You got any kids?"

"Boy, please." Tiara sucked her teeth.

"Well, I had to ask," Lionel chuckled. "So, what does your father do for a living?"

She paused a moment, suddenly once again embarrassed by her father's occupation. "He's a sanitation worker."

"They make pretty good money, don't they? How do you guys qualify to live in the projects?"

"This is New York City," Tiara giggled. "People here inherit apartments. My grandmom used to live there, and when she died my dad moved in so he didn't have to pay a lot of money for rent."

"And the housing people don't care?"

"Not really. The apartment's still in my grandmom's name, and all. The rental office knows, but everyone does it. They get a nice Christmas present from my dad, and that's that."

"Cool," Lionel started laughing.

"Yeah, well," Tiara chuckled.

"So, which building?" Lionel was pulling up to her corner. *Dang, the ride was over so fast,* Tiara thought. "Right here." She pointed to her building.

"Well, I'm glad I got you to your place all safe and sound." Lionel turned to her and flashed a wide smile.

"Yeah, thanks." *This guy had better ask my phone number,* she thought.

"So, would you mind if I get your telephone number? Maybe I can take you out some time?"

"Yeah, that would be great." Tiara tried to hide her relief. Lionel took out his Palm Pilot hand-held computer and tapped in the telephone number she gave him.

"Hold on a sec," Lionel said as she reached for the car door handle. He jumped out of the car and quickly came around to open the door for her.

"Well, thanks for the ride," she smiled up at him while noticing, out of the corner of her eye, the usual scrubs hanging out in front of the building. *Them ho's were jealous before, I know they're going to die from jealousy now.*

"So how about I take you out tonight? We can go out to eat and then catch a movie." Lionel smiled back down at her. "I know it's short notice, but if you're free, I'd love to get with you."

"Yeah, I think I'm free," Tiara stepped closer to Lionel, for the oglers' benefit. "What time?"

"Say, seven?"

"Cool."

"Should I walk you to your apartment so I know where to pick you up?" Lionel pushed a stray strand of hair from Tiara's face.

"No, that's all right. I'm in apartment 1G, but don't worry about it.

I'll just meet you outside, okay?" Tiara said quickly. With her luck Aunt Charlie would be sitting watching television or something with her non-working self, and Tiara didn't want her messing up her roll with Lionel.

"You sure?"

"I'm sure."

"Okay. I'll see you at seven, okay?" Lionel bent down and gave Tiara a small peck on the lips. Oh God, he smelled good, Tiara thought as she strutted into her building. Smells good, looks good, and got money. Just the kind of guy she deserved. Fuck that old stupid broke-ass Rashad.

He was leaning on his car, his arms crossed, when she emerged from the building at 6:55 that evening. His mid-calf-length butter-soft gray leather coat was open, revealing sharply creased black trousers from Hugo Boss, and a matching black turtleneck. His black slip-on shoes were Kenneth Cole. The gray leather gloves he held in one of his hands were a little over the top, in Tiara's opinion, but she had to admit he was impressive. The three girls hanging out on the stoop must have thought so, too.

"Fuck that! I seen him first," a girl with pink and white butt-length braid extensions was saying as Tiara stepped out onto the stoop.

"Bullshit, Niecie. We seen him at the same time," another with an ultra-short blond curly perm retorted.

"Y'all just stand there and argue if you want. I'm on the brother." Shakira took long strides toward Lionel. Tiara, who had made eye contact with Lionel, followed quietly behind the girl.

"Hey, what's up?" Shakira said when she reached him. "You waiting on someone?"

Tiara stood off a little to distance, and watched Lionel give Shakira a slow look up and down—from her cheap weave, which needed to be redone, to her knock-off Prada boots with rundown heels.

"Yeah, I'm waiting on someone."

"Well, if you want, I could wait with you," Shakira batted her eyes. "That is, unless who you're waiting for might get jealous when they see me out here with you."

Lionel guffawed. "Yeah, well, I don't think she'd have any reason to be jealous, but just to be sure, why don't we just ask her?"

Oooh, nice diss, Tiara thought as she stepped forward and into Lionel's embrace. Normally, she wouldn't be hugging on a dude like that until he earned some attention, but she was willing to make the exception for Shakira's sake. Anything to make the skank feel worse than she must already be feeling.

"Girl, you're looking good!" Lionel kissed her on the forehead.

"Yeah, you know how I do," Tiara answered. She knew she was looking good, with her J-Lo purple button-up blouse, and black Bebe jeans with purple highlights, topped off with her black leather shirt-waist jacket. She turned to Shakira, and batted her eyes in the same manner she had treated Lionel. "Hey, girl. How's it going?"

"It goes," Shakira said sweetly.

"Ai'ght then, I'll catch you later. We gonna move on up outta here." Tiara looked at Lionel. "You ready?"

"Yeah," Lionel pushed a button on the car remote to unlock the car, then reached over and opened the passenger door.

"Yo, girl . . . you ain't even going to give me no intro?" Shakira demanded as Tiara prepared to step into the car.

"My bad. Lionel, this is Shakira," Tiara said flippantly.

"Yeah, okay. How you doing, Lionel?"

"All right." He answered without looking at her. "Come on, girl, let's roll." He took Tiara's hand and helped her to the car, then walked around to the driver's side and got in.

Uh huh, she's trying to figure out a way to save face 'cause she knows her girls are going to bust on her for getting dissed, Tiara thought when she saw Shakira was still standing by the car. *It's her own fault for trying to step outta her league.*

Tiara pushed the button to roll down her window when Lionel started the car. "What?" she asked the girl.

"What, what?" Shakira answered.

"Why you still standing there and shit?" Tiara said irritably.

"Oh, it's like that," Shakira caught an attitude. "Well, I was just wanting to tell you that Marcus was up in here looking for you a minute ago. He said he was supposed to be getting up with you tonight."

"You a fucking liar," Tiara snapped. Leaving the window open, she turned to Lionel. "I'm ready when you are."

Lionel nodded, then peeled off with his usual squeal of tires.

"So who's Marcus?" he asked after they driven a couple of blocks.

"Some retard, trying to get there with me. I ain't even thinking about him and Shakira knows it. She's just trying to start some shit."

"Yeah, I could see that. She's just mad and shit because you're in my car and her ass is on the sidewalk." Lionel threw his head back and laughed. "Like I was going to settle for some half-done pork chop when I can have prime rib."

"You got that right," Tiara grinned.

"But for real, mama, you must have a lot of dudes trying to get with you as fine as you are. And them eyes. I mean, damn. I ain't trying to blow up your head or anything, but shit." Lionel shook his head. "You got it going on."

"Yeah, well, there's always a few guys trying, but I ain't got time for most of them. Especially the guys around here. I ain't looking for no gangsta love and shit." Tiara shrugged, then started moving her shoulders to the Nelly song coming out of the car stereo. Same old shit, and she was used to it. Whenever she went out with a guy for the first time he asked who else was pushing up on her, because they knew as fine as she was they had competition. It tickled her, though, that someone as fine as Lionel, and with money and a car like his, was worried.

"So this Marcus dude thinks he's some kind of gangsta or something?"

"He thinks he is, but he ain't making no money. Like I want to be with someone scrambling on the corner. Please."

"Yeah, I know you got too much class for that kind of shit."

"For real." Tiara noticed that Lionel was pulling onto the FDR Drive, heading downtown. "Hey, where we going?"

"I thought I'd take you to a restaurant I like in the Village. You ever heard of One If By Land, Two If By Sea? It's on Barrow Street. My dad and I go whenever he's in town."

"Yeah, I've heard of it." Tiara had to stop her eyes from widening. She'd read about it in a couple of swanky magazines. Talk about classy! Just wait until she told her father!

She was even more impressed when she got there. The dimly lit restaurant was filled with roses, and a fire cackled in the foyer's large fireplace. Long tapered candles burned on every table, and the light tinkling of a piano player added to the romantic atmosphere.

When the stately waiter handed them their menus, she found that hers had no prices next to the selections. She'd heard about restaurants like that, where only the man's menu had the prices, but she'd never been to one.

"Would you like me to order for you?" Lionel asked.

"No, I can handle it," she answered.

They placed their orders: She had the wild mushroom tart as her appetizer, and the crisped Muscovy duck breast as an entrée; he ordered a mosaic of yellowfin and Hamachi tuna to start, followed by rack of Australian lamb.

"And would the gentleman like to look at our wine list?" the waiter asked.

To Tiara's disappointment, Lionel shook his head. Damn, it would have been nice to sip on some pricey wine. But it wasn't like she should complain. Their meal was probably going to cost about two hundred bucks without drinks.

Tiara took a good look around. Almost all of the male diners wore expensive suits, and she saw more than a few furs draped over the chairs of women wearing evening gowns. *How tacky. You'd think they'd check their coats, but no, they just want to show off the fact that they have furs,* she thought.

"So, how do you like this place?"

"Really, cool," Tiara didn't even bother to try and hide the fact that she was impressed. There wasn't that much playing it off in the world.

"I thought you'd like it," Lionel smiled.

"I do." Tiara took a sip from the crystal water glass. "I've always wanted to come here."

"Well, see," Lionel lifted his own glass in a mock salute. "Your wish is my command."

Tiara giggled and clinked her glass against his.

"Seriously, though," Lionel said after taking a long sip. "I do aim to please."

"So, do you take all your dates here?" Tiara teased.

"No, only the ones that I think would know how to act. You're not going to believe this, but I took one girl to see *The Producers* on Broadway, when Matthew Broderick and Nathan Lane were playing the lead; the tickets cost almost a thousand dollars, and you know after the show she wanted me to roll some white guy?"

"What?" Tiara started laughing. "Why?"

"Just because she thought it would be fun," Lionel shook his head in disgust.

"You've got to be kidding. Where did you find this chick?"

"Oh, you're really not going to believe this. It was a blind date. She was an ambassador's daughter or some shit, and her mother knows my mother and you know how that goes." Lionel took another sip of water and looked around for the waiter. "I guess I don't need to tell you I never took her anywhere again."

"I hear that."

"I really woulda been pissed if I had to pay for the tickets myself. But my mom gave them to me. She's always getting tickets and shit because of all her fundraising activities," Lionel grinned.

"Damn, it must be nice," Tiara sighed.

"Yeah, it is. Maybe I can convince you to come with me to see *Hairspray* next week."

"Depends on what day," Tiara said nonchalantly although her heart was racing. *Damn, that's the hottest show out right now. Like I care what day, shit, I'm there.*

"Next Friday?"

"Sounds good. I guess that means you think I know how to act." Tiara smiled.

"Yeah, you know how to act, you know how to dress. You just know, girl."

"Well, if you told me you were going to take me to a fancy restaurant I wouldn't have worn jeans." Tiara looked again at the other women in the dining room.

"Girl, you look fine," Lionel scoffed. "You look better in those jeans than half these women in here."

"Half?" Tiara teased.

"Better than all these women in here," Lionel corrected himself. "Believe me, with all these gorgeous women in here, there's no one here I would rather be with than you. You're my kind of lady."

"And what kind of lady is that?"

"You got brains, you got looks, you got a confident attitude, and you're doing something for yourself. Going to school and all."

"Yeah, but I know in your circle, there's a lot of girls in school and shit, and at least some of them have to be pretty," Tiara said suspiciously.

"Yeah, but I want someone with some street smarts, too," Lionel leaned back in his chair.

Tiara sucked her teeth. "Boy! What you know about street smarts?" She started giggling. "Your dad's a millionaire. You take girls out to Broadway shows. You're getting your degree from NYU, and you talking about you want a girl with street smarts. Give me a break."

"Oh, now you going to try and play me and make like I'm some rich kid who don't know what's going on?" Lionel actually seemed to be hurt. "Just because my family has some cash doesn't mean I ain't been around the block a few times, you know."

"Oh, you have, huh?"

"Yeah, me and my boys hang out in the Southeast, the toughest part of D.C.," Lionel said defensively.

"You and your boys, huh?"

"Yeah, me and my boys."

"Whatever," Tiara shrugged. It seemed pretty stupid to her, him wanting to play like he knew how to thug. *I mean it's not like he's a nerd, far from it. He's pretty cool, as a matter of fact.* She looked up as the waiter approached the table with their appetizers. *But if he wants to play like a thug from the projects, then I can play like the millionaire from D.C.* "Excuse me, waiter, we would like to see that wine list."

5

So where's that oldest daughter of yours? Out with the rich kid again?"

"Yeah, Charlene, she's out with the rich kid," Reggie said wearily. He lay the newspaper he had been reading down on the kitchen table, leaned his head back, stretched his arms out, and let out an expansive yawn. As good as Charlene's spaghetti sauce smelled, he was seriously considering going to bed without eating. Only he knew if he did Charlene would kill him. She took their Thursday "Family Nights" seriously. Which was why Reggie knew Charlene was about to start bitching about Tiara being out on a date.

"What's she known him . . . a week now? A week and a half?" Charlene riffled through a grocery bag on the counter, pulled out a bottle of olive oil, and slammed it down on the table hard enough to make the aluminum legs shake. She grabbed her glass of Johnny Walker Black off the counter and took a gulp before resuming her kitchen activities. Reggie let out a deep sigh, knowing his older sister was about to go on a tear. He watched her as she bustled around the tiny kitchen, opening and shutting cabinets in a fury. But then again

Charlene was always in a fury, or about to be in one—at least since the disfiguring car accident. She'd won a huge settlement from the driver's insurance company, but though it allowed her to buy a co-op in the Bronx, and ensured that she never had to work another day in her life, it didn't compensate for the loss of her looks. Even after more than a dozen surgeries, the nerve damage on the left side of her face couldn't be fully repaired. Anyone seeing her from just her right side would think she was still one of the most beautiful women in the city, with her golden complexion, long wavy auburn hair and green eyes. It was precisely because her right profile was so perfectly beautiful that her frontal view was all the more disturbing, when her drooping left eye and lips came into view. It wasn't that she looked grotesque, but it made people shake their heads that such a thing of beauty could be so marred.

"I mean, what does she know about him?" Charlene demanded as she tossed the spinach salad. "So, he told her that he gets his money from his family, but for all she knows he could be a drug dealer or something. I don't care how much money your family got, they ain't going to be buying some boy a car like that. You know how much that car cost?" She placed a loaf of frozen garlic bread in the oven. "One hundred and fifteen thousand dollars. I called the dealer and asked yesterday. You going to tell me his family bought him that car? I don't think so. I bet that boy's dealing drugs. Probably some big-time coke dealer."

"The boy ain't no drug dealer, Charlene. He's a student at NYU." Reggie rubbed his eyes. He really wasn't in the mood for all of this. He watched as his sister drained her drink and poured herself another. He still found it amazing that the woman could drink like a fish and never get drunk. She never even slurred her words.

"So, what you trying to say? That a coke dealer can't go to NYU? Please!"

"No, I'm just saying that I don't think we should be assuming that he's dealing," Reggie grimaced. "And what you calling the car dealer for? You just bought a brand-new Camry."

"Shit, Reg, pay attention. I'm not buying another damn car." Charlene sucked her teeth. "I called because I'm checking up on the boy. And I don't know why you ain't. Tiara's your daughter, not mine."

"'Cause I talked to the boy—and his name is Lionel, by the way— and he sounds legit to me. And I trust my judgment, and my daughter's judgment." Reggie got up from the table and moved toward the living room, which was adjacent to the kitchen. "Damn, you can try a man's patience, Charlene. Just leave it alone, okay?"

"Uh huh, go ahead and tell me to leave it alone now. You weren't saying that shit when Sharon left you with two kids on your hands and you ain't even know how to change a fucking diaper." Charlene swished her drink, her hand on her hip. "But now it's leave it alone, huh? Yeah, okay. You got that." She took another sip of her drink. "I guess you want me to just go on home, huh? No problem. It's not like I got to be up here cooking for you and the kids every week. I just do it as a family kind of thing, because we supposed to be family and shit. But I guess I don't count as family no more since the kids can take care of themselves, huh?" She sniffed and wiped a tear from the corner of her eye, then brushed by her brother and into the living room, her drink still in hand. "So, cool. I'm outtie. Call me the next time you need me. Maybe when you need someone to change your grandkids' diapers or something."

Reggie sighed and shook his head. He was used to Charlene's drama; it was played out at least once a month. He walked over to her and took her coat from her. "Come on, Charlene, you know I don't want you to leave," he said soothingly. "I'm just tired from doing all this overtime and everything. I'm sorry if I hurt your feelings."

"I know you're tired, and that's why I'm here," Charlene whined. "I'm trying to make things easy for you and everything."

"I know, Sis." Reggie hugged her. "I don't know what I would do without you."

"Well, I'm always here for you," Charlene said softly as she buried her head in his shoulder.

"And you know I'm always here for you," Reggie said. "We're family."

"That's right." Charlene pulled away and looked at her brother. "That's the only reason I'm worrying about Tiara. I know you don't think she and I get along, and I know we do argue sometimes, but I do care about that girl. And I don't want her to get caught up in some shit she can't handle."

"I know, Sis." Reggie pulled away slightly. "But you don't have to worry. I'm monitoring the situation."

"No, you're not. You're more crazy about that boy than she is. I hear you telling everyone about your daughter going out with a millionaire's kid."

"So, I'm proud, I admit it," Reggie shrugged. "It's better than her going out with these knuckleheads out here in the projects."

"Ain't everybody coming out of these projects a knucklehead, you know. You came outta here." Charlene rolled her eyes and headed back to the kitchen. "And I ain't even saying she should hook up with someone from around here. I liked that cabbie guy."

"What cabbie guy?" Reggie asked as he trailed behind her.

"That Ahmad guy. Or Muhammad guy. Whatever his name was."

"Rashad, Aunt Charlie." Jo-Jo walked into the kitchen, peeling a hooded sweatshirt off over her head. She threw the hoodie on one of the kitchen chairs, and started scratching under her arm.

"Girl, go get washed up." Aunt Charlie grinned at her young niece. "You coming in here stinking like a man and scratching under your arm. And get that funky sweatshirt outta this kitchen, too."

"How was practice, Sport?" Reggie asked as Jo-Jo stood on her tiptoes to plant a kiss on his cheek.

"It was cool. Coach made us run thirty laps around the gym because we kept messing up our drills," Jo-Jo said nonchalantly. "Hey, Aunt Charlie, we playing Monopoly tonight?"

"You can count me out. I'm too tired," Reggie said.

Charlene made a face. "Your daddy's too tired, and your sister's running the street, so let's just pass tonight. It's just not as much fun when there's only two people playing."

"Cool. I'll just do some studying after dinner, then."

Reggie gave a low grunt. He knew Jo-Jo hadn't wanted to play Monopoly. She complained just as much as Tiara about Charlene forcing them into their family nights, playing Monopoly or charades or Trivial Pursuit every Thursday. The girl probably only brought it up to rub it in that Tiara wasn't around. As close as the sisters were, they couldn't help trying to get each other in trouble from time to time, just for the hell of it.

"Now, see, at least one of your daughters has her head on straight. You watch. Jo-Jo's going to get a full basketball scholarship to some fancy school." Charlene smiled as Jo-Jo left the kitchen, then turned and saw the sweatshirt still on the chair. "Girl, get back in here and get your stank clothes and put them in the dirty clothes hamper!" she yelled.

"Sorry, Aunt Charlie." Jo-Jo scooped up the hoodie, then walked back out whistling.

"Yeah, she's going to be okay," Reggie said in almost a whisper as he watched Jo-Jo disappear into the bathroom. She was going to be something—athletic as all hell, and just as smart as her sister. He was raising some good kids, he thought proudly.

"Yeah, it's Tiara you have to worry about. You got her all souped up thinking she's the shit and too good for everybody," Charlene chuckled then took a sip of her drink. "She's sure crazy for that Rashad guy, though."

"What are you talking about?" Reggie said irritably. Here she goes again, he thought.

"Oh, please. Up until she started going out with that rich kid, the first thing she did when she came into the house is ask if he called."

"I don't remember any of that."

"Because you don't want to remember. But that girl ran for the telephone every single time it rang. And then if anyone was on the phone for more than five minutes she was all up in their mouth talking about they better click over if someone else was trying to call." Charlene laughed.

"Yeah, she was, Daddy," Jo-Jo chimed in. "Got all on my nerves with that stuff."

"I thought you were taking a shower," Reggie said gruffly.

"I am. I'm waiting for the water to get hot."

"Go wait in the bathroom, then."

"Hurry up, 'cause I'm getting ready to serve dinner," Charlene said. "Anyway," she said turning back to her brother. "Your daughter's got the hots for that Rashad guy."

"Who?"

"Very funny. The cab driver."

"You're the one being very funny," Reggie retorted. "Tiara ain't interested in no cab driver. She's in college. What does she want with some cab driver? If he had anything going for him he wouldn't be driving a cab."

"Damn, Reggie. Just because he doesn't have a lot of money doesn't mean he ain't no good. And driving a cab is an honest living. And he seems like a nice guy."

"Charlene, you didn't say but two words to the guy when he was here. How do you even know he's a nice guy?"

"Because," Charlene said as she spooned sauce over the three plates of spaghetti she had already placed on the table, "I'm a good judge of character."

"Why are we even talking about this?" Reggie said in an exasperated voice. "If she did like him, she doesn't anymore. She's dating Lionel, she likes him, I like him, and they seem happy. What say we drop the subject and let's eat. Jo-Jo! Just wash under your arms and wash your hands and come on in here and get your grub on."

"You know what your problem is, Reggie Bynum?"

"No. What is my problem, Charlene Bynum?" Reggie lay on the couch, his eyes closed, half listening to the Knicks game Jo-Jo was blasting on the television in the girls' room, and half dozing off. Usually he offered to help Charlene clean up in the kitchen, but as much as he loved her, tonight he really didn't feel like hearing her mouth off anymore. Now that she was finished, though, she was standing over him, ready to start in on him again.

"Your problem is that you're a wimp."

"Oh, really?" Reggie yawned.

"Not when it comes to men. You can fight your ass off and everyone knows it, and you don't take any shit from a man. But when it comes to women, you're a pure wimp."

"Is that right?" Reggie said indifferently.

"Hmm . . . let me rethink that."

"Please do." Reggie smiled in spite of himself.

"Okay, when it comes to your women folks you're a wimp, 'cause God knows you treat all them women chasing you like shit."

Reggie sucked his teeth. "Charlene, please!" This was too much even for him. He went out of his way to treat every woman he'd ever been involved with like a lady, and Charlene knew it.

"Well, you don't give them the time of day."

"That doesn't mean I treat them like shit."

"Whatever," Charlene shrugged. "The point is, when it comes to the women you love, you're a pure wimp."

"If you say so," Reggie said irritably.

"Look at how you treated Mama. Anytime she said she wanted anything, even before she said it, you were right there with it."

"Oh, so because I tried to make my mother happy I'm a wimp, huh? That's a new one on me."

"You know what I mean."

"No, I don't, Charlene. And I swear you're getting on my nerves." Reggie sat up and looked at his watch. Ten o'clock, and he had to be up at 5:00 A.M. for work. "Come on, let me walk you to your car."

"I'm not ready to leave yet, and don't try to change the subject," Charlene snapped. "You treated Mama like she was your woman or something. There's being a good son, and then there's acting like you were responsible for her every little comfort."

"Damn, Charlene. The woman had a hard life. After our no-good father fucked her over like that she deserved for some man to treat her like the queen she was. She busted her ass day and night to make a good home for us, the least I could do when I got older was to show her that she was appreciated."

"Oh, so you think you treating her good was supposed to make up for him treating her like shit?"

"Well, yeah in a way."

"It doesn't work like that."

"Okay, if you say so." Reggie shrugged. What the hell was wrong with Charlene tonight, he wondered. And when the hell was she planning on going home?

"And look at your relationship with that wife of yours."

"Charlene, don't start your—"

"I'm not going to talk about the tramp, okay?" Charlene cut him off. "I'm just saying that you treated her way better than she deserved. You ain't had no business even marrying her. Everyone knew she only got pregnant just to trap you because you were making all that money on the gambling circuit. And like an idiot you walked right into the trap."

"I didn't marry her because I was trapped, I married her because I loved her," Reggie snapped.

"Yeah, and she loved you, too, huh? That's why she left your ass when you decided to get off the circuit and get legit."

Reggie frowned but said nothing. She was right, of course. He had only wanted to do the right thing by getting a job with the city. The year he spent in jail had been a wake-up call. He was making big money on the circuit, traveling city to city playing poker, and they were able to save a hefty sum in the bank, while at the same time living the good life—fancy clothes, expensive jewelry, and going out on the town—but it wasn't worth risking him being sent up the river for some real time. What kind of man would he be to leave his wife and children to fend for themselves while he was in prison? He had tried to explain that to Sharon, and she said she understood. But just a few months after Jo-Jo was born he came home from his sanitation job one evening and found seven-year-old Tiara trying to heat a bottle of formula for her baby sister, who was crying bloody murder because of her soaking wet Pampers. When Reggie asked Tiara where her mother was, the little girl said Sharon had told her to take care of Jo-Jo while she went to the store, but she never came back. Reggie was frantic as evening turned into night, and then into day, and there was still no sign of Sharon. He called in sick, and then reluctantly called Charlene, who rushed over to watch the children while he combed the city looking for his wife. It was when he called home that afternoon to see if Charlene had heard from Sharon that he found out the truth. Charlene told him that a woman who lived down the hall had knocked on the door to tell Reggie that everyone was talking about Sharon leaving Reggie for a coke dealer in the Johnson Projects. Charlene advised him to head straight to the bank and withdraw everything before Sharon did, but it was too late. Their joint account that had once held $65,000 suddenly held only $150.

"See, it's like Mama used to say. How you start is how you better end. You started out showering Sharon with all those gifts and shit, and then when you couldn't afford it anymore she left your ass," Charlene said now. "You never should have spoiled her like that. You'd better believe none of the other men she had treated her like that."

She walked over to the hallway closet and to Reggie's relief started putting on her coat. He jumped up and grabbed his jacket and his keys before she could change her mind.

"But you know? I just got it figured out," Charlene said thoughtfully as they headed out the door. "Like you just said, you treated Mama real good to make up for Daddy leaving her. So now, I'm thinking you treated Sharon like that to prove—to God knows who—how a man is supposed to treat his wife. And that's why you spoil your kids too. To prove how a good father is supposed to act. It's like you spoil every woman in your life because Daddy left us."

Reggie nodded, but he wasn't really listening.

6

So when are you going to finally stay the night with me, Sweet Pea? I'm crazy about you, but I'm getting kind of tired of taking a quick nap after we take care of business, then having to get up in the middle of the night to take you home."

Tiara reached over and stroked Lionel's knee as he drove her home from school. "Yeah, I feel the same way," she said softly.

"So then why don't you pack some clothes the next time we go out so you can just go to school from my place the next morning?" Lionel looked straight ahead as he spoke, but Tiara could see his jaw tighten as he awaited her answer. She sighed. They'd been seeing each other a month now, and been sleeping with each other for the past two weeks, and the sex was damn good. And she even thought she was falling in love with him. She was sure he must be in love with her with all the stuff he was buying her. The tennis bracelet he gave her just a few days before had to cost a cool grand, and the diamond pendant he'd given her the night before that probably cost even more. He had never given her any cash, but she was sure if she asked he wouldn't have a problem with it. And to make it more perfect, her father adored him and, God knows, he didn't like most of the guys she dated. No one was ever good enough for his little girl. Yeah, Lionel was a real catch. The only thing they ever argued about was the fact that she wouldn't spend the night with him.

"Lionel, I told you, Daddy would have a fit if I spent a whole night out."

"You act like he thinks you're a virgin or something, girl." Lionel grunted. "Come on, you're eighteen, he knows you're giving it up."

"That doesn't matter. He still wouldn't want me staying out overnight," Tiara said, a little irritation creeping into her voice. She didn't bother telling him that Reggie probably did think she was a virgin.

"How do you know unless you try?"

"Because I know my Daddy," Tiara huffed. "Why you gotta keep sweating me on this?"

"Girl, please, I know you're not getting an attitude with me about this." Lionel stopped for a red light. "You act like I'm asking for something unreasonable. I'm a grown man, and you're a grown-ass woman, and we can't even sleep together overnight because you're afraid of upsetting Daddy. You'd better grow the hell up."

"Yeah, all right, I'll show you just how fucking grown I am." Tiara threw open the car door and jumped out.

"Tiara, get your ass back in this car," Lionel yelled as she started walking away.

Tiara flipped her hair and kept going. It was only six blocks to her building, but if she knew Lionel, she wouldn't be walking it anyway.

Just as she anticipated, Lionel pulled his car over and trotted up to her.

"Tiara, come on, get back in the car." He gave her arm a light tug.

"No!" She jerked away.

"Tiara, come on now. Quit playing."

"Playing? Boy, do I look like I'm playing with you?" She whirled around to face him. "You insult me and my father and you think I'm going to get back in your car so you can do it again? I don't think so."

"How did I insult your father?"

"By not respecting the fact that he doesn't want his daughter spending the night out with some man," Tiara snapped.

"Tiara, I'm not *some* man. I'm supposed to be *your* man."

My man. Oooh, that sounds good, Tiara said to herself. *Yeah, I got it like that.* It took all of her willpower not to break into a large grin. Instead, she fixed her mouth into a pout. "Yeah, I know you're my man, and I understand where you're coming from, but damn, all I'm saying is give it a little bit more time, Lionel. I just need to work on Daddy a little."

"Yeah, all right, I hear you." Lionel gave her arm another short tug. "Now come on and get back in the car. You got people out here looking at us like we're a couple of nuts or something."

"Okay, I'm sorry," Tiara gave a quick smile as she allowed him to lead her back to the car. She was secretly hoping someone had seen this fine man trying to cajole her back into his fine Porsche Turbo. *'Cause I got it like that.*

"You know what?" Lionel sat behind the wheel, but he hadn't turned the key in the ignition.

"What?"

"You are really high maintenance." Lionel shook his head and sighed.

Words from one of the old songs her aunt played at the apartment suddenly popped into Tiara's head. "Well, you know," she said, "I'm a helluva woman, for me it takes a helluva man."

"And I'm the man for the job." Lionel chuckled as he pulled off. "But you know, I just want you to know I'd really be pissed if you pulled that little stunt, jumping out the car and shit, if I was with my boys."

Tiara snorted. "Well, it wasn't a stunt. You pissed me off and I reacted."

"Yeah, I wish you'd control your reactions. I'm not kidding. I don't mind when we're alone, but don't play around like that when we're in front of people."

"Oh, Lionel, please!" Tiara rolled her eyes. "Why should you care what people think anyway?"

"I don't want my boys to think I'm pussy-whipped or anything." Lionel was scowling.

"Well, it's not like we're really around your friends anyway. I keep hearing about your boys, but I ain't met none of them." Tiara shrugged her shoulders. And if he thought he was going to control her actions, he was crazy. She was her own woman. *Hmmph! If he doesn't like the way I act when I'm pissed off, he'd better work harder not to piss me off.*

"Okay, babe," he leaned over and kissed her when he pulled up in front of her building. "I'll call you later, okay?"

"Okay."

"And I love you."

"I love you, too."

She grinned when she got out of the car and saw Shakira hanging out on the stoop looking jealous as shit as Lionel peeled off.

"What's up, girl? Too good to hang out with your friends these days?" Shakira asked a little too casually.

"You know how it is," Tiara said just as casually. She leaned against the railing across from the girl. "What you been up to?"

"Nothing as good as what you been up to." Shakira squinted her eyes as she peered at Tiara's wrist. "Is that a new chain?"

Tiara shook her wrist, allowing the bracelet to fall into full view. "Chain, shit. My man bought me a tennis bracelet, girl."

"Damn! That is nice," Shakira gaped. "Let me borrow it tonight?"

"Girl, don't even trip." Tiara laughed. "I ain't letting your broke ass borrow my shit. How you going to pay me if you lose it or something?"

Shakira snorted. "Whatever, Tiara. I was only joking anyway."

"Yeah, well whatever." Tiara rolled her eyes. "Bad joke."

"Aw, to hell with you. I could get my man to buy me one if I wanted, but I don't need to be flashing jewelry and showing off, trying to make people jealous."

"I ain't trying to make anyone jealous. Why? You jealous?"

"Did I say I was?"

"It's not what you be saying, it's how you be saying it."

Shakira sucked her teeth. "Forget it, Tiara. I ain't trying to be messing with you. You my girl even if you are fucked up as shit."

"Whatever."

Shakira leaned back on the railing again, popping her chewing gum. She was silent for a moment, but Tiara could see there was something up.

"So, Alice tell you she been going out with that cab driver you liked?"

Tiara's mouth flew open before she could catch herself. "What?"

"Oh, I thought you knew. I saw them the other day getting in his car." Shakira said nonchalantly. "Actually not the other day. The other night. It had to be about eleven or so. Might of been like last week or something."

"Get outta here. Well, good for her," Tiara said quickly. "It's about time Alice got herself some. I'm just surprised 'cause she ain't mentioned it to me. But then again she did call me a couple of times last week and I just ain't had time to call her back to see what she wants."

"Oh, yeah right," Shakira nodded her head sarcastically. "She's been trying to call you."

"Girl, what you think I'm lying or something?" Tiara snapped.

"Hey, I ain't saying nothing." Shakira gave an exaggerated shrug. "She just oughtta been calling you seeing that she knows you like him and shit."

"I ain't ever said I like that boy." Tiara glared at Shakira.

"Like you said, it's not what you say, it's how you say it." Shakira smirked. "And anyway, I was right there when you was trying to push up on him and he was dissing your fast ass."

"Oh, shut up, I was not," Tiara made a face. "And why would I want some stupid cab driver when I already got a man?"

"You ain't had one back then."

"Shakira, whatever, I didn't want him then, and I don't want him now."

"Then why you getting all upset and shit?"

"Shakira, I'm telling you, you're working my nerves." *This fucking girl is probably making it all up to piss me off 'cause she's jealous 'cause I'm with Lionel.*

Shakira shrugged her shoulders. "I ain't studying you or your nerves. I was just trying to be a friend and telling you your girl's stepping out with a guy you like. But you say she's blowing up your phone like she wants to tell you anyway, so I ain't got nothing else to say."

Tiara turned to stomp into the building, but whirled back around. "You trying to say there's more to say?"

"Why you asking me?" Shakira rolled her eyes. "Why don't you just ask Alice since you say she's been trying to call you and shit."

"Ask me what?" Both girls turned around to find Alice standing there, an eager smile on her face.

"How you doing, Tiara?" Alice dropped the book bag that had been slung over her shoulder onto the ground and grabbed Tiara in a great big bear hug. "Girl, I been trying to call you for weeks!"

Tiara gave Shakira an "I told you so" look over Alice's shoulder, before extricating herself from the girl's massive arms. "I've been okay, Alice. What you been up to?"

"Nothing, nothing, I've just been worrying about you!"

"Worrying about me, why?"

"Well, Rashad told me you had twisted your ankle, and I just wanted to make sure you were okay."

Tiara's eyebrow shot up. So Shakira wasn't joking to piss her off after all. She glanced at the girl, and saw it was Shakira's turn to gloat.

"Yeah, I heard you and the brother got something going on." Tiara tried to keep her voice as nonchalant as possible.

"Me and what brother?"

"Rashad," Tiara said impatiently.

"What?" Alice said incredulously. "I'm not messing with Rashad! What gave you that idea?"

"Well, I saw you getting in his cab last week, and you was all giggly and shit." Shakira stepped in front of Alice. "So you can't tell me ain't nothing going on."

Alice gave Shakira a look of contempt. "First of all, it was like three weeks ago. Second, I wasn't talking to you. And I don't know why you think you can speak to me in that tone of voice." She sidestepped Shakira and addressed Tiara. "Please don't tell me you're going to take anything she said seriously."

Tiara shrugged. "I was just going by what I was told, but you now telling me something else, so cool. You ain't messing with Rashad, it don't matter to me anyway. I was just commenting."

"Oh, yeah, yeah, I mean I know you probably don't care, or anything, I just didn't want you to get the wrong impression," Alice stammered.

"So, just outta curiosity, why were you getting in his cab the other night?" Tiara asked.

"He came over to my house because he found my driver's license in the back seat of his cab. He couldn't call because he didn't have the telephone number, but my address was on the license," Alice explained quickly. "I didn't even know my license was missing. It must have fallen out when I was getting the money out to pay him."

"So why were you getting in his cab, then?" Tiara asked suspiciously. "He had to take you to the license or something?"

"No, no . . . he came over to my place just as I was walking out to grab a bus to the Schomburg Center on 135th Street to do some research for a paper for my African-American Literature class. When he asked me where I was headed and I told him, he said he'd give me a ride since he was heading uptown."

"Oh, you were going to do research on your paper at midnight, huh?" Tiara shot Shakira a knowing look. "Yeah, all right, tell me anything."

"Midnight? What do you mean? It wasn't midnight." Alice's head jerked back in surprise. "It was the middle of the afternoon. Like maybe two or three."

Tiara glanced over at Shakira who pointedly looked the other way.

"Oh, well, sorry. I got some bad information from a very bad source." Tiara shrugged her shoulder. "It figures."

Alice turned around to face Shakira. "I don't know why you're trying to make trouble between Tiara and me, but I sure don't appreciate it." She placed her hands on her hips and glared at the girl.

"Oh, shut up, you old fat slob," Shakira jeered.

Alice's face reddened. "I'd rather be heavyset than be as skinny as a crackhead like you."

"Shit . . . I wouldn't call five hundred pounds heavyset. I would call it Dumbo-size."

"I'm not five hundred pounds," Alice said between clenched teeth.

"Oh, have you gained more weight since you broke the scale at Coney Island?" Shakira giggled at her own joke.

Alice's face changed from red to purple, and her breath was coming in short pants. It looked like she was about to take a swing at Shakira. *Good, I hope she kicks that bitch's ass,* Tiara thought. *But, naw, for all her shit, Shakira can duke, and I don't want to take the chance that she beats the crap outta poor Alice. Let me break this shit up.*

"Alice, don't even worry about this chick." Tiara reluctantly tugged on Alice's arm. "Come on, girl."

"Why, you taking her side?" Shakira jerked her back in surprise. "You supposed to be my girl, and you siding with Dumbo over me?"

"Shakira, I'll talk to you later, I gotta go." Tiara tugged on Alice's arm again. "Come on, pick up your bag and walk me upstairs, Alice. I want to talk to you."

"Be like that, then," Shakira called after them.

Alice was still puffing as she followed Tiara into her first-floor apartment. Tiara threw her school bag on the couch, as Alice eased into the armchair. "You want a soda? We got Wild Cherry Pepsi and Sprite," she said as she walked into the kitchen.

"No, I don't want anything."

Tiara walked back into the living room and plopped down on the couch next to the school bag. "So, anyway, you said Rashad told you about me twisting my ankle?"

"Yeah." Alice nodded her head, but she was still puffing in anger.

"So what else did he say?"

"Nothing."

Tiara propped her legs on the coffee table and looked at the girl. Here she was trying to get some important information, and Alice was still dwelling on a fight that didn't happen. Maybe she should have let Shakira kick her ass.

"Well, did he ask about me or anything?" she tried again.

"No. I mean, yeah," Alice huffed. "I mean, I really don't remember right now."

"Look, let that shit with Shakira go, Alice. It's over, okay?" Tiara sucked her teeth. "So, now focus for a minute. What did Rashad say about me?"

Alice leaned back in the chair, swiping her hand over her perspiring forehead. "I'm sorry. All he did was ask how you were doing, and wanted to know if your ankle had healed."

"What did you tell him?" Tiara demanded.

"I told him I hadn't seen you in a few days, but that the last time I saw you you seemed okay."

"So what did he say to that?"

"That was it." Alice shrugged her shoulders.

"What do you mean, that was it? He didn't ask for my telephone or anything?" *Damn him.*

"Well, no, but, um," Alice hesitated. "Well, he did kind of seem happy when I said you were doing okay," she offered.

Oh, great, now Alice thinks I like him because I'm asking all these questions. Tiara inwardly groaned. *Why am I doing this crap? Why should I care whether he asked about me or not? I gotta stop tripping like this.*

She stood up and stretched expansively. "Look, I'm going to take a nap before Jo-Jo comes in or my aunt stops by. I'll talk to you later."

"Okay," Alice said reluctantly. She slowly lifted herself out of the chair. "I gotta go finish my paper anyway. It's due tomorrow."

"All right, see you later." Tiara held the front door open and Alice obediently walked out. "Hey, wait a minute," Tiara called out when Alice was halfway down the hall. "What's Rashad's last name? Do you know?"

"You know what, I do!" Alice said excitedly. "He knew my last name is Garrison, because of my driver's license, you know? And he mentioned that his last name was Harrison."

"Oh, cool. So, um, did he mention anything else about himself? Like where he lived or anything?" Tiara hated herself for asking.

"No." Alice sighed, as if she knew she had outlasted her usefulness.

Should I, or shouldn't I? Tiara debated after she returned to the sofa. She picked up the remote from the coffee table and clicked on the television. It was CBS, which meant that Aunt Charlie had been there earlier watching her soaps. Why couldn't the woman stay in her own house? Tiara switched the station to BET. The latest Nelly video was just coming on. *I bet the only reason he actually came down to the projects to give Alice that license back was because he had hoped to run into me. I mean, otherwise he could have just dropped it in the mail. And why did he make it a point to tell Alice his name? He wanted her to mention it to me because he was embarrassed to ask her for my telephone number and he didn't want to just pop in here without calling. I know he told her his name because he wanted her to mention it to me. So should I, or shouldn't I?* She went to the hallway closet and pulled the Manhattan white pages from the shelf, then placed it unopened on the coffee table. *I don't even know why I should be debating. If he's too stupid to figure out a way to get in touch with me, then he ain't even worth me worrying about.* She tapped her fingers on her knees as she stared at the telephone book, then finally sighed and opened it to the H's. There were ten Rashad Harrisons listed in the Manhattan telephone directory. Two of the numbers were disconnected. She reached an answering machine on four others, and none of the taped voices sounded like Rashad. A woman answered the seventh number, and Tiara hung up without asking for anyone. A man's voice answered the eighth number. It was undoubtedly Rashad's.

"Peace."

Tiara gripped the telephone receiver tightly trying to figure out what to say.

"Peace," Rashad said again.

"Hi, Rashad, this is Tiara. How are you doing?" Tiara said breathlessly.

"Hey, little sis! I'm doing fine, how are you?"

Rashad's voice was pleasant, and he seemed happy to hear from her. That was a relief. She had half expected him to pretend he didn't remember who she was.

"I'm doing fine," Tiara smiled into the receiver. "I was just calling to see how you were. Alice told me you were up my way the other day."

"Yeah, I had to return her license."

"Yeah, she told me."

There was a short silence as Tiara tried to figure out what to say next. It would sure help if he would hurry up and ask if he could see her, but he was just not cooperating.

"So, like, how's it been going?" she asked awkwardly.

"It's been going fine," Rashad said slowly. "Listen, how did you get my telephone number?"

"Um, I looked it up." Tiara squeezed her eyes shut. Damn, she hated admitting that.

"Oh, okay," Rashad said simply.

Another silence.

"Well, listen, I've gotta go. I just wanted to give you a holler."

"Okay, peace," Rashad's voice turned pleasant again. "You take care of yourself, little sis. Tell your father and your aunt I said hello."

Tiara hung up. *Damn. Could that have gone any worse?* She was never going to talk to him again, she decided. If he wanted to play hard to get, fine. She didn't need him. She didn't want him. In fact, she was beginning to really dislike him. She picked up the telephone and redialed his number.

"Peace."

"Hey, Rashad, I just wanted you to have my telephone number in case you needed it for some reason," Tiara said quickly. "You know, in case something comes up and you need to get in touch with me."

"Something like what?"

"Something like whatever," Tiara said impatiently.

"Okay, hold on . . . let me get a pen. Okay, what's the number?"

"Two-one-two, five-five-five, one-oh-three-four."

"Okay, thanks."

Damn, why did I do that? He must be laughing his ass off at the way I just played myself. Tiara sighed, closed her eyes, and lay across the couch.

Riiiing.

Tiara didn't bother to sit up or open her eyes as she reached for the receiver and brought it to her ear. "Hello," she said tiredly.

"Peace. Tiara?"

Tiara's eyes flew open at the sound of Rashad's voice.

"Yes. Hi. It's me," she said quickly.

"Listen, there's this play tonight. I know it's short notice, but if you're not busy would you like to go?"

"Sure."

"Okay, how about I pick you up around six-thirty tonight, then."

"Sure."

"Okay, see you then."

Yeah, Tiara thought happily as she lay back across the couch and drifted off to sleep. *I got it like that.*

7

What to wear, what to wear, Tiara worried as she ruffled through the bedroom closet crammed with clothes. He hadn't said what kind of play, but since it was Rashad it was probably going to be some kind of Afrocentric something or other, or maybe some kind of show about world peace, or overthrowing the government. He looked the type to like shit like that. A real anarchist. He probably lived in a commune or something.

She finally decided on a mid-calf brown suede skirt and cream-colored turtleneck. Good, that was settled. Now she had to go about thinking what excuse she was going to give Lionel. Not that they had made any concrete plans, but he often called around seven to ask if she wanted to go out to dinner. Sometimes they'd catch a show, or a concert, but usually they would simply go to a nice restaurant in the Village, walk around for a bit looking at the sights if it wasn't too cold, then head to his huge apartment on Varick Street. They would listen to music, drink a glass of wine or two, and then get busy.

She wasn't exactly cheating on him, because it wasn't like she wanted a relationship with Rashad, or to go to bed with him or anything. She just wanted to hang out with him and get to know him a little better. Shit. She just wanted to go out with him this one time so she could get him out of her system.

But, oh man, Rashad. He had this thing . . . this calmness, and this confidence that had nothing to do with arrogance. Like the world wasn't his to conquer, but for him to enhance. It was such a wonderful thing. Like he had nothing to prove to anyone. It's what made people think they had to prove themselves to him. *People like me.* Tiara shocked herself with the thought.

It was so weird that he stayed on her mind so much, even now that she had a great guy like Lionel.

"Okay, who's home?" a loud voice trumpeted through the apartment.

Damn. Just because Aunt Charlie has keys to the apartment shouldn't mean that she could come in and out as she pleased without knocking, Tiara shrugged. *Shoot, if she did knock I wouldn't let her in.*

"Tiara? Jo-Jo?" Charlene's voice got louder as she approached the girls' bedroom. Tiara rushed over to lock the door, but she was too slow, and her aunt was already pushing the door open.

"Girl, you can't answer when someone calls out to you?" Charlene walked in and strode to the middle of the floor looking around.

"I was about to answer you when you came busting through my door," Tiara answered sullenly. "You don't know how to knock when a door's closed?"

"I called out and you didn't answer, so I didn't know you were home." Charlene walked over to Jo-Jo's side of the room and started folding clothes strewn on the bed. "And watch your tone, little girl. Don't make me slap the shit out of you."

Yeah. Right. Like I'm going to just sit here and get slapped. Like I couldn't give your ugly ass a beat down. Tiara scowled, but wisely kept her thoughts to herself. Whatever Charlene might be, she wasn't to be taken lightly. *Look at her cleaning up after Jo-Jo like we're babies or something. Damn, I wish she would get a man and have a couple of kids so she could aggravate the hell out of someone else for a change and leave us alone.*

"I don't know why you always have to be so damn hostile all the time, anyway," Charlene said as bustled around the room, putting clothes in the bureau and hanging others in the closet. "You act like you think I'm going to come in here and go through your stuff or something."

"It isn't like you haven't done it before," Tiara said grimly.

"That was ten years ago." Charlene sucked her teeth. "And you shouldn't have left your diary out for everyone to see if you didn't want anyone to read it."

"It was under my pillow, Aunt Charlie."

"Well, if you had made your bed I wouldn't have found it, now would I?"

"That didn't mean you had to read it."

"Oh, girl, please. Like I cared that you were kissing some little stupid boy at some little stupid party." Charlene chuckled. "And it taught you a lesson. Now you make your bed every morning before you leave the house, don't you?"

"Aunt Charlie, do you mind? I have to make a telephone call." Tiara sat on her bed, her arms folded, tapping her foot.

"I don't mind at all, go right ahead."

"Aunt Charlie!"

"I'm leaving. I'm leaving. Just let me gather up this dirty laundry." Charlene started stuffing things in a pillow case. "I'll be finished in just a minute."

Tiara sighed but said nothing. She could use the time to think of an excuse to offer Lionel anyway. Maybe she shouldn't even make the call. Maybe that would seem suspicious. It might be that Lionel didn't even call. And if he did, she could just tell Jo-Jo to tell him that she was visiting a friend or something. Yeah, that might be the way to go.

KAREN E. QUINONES MILLER

"That's a nice skirt." Charlene pointed to the brown suede that lay on Tiara's bed. "Where did you get it?"

Tiara smiled in spite of herself. "That's funny. I was going to ask you the same thing. You bought it for me a couple of years ago for my birthday."

"Oh yeah, that's right. Lord and Taylor's. You got to admit your Aunt Charlie got good taste, doesn't she?"

"Yeah, you know how to pick out some clothes," Tiara admitted. It was true. Aunt Charlie could dress her ass off, and as tight as her body was for a woman of forty-something, she never wore clothes inappropriate for her age, like so many older woman did. Aunt Charlie dressed with class. Not stuffy like a lawyer or anything, but like a CEO. Nice dresses and skirts that hung just right on her. And she could accessorize better than anyone Tiara knew.

"Hey, Aunt Charlie . . . what kind of jewelry would you wear with this outfit?" Tiara held up the turtleneck she was planning on wearing with the skirt.

"Hmm . . . depends. Where are you going?"

"To a play."

"A play? You sure you don't wear something a little flashier than that?"

"Naw, I'm going for the conservative look."

"Well, that is really understated for a Broadway play. But I would just wear a simple gold chain, maybe with a small pendant, and half-shell gold earrings." Aunt Charlie said thoughtfully. "Or . . . hmm."

"What?"

"Well, you could even do a whole other look if you want. You could wear a thick cowrie shell necklace and nice cowrie earrings in a gold setting."

"Ooh, that would work!" Tiara said excitedly.

"What kind of shoes are you wearing?"

"My brown leather boots with the square heel."

86

"Okay. You know what I would do? I'd wear a nice cowrie anklet."

"An anklet with boots?" Tiara was skeptical.

"Yep. It would look different, but not wrong. Just wear it with confidence. You know how to do that. You're a Bynum woman." Charlene grinned. "You'd be making a fashion statement."

"Yeah, that would work." Tiara nodded her head. "Real Afrocentric, too."

"Afrocentricity with class."

"Works for me!"

"Well, then," Charlene tossed her head proudly, "my work here is done."

"Thanks, Aunt Charlie."

"No problem. You got any laundry you need done?"

"No, I'm okay."

"All right. I'm out of here then. Tell Jo-Jo I'll drop off her clothes this evening." Charlene headed out the door, dragging the bulging pillowcase behind her.

"Aunt Charlie?"

"Yes?"

"Umm, do you have a cowrie shell necklace, earrings, and anklet?"

"Of course," Charlene grinned. "I'll bring them by when I drop off Jo-Jo's laundry. I'll be back around seven."

"Umm, could you make it a little earlier? Say around six?"

Charlene frowned. "That early? Well, yeah, I guess so. I was going to stop by the—"

Riiing

"Hold on a sec." Tiara reached for the telephone on the nightstand near her bed. "Hello?"

"Hey, Sweet Pea. What's my baby doing tonight?"

Tiara grimaced at the sound of Lionel's voice, but answered with a smooth, "Hey, baby."

Dang, she still hadn't fully thought out her excuse. Now what was she going to say again? Oh yeah, visiting a friend. But what friend? She could say she was going over to Alice's house. Yeah.

"Guess what?" Lionel's voice was excited.

"What?"

"My father's in town. He wants to take us out to dinner. I'll pick you up around seven, okay?"

"Oh, shoot. Um, no, I can't make it tonight," Tiara stammered.

"What? Why not?"

"Um, I promised Daddy I was going to hang with the family tonight." Tiara said quickly, forgetting about her half-prepared lie.

"Oh, Tiara, come on! Just tell him that my father's in town. He'll understand!"

"Well . . . I mean . . . he was really looking forward to us spending some time together, and I think he would be real upset if I canceled at the last minute like this. Because, you know, I've been spending so much time with you lately."

"Tiara, my father's only going to be in town for one day. Explain to your dad this is important," Lionel insisted.

"WILL YOU HURRY UP!" Charlene shouted.

Tiara jumped. She'd forgotten her aunt was still in the room. She turned around with a questioning look, wondering what was wrong with Charlene.

"I SAID HURRY UP! YOUR DADDY'S GOING TO BE PICK-ING US UP IN TWENTY MINUTES AND YOU'RE NOT EVEN DRESSED YET. YOU KNOW HE'S GOING TO BE PISSED IF YOU'RE NOT READY FOR GRANDMA EULA LEE'S BIRTH-DAY PARTY!" Charlene's hand was cupped around her mouth, and she was pointing to the telephone receiver with the other.

Oh, cool, Tiara thought. She took the telephone from her ear, but, following her aunt's cue, she spoke loud enough for Lionel to hear her. "I'M HURRYING, AUNT CHARLIE." She returned the telephone to her ear.

"Lionel, I'm really sorry, but there's no way I can get out of this at the last minute like this. Daddy would have a fit. Can't you just tell your father I'm very sorry I can't meet him tonight?"

Lionel sighed. "Yeah, okay. I'll give you a call tomorrow." He hung up without saying good-bye. Man, is he pissed, Tiara thought. I'm going to have to find some way to make it up to him.

"Ahem!"

"Oh! Thanks a lot, Aunt Charlie," Tiara said quickly. "I owe you big time."

Aunt Charlie chuckled as she walked out the door. "Girl, you been owing me all your life. You just realizing it now?

"And you notice I ain't ask you who you're going out with, right?" she yelled from the living room. "I have a pretty good idea who it is, though. See you at six!"

8

Y ou're always yelling about me spoiling the girls, and look at you. Every week coming over here and doing their laundry." Reggie grabbed the bag of clean clothes from his sister. "Why didn't you call me so I coulda helped you from the car?"

Charlene shrugged. "It wasn't all that heavy." She glanced at her watch. "Where's Tiara?"

"In her room."

Charlene took a few steps toward Tiara's room then stopped. "Whoa! What are you celebrating? What's that, a gallon bottle of Chivas?"

"I'm not celebrating anything," Reggie grinned. "I just came into a little extra money so I thought I'd get a little something-something to unwind. You gonna stick around for awhile? I picked up a bottle of Johnny Walker for you."

"Yeah, I ain't got nothing else to do," Charlene looked at her brother quizzically. "So how'd you come into some extra money? And how extra is extra?"

"Oh, only about thirteen thousand, five hundred extra." Reggie started dancing to imaginary music.

"What! From where?"

"Richard called me last night and asked me to come over to play poker."

"Get the hell outta here. I thought you weren't playing anymore."

"I'm not. But he begged me because this stupid-ass brother, Jacob, invited some dude from South Carolina over last week who cleaned the crew out. Richard thought dude was cheating, but they couldn't catch him at it, so they invited him over again this week. But meanwhile, Red Oscar did some checking up on the guy. Turns out he was a pro. And Red also found out that the dude won about seventy-five grand playing some hustlers over at The Stop on 127th Street on Tuesday. And dig, since Jacob was supposed to be driving with the guy back to South Carolina right after the game at Richard's, they knew dude was going to have his roll on him. So they called me, because they wanted me to kick his ass." Reggie did a full twirl, then started the James Brown moonwalk. "So, I felt it was my duty to comply."

"But he had to know from last week that Richard and them don't play for big stakes." Charlene cocked her head in puzzlement.

"I'm sure he did. He was probably planning on just taking a couple of hundred from them like he did last week. But before I went over there I gargled with rum, and splashed some on my face. Then when I got there I started boasting that I just cashed a twenty-thousand-dollar settlement from the city."

"Yeah, yeah, boy. You're the shit!" Charlene clapped her hands excitedly.

"We started playing, and dude was cheating big time. I peeped his game, though. I lost about fifty dollars in the first two hands. So, then I pulled out six hundred dollars and lost every penny to dude. Richard and them were playing along with me, so they kept telling me to take my drunk ass home, but I made a big deal about I was going to go home and get some real money and come back and win my dough back. I was slurring my words and shit, and you should have seen dude's eyes light up. So I went out and came back about fifteen minutes later, and dude was ready. You hear me? He was ready. The motherfucker was salivating. He let me win a couple of hands to soup me up, then suggested we raise the stakes. So I made like I was real cocky and shit, and said I could handle whatever he wanted to throw at me. The shit was on."

"Aw yeah! Aw yeah!" Charlene started bopping her head to Reggie's imaginary music.

"So Richard and them said they were going to sit the shit out, because they felt bad about me getting ready to lose all my money. So me and dude were playing one on one, and I lost ten thousand in three hands. So I get up from the table, like I was all upset and shit and said I was going home. So dude acted like he was all sorry and shit and said we should play one more hand, straight up, double or nothing."

"Go Reggie! Go Reggie!" Charlene was dancing around the living room like there was a party going on.

"Richard started tugging on me and shit, saying he wasn't going to let me blow my whole settlement like that. Dude was like, 'let the man make his own decisions,' and shit. So I told Richard to get the fuck off of me, and I sat down. You should have seen dude. He was fucking drooling, you hear me? And then dig this. All night dude was palming cards and shit, cheating his ass off. But his hand, his cards were so good, he played on the up and up. The motherfucker laid down a straight in spades, king high. He started howling like a wolf and shit."

"Oh, no he didn't!" Charlene hooted.

"Oh, but I was cool." Reggie brushed his hands over his chest in a congratulatory manner. "I kind of sniffed a couple of times. Then I wiped my brow, and leaned back in my chair and started chewing on my lips like I was trying not to cry. Then I put my cards down on the table face down, I shook my head, and I said, 'I don't believe it.' Dude was like, 'You'd better believe it.' He reached for the pot, and I said, 'Hold up. Let me at least turn over my cards. Let me leave the table like a man,' and he started acting all gracious and shit, and said for me to go ahead. I turned them over one by one. Ace of diamonds. Bam! King of diamonds. Bam! Queen of diamonds. Bam! Jack of diamonds. Bam! Dude's eyes were as wide as dinner plates. So then I turned over the last card, and slammed it on the table so hard I almost broke the motherfucker. Ka bam! Ten of diamonds. Royal fucking flush! Whoo hah! Dude almost had a heart attack."

"Damn, I wish I was there!"

"He started sputtering and shit, calling me all kind of cheating motherfuckers. I told him I didn't know what the fuck he was talking about, and I reached over and grabbed the pot. Do you know that motherfucker pulled a gun on me?"

"What?"

"Yep. I told him he was going to have to shoot me, cause I was claiming what was mine. He put the gun up in my face, but he didn't have the trigger pulled back and his hand was shaking, so I wasn't even sweating it. I was getting ready to slap the shit out of his hands and coldcock the bitch, but Red was already on it. My man put a glock to dude's head and told him to drop the gun or he'd blow his head off."

"Oh my God!"

"Dude laid the gun down on the table and his whole body started shaking. I almost felt sorry for him. Not sorry enough to give him back his money, of course," Reggie chuckled. "Imagine someone coming out town, to my projects, and thinking he's going to go home with my cash. That shit wasn't going to happen!"

"That bitch didn't know who he was fucking with," Charlene hooted.

"Damn tooting. Sugar Reg was on the real." Reggie stretched out his hand, and Charlene gave him a hard five.

"Ooh, baby . . . don't slap them too hard," Reggie shook his hand like it was in pain. "How you expect me to palm a royal flush with sore hands?"

"I knew it! Ooh, Sugar Reg. Youse a cheating sonuvabitch!" Charlene started jiggling her shoulders in delight.

"Rich cheating sonuvabitch, thank you very much." Reggie pulled out a wad of hundreds. "I laid a thousand on Richard for turning me on to the game, gave Jimmy five hundred just 'cause he was there, and two thousand to Red Oscar because my man was willing to blow dude's head on my humble behalf. The rest is mine."

"I love it!"

"Yeah, baby!" Reggie started dancing again.

"Wait a minute, wait a minute. Let me put some music on so you can really get your groove on proper, Sugar Reg!" Charlene ran over to the CD player, and seconds later Kool and the Gang's "Celebration" was blasting through the apartment.

"Pass me that bottle, little brother," Charlene shouted over the music. "We gonna have a party going on tonight!"

"Oh, yeah, oh yeah," Reggie snapped his finger. "That reminds me. Red Oscar invited me to his birthday party next month at Perk's. I can't wait. I know there's going to be a bunch of guys from the circuit there. Guys I ain't seen in years."

"Cool. But I'm concentrating on the party up in here tonight!" Charlene shouted, bopping hard to the music. "Whoo hah!"

"Daddy, you got that thing up so loud I can't even hear my own music." Tiara came out of her bedroom. "Oh, man, I didn't even know you were here, Aunt Charlie."

"I'm sorry, honey. I got so caught up with your daddy's good news I forgot all about you." Aunt Charlie gave Tiara a quick hug. "He told you what happened, right?"

"Yeah, he woke me and Jo-Jo up about three o'clock this morning when he came in to tell us."

"How come you didn't tell me when I was over here this afternoon, then?" Charlene demanded.

Tiara shrugged her shoulders. "I forgot. I had other things on my mind."

"Other things on your mind," Charlene said, shaking her head. "Girl, you bring a new meaning to the word egocentric."

"He told you he isn't planning on spending it, didn't he? Don't you think he should take me and Jo-Jo to Hawaii for vacation or something?" Tiara gave her father a pouting look. "I'm not saying he should spend all the money, but he could break off a little cash to show his children a good time."

"Princess, this is going in the brownstone fund," Reggie said. "The way we're going we're going house hunting in another year or so."

"Yeah. Yeah," Tiara turned back to aunt. "Did you bring the jewelry, Aunt Charlie?"

"Here," Charlene reached into her pocketbook and threw a plastic bag at Tiara. "Now get out of my face. I can't believe how selfish you are."

"Whatever." Tiara shrugged. "Thanks," she said over her shoulder and disappeared back into her room.

"What's going on out there?" Jo-Jo asked. She was lying across her bed with a math book open in front of her.

"Daddy's going crazy," Tiara snapped. She sat down in front of her bed while putting in the earrings. "Jo-Jo, go out there and tell Daddy you can't study with him blasting that old-ass music."

"It ain't bothering me. You make me study while you blast your music in here."

"Oh shut up."

"You're just mad because I ain't on your side."

"I thought I told you to shut up." Tiara stood up and started posing in the full-length mirror. Yeah, she looked good. Rashad's eyes were going to pop out when he saw her. She glanced at her watch. She had twenty minutes before Rashad got there. She grabbed her jacket. She wanted to go outside and meet him so he didn't have to come in the apartment. She didn't want the third degree she knew she'd get if Reggie saw she was going out with someone else besides Lionel. She took another quick look in the mirror, and suddenly decided to pull her hair into a ponytail so the earrings were easily seen.

"Now you done messed yourself up," Jo-Jo said after she had finished. "You look better with your hair down on your face."

"Like you know what looks good, and what doesn't." Tiara said. But then she paused in front of the mirror. Jo-Jo was right. She snatched the ponytail holder out, and shook her hair loose.

"Told you."

"Whatever." Tiara headed out. Aunt Charlie was in the middle of the floor with a drink in her hand, dancing to a Funkadelics song, while Reggie sat on the couch bopping his head to the music.

"I'm leaving! See you when I get back." She had to almost yell to be heard over the music.

"Whoa there, young lady." Charlene stopped dancing. "Your gentleman friend isn't picking you up?"

"I'm going to wait outside for him. We probably wouldn't be able to hear him knock with the music being so loud," Tiara said quickly. Leave it to Aunt Charlie to try and bust her shit out.

"Oh, well, then, I'll just turn the music down." Charlene walked over to the stereo.

"That's okay . . ." Tiara started, but just then to her dismay, there was a quick three knocks on the door. "I'll get that. See you later, Daddy!" She rushed to the door, but Aunt Charlene was faster.

"Well, well, how nice to see you again!"

Rashad stood there wearing his green army jacket and brown corduroy slacks and combat boots. "How are you, Miss Bynum?" he said with a smile.

"Come right on in," Charlene stepped to the side to allow him to enter. "Tiara, sweetie . . . your date is here," she said innocently.

Reggie's head snapped up, and he got up and turned off the stereo completely.

"Daddy, you remember, Rashad, don't you?" Tiara said before her father could speak. "He was the guy who helped me out the night I twisted my ankle. You do remember, don't you?"

Rashad reached out to shake his hand. "How are you doing, sir?"

"Yeah. Yeah. I remember," Reggie said absently. "I'm doing fine, son," he addressed Rashad. "How are you?"

"I'm doing fine, thanks."

"Why don't you sit down for a minute?" Reggie waved him over to the couch.

Tiara glanced over and saw Charlene leaning against the wall, grinning from ear to ear as she twirled her drink. *Dang, she's really getting a kick out of this. This is all her fault.*

"Daddy, we gotta go. We're going to be late for the play." Tiara gave Rashad's arm a slight tug. "Come on, Rashad. Night, Daddy."

"You have a few minutes," Charlene clinked the ice in her glass. "Didn't you say Rashad was supposed to pick you up at seven? It's only like six-thirty."

"It's six forty-five." Tiara cut her eyes at her aunt.

"It's not a problem, we have a few minutes," Rashad said as he sat down on the sofa. He casually looked around the room. "You have a really nice apartment here."

"Thanks," Reggie mumbled.

"So, Rashad, would you like a drink?" Charlene asked.

"No thanks."

"Are you sure? We have Chivas, Johnny Walker Black, and I'm sure there's a bottle of wine in the kitchen."

"No, that's okay," Rashad assured her. "I don't drink."

"Oh, okay," Charlene said graciously. "How about a glass of juice, then?" She turned and smiled sweetly at her niece. "Tiara, honey, why don't you go in the kitchen and see what kind of juice we have?"

"He didn't say he wanted juice, Aunt Charlie," Tiara snapped.

"So, Mr. Bynum, are all these trophies yours?" Rashad turned to Reggie.

"Those four over there belong to my youngest daughter, Josephine." Reggie pointed to the top of the television. "She's a basketball champ."

"Cool." Rashad nodded his head. "Tiara, do you play, too?"

Charlene threw back her head and gave a hearty laugh, ignoring the dirty look Tiara threw her way. "Yeah, she plays, all right. Not basketball, though."

"No, Tiara doesn't play sports." Reggie ignored his sister. "Jo-Jo's the athlete in the family."

"Doesn't look like she's the only one." Rashad got up and walked over to the small black lacquer entertainment unit near the window to admire almost a dozen trophies showcased in the glass center. "You box?"

"Yeah, I was pretty good with my hands back in the day," Reggie said proudly.

"Oh, he's being modest." Charlene walked over and stood next to Rashad. "See this one?" She pointed to the tallest trophy in the entertainment center. "He got this one when he won the Golden Gloves championship. He was supposed to go to the Olympics, but our mother was sick, and he didn't want to leave the country."

Rashad let out a whistle as he took a closer look. "Wow, a Golden Glove champ."

"Yeah. I had my day."

"Oh, man, this is great." Rashad turned to face Reggie. "Do you still fight?"

"Naw, I gave that up years ago. I still go down to the gym to punch a bag every now and then to stay in shape, but that's it."

"You ever thought about coaching?"

"Coaching?"

"Yeah. I volunteer at a rec center on Eighth Avenue, and the kids up there could use a boxing coach. We got a little equipment there, not much, but a bit. The kids could use someone to come down once a week to give them some pointers. I mean, there's no pay involved or anything, but if you have some spare time it would sure be great. Help those little brothers expend some of their frustrations out in the boxing ring rather than on the streets cutting and shooting each other up."

"Or getting caught up in all this drug shit out here," Reggie snorted. "It pisses me the hell off when I see these little punks on the corner selling crack. I can stand a lot, but I can't stand some dude selling crack to kids. They should take them all and line them up against the wall and just gun them down. Forget about putting them in jail."

"Oh, Lord, you got Reggie started on his favorite subject," Charlene laughed. "Now see, Tiara, you guys really won't get out of here anytime soon now."

Tiara sighed and rolled her eyes.

"Look, you know how I feel about the subject. It was bad enough with heroin and cocaine, but this crack thing is a whole other animal. Got women selling their bodies in the street. Kids getting shot in drive-bys. Babies being born addicted to that shit." Reggie shook his head in disgust. "I tell my daughters they can hang out with whomever they want, but they know I better never find out they're hanging with any dope dealers."

"Mr. Bynum, I feel the same way," Rashad nodded. "They're out here and killing their own people with that poison. Even my own godbrother, Alvin. Lives right in my building and was a real stand-up guy until a few years ago. Then he did a complete one-eighty. Quit school and decided he was going to make his money dealing."

"This is some crazy shit out here." Reggie shook his head in disgust.

"You got that right," Rashad sighed. "I try to keep the lines of communication open between me and Alvin, because I don't want to give up on anybody, but then I found out a couple of weeks ago that he recruited a ten-year-old kid to work for him. That did it for me. I have no more words for my man. He's dead in my eyes."

"He's got a ten-year-old working for him? Jesus Christ." Reggie shook his head.

"Well, believe it or not, I managed to talk to that little brother and set him straight. But that's one little boy off the street; there's plenty more out there. That's why we try to get as many kids as we can involved in sports so they don't get caught up in drugs."

"Boxing coach, huh? Yeah, I might be interested in something like that." Reggie rubbed his chin. "I could get over there on Saturday mornings, maybe."

"Mr. Bynum, that would really be too cool for words. The kids would really appreciate that," Rashad said eagerly. "Why don't you come over and check it out tomorrow morning so you can make up your mind for sure?"

"Yeah, yeah, I'll do that," Reggie nodded. Tiara could see he was getting just as excited about the idea as Rashad. "What time?"

"Say about ten thirty?"

"That'll work."

"Daddy, we really have to go now," Tiara said impatiently.

"What's wrong with you, girl?" Charlene snapped. "Give them a few minutes to talk."

Tiara struggled to contain herself, not wanting to argue with her aunt in front of Rashad, but she wanted to tell her to shut up and mind her own business. Damn, that woman.

"Actually, ma'am, we really do have to get out of here if we want to make it before curtain time," Rashad said apologetically. "I hope you don't mind," he said turning to Reggie.

"No, you kids get on up outta here," Reggie said. "I'm going to be up late, so I'll see you when you drop Tiara off and you can give me the address to the rec center then, okay?"

"And stop calling me 'ma'am.' I'm not your mother," Charlene said almost flirtatiously. "I'll probably still be here when you bring Tiara home, so I'll see you then."

Oh great, Tiara thought as she and Rashad left the apartment. *A send-off committee and a welcome home committee. It would serve them right if I didn't come home at all tonight.*

9

"Where are you parked?" Tiara rubbed her hands together, wishing she had brought gloves. They had already walked two blocks, and the cold November wind made her eagerly anticipate the warmth of Rashad's cab. He, on the other hand, seemed oblivious to the biting weather. His army jacket was open, and his ever-present smile was plastered on his face. He was a fast walker, but had courteously slowed down when he realized Tiara was struggling to keep pace. He stopped now to face her.

"I don't have a car, sis," he said slowly.

"What about your cab?"

"I rent the cab to work. I have to return it to the depot when my shift is over."

"Well, how are we going to get to the play?"

"I thought we'd just walk."

"You expect me to walk from Harlem to the theater district?" Tiara was incredulous. He had to have lost his mind. It would have been bad enough if he had suggested a subway, or the slow-ass bus. But he expected her to walk sixty city blocks? She might have wanted to spend time with him, but not damn much.

"No, no, we're not heading downtown, sis. I should have made that clear," he chuckled. "The play is being held right here in Harlem. At a friend of mine's house."

"A play in someone's home? What the hell is that?" Tiara demanded. Here she was all dressed up, and he was taking her to some dinky apartment. She could have been having dinner with Lionel and his millionaire father in a swanky downtown restaurant, but no . . . she had to opt for some stupid amateur play with Rashad. And for what? He hadn't even complimented her on the way she looked, or shown any kind of romantic interest in her at all since they'd left her apartment. And she wished he would stop with that "sis" shit. At least he wasn't calling her "little sis" anymore, but still . . .

"Oh come on, you'll enjoy it," Rashad put his arm over her shoulders and gently pulled her back into a walk. "Just give it a chance."

Tiara screwed up her face, but Rashad didn't seem to notice. "It's only two blocks away from here, on 119th Street." His arm slid down her shoulder, and he gently took her hand into his.

"Whew, your hands are cold. Poor baby, are you anemic or something. You need to take vitamins."

"So how long have you been driving a cab?" Tiara changed the subject. She didn't feel like hearing a lecture about how she should be eating health food or some such shit.

"About two years now. It's not the best job in the world, but it'll do for now. Got to do something to keep food on the table, you know." Rashad chuckled. "What about you?"

"What about me what?"

"Do you work?"

Tiara snorted. "No, I'm a student."

"Now, that's cool." Rashad nodded his head approvingly. "Where do you go?"

"City College. I'm studying pre-law. I'm probably going to be attending Columbia Law when I finish. Probably on scholarship. I have an A-minus average going on two years now." She was going to show this guy she wasn't just a great-looking babe, but also an intellectual woman. She was going to make him respect her one way or another. "I was thinking about going to Harvard or Yale for graduate school, but I've decided to stick to my roots here in Harlem. You know, give back to the community and all."

"Oh, cool. You plan on doing volunteer work up here then?"

"Volunteer work?" Tiara acted as if she had been insulted. "I'm all about getting paid for my time. That's why I'm going into corporate law instead of criminal. I plan on making the benjamins," she laughed.

"Well, what do you mean about giving back to the community then?"

"Just by my sticking around," Tiara explained patiently. "I'll be a role model for the young girls in the community. They'll see they don't have to wind up like some of these chicken heads out here, but they can grow up like me, and make something out of their lives by going to school and becoming a success."

"Okay, that makes sense." Rashad shrugged.

"Yeah, you should see how some of my so-called friends from high school try to diss me now because I'm doing something for myself," Tiara continued. "They're just jealous because they know I'm going places, and they're going to be stuck in the projects for the rest of their lives just popping out babies."

"I guess they must be jealous of Alice then, too?"

"What do you mean?"

"Well, she's going to college. She's at Hunter College, right?"

"Yeah, but that's different." Tiara waved her hand dismissively.

"And why's that?"

"Because Alice is Alice. I mean, not to be funny, but who's going to be jealous of her? I mean, she's a nice person and all that, but, well, you know." Tiara tried to pick her words carefully. "She just doesn't look like someone other people would be jealous of."

"But you do?"

"Now, see, you're trying to make like I'm conceited or something," Tiara protested. "Alice is my girl, and I ain't saying she's ugly or anything. So don't be trying to make like I'm busting on her."

"No, I'm just trying to understand, is all."

"Well, I'm just saying I've got some looks, and some smarts, and I'm going places, and that makes some of these peeps out here jealous," Tiara said angrily. "It's not my fault."

"I hear you."

"I mean, people can just talk to me a few minutes and see I've got it going on, you know? So what you think? I'm supposed to try and make myself look ugly, or act like I ain't got no brains to make people happy? I don't think so," Tiara said huffily. "I'm going to be me, and if they don't like it, they can kiss my ass, and then just get the hell out the way and watch me step."

"Here we are." Rashad stopped in front of an impressive brownstone.

"Good, because my feet hurt," Tiara grumbled, her mood darkened because of the conversation during the four-block walk. It was obvious to her that Rashad was jealous because she was going to be a lawyer and he was nothing but a cab driver, but she was damned if he was going to make her feel bad. Shit, if he had any sense he should be trying to hook up with her so he could have a lawyer for a wife. The boy obviously didn't have the brains he was born with.

"So, what do you think? Is it something we can do?" The tall light-skinned blond-haired man sitting in the wooden folding chair behind

Rashad's leaned forward, his arms folded commandingly across his chest. "The girl playing the lead, Charnelle Thomas, has been in an indy before, so I know she can act in front of the cameras."

Rashad finished applauding the bows of the seven-member cast before answering.

"Yeah, yeah, it's doable," he said thoughtfully. "What about the playwright? Can he turn the script into a screenplay?"

"I don't know, but it shouldn't matter. We can get someone else to do it if he can't." The blond-haired man sniffed a couple of times, then sat back in his chair, pulled out an already soiled paper napkin from his pants pocket and wiped his nose, then—to Tiara's disgust—stuffed it back into his pocket. However Rashad, she noticed, didn't even flinch. Really classy guy, she thought, as the man then got up and shuffled off without saying a word. She shifted uncomfortably in her seat, trying to signal Rashad that she was ready to get up.

"Would you like something to drink?" Rashad stood up and stretched. "Did you like the play?"

"It was pretty good," Tiara answered simply. It was, in fact, great, she had to admit, if only to herself. It was about a young mother of three who decided to kill herself because her oldest son had been left a paraplegic after an accidental shooting. She reasoned her life insurance could be used to give the child the best medical help available, something she could not otherwise afford. The woman had to make her death appear accidental to get around the insurance policy's suicide clause, so she had to persuade her reluctant husband and parents to help. The closing scene, where the family gathers for a final goodbye to the courageous woman was so emotional, that Tiara—and almost everyone in the audience—had tears in their eyes.

Tiara followed Rashad to the back of the enormous living room that had been the theater of the evening. Six rows of folding chairs had been set up on the shiny hardwood floor, only four of which had been occupied. The play itself was conducted in the very front of the living room, only a few feet away from the first row where Tiara and Rashad were seated. The room had already been darkened when Tiara and Rashad entered, except for a set of portable flood lights that shone on the players. Now that the room's overhead lights were turned on Tiara could see that the ivory-colored walls were lined with artwork. One wall held framed movie posters, old movies that she had seen late at night on BET. *Uptown Saturday Night*, *Blazing Saddles*, *The Learning Tree*, and *The Great White Hope*. Another wall had framed posters of jazz musicians, including Thelonius Monk, Miles Davis, John Coltrane, and the well-known Great Day in Harlem photograph, which featured dozens of jazz artists from the fifties. Hung on yet another wall were pictures of writers from the Harlem Renaissance. There was no furniture in the room, except for the folding chairs and a small drink bar, making Tiara wonder if artsy folks didn't bother with furniture, or if it had all been moved out for the evening.

"Rashad, my man!"

Tiara turned and saw her date being enthusiastically hugged by a medium-height man with short hair and cherubic cheeks.

"Didn't I tell you? Wasn't it brilliant?" The man's smile was so wide, Tiara was sure his face had to hurt. "Freddy has himself a real winner with this one. What do you think?"

"Yeah, I was blown away." Rashad nodded gravely. "I was just talking to Ed. We're thinking we might want to do something with this. You think Freddy would be game?"

"Oh, hell yeah! Let me go get him!" The man turned away.

"No, no, let him bask in his glow for a little bit." Rashad grabbed his arm. "Here, let me introduce you to a friend of mine. Roy Johnson, this is Tiara Bynum. Tiara, this is Roy, our host for the evening."

"Pleased to meet you." Tiara extended her hand.

"Pleased to meet you, too." Roy shook her hand. "Are you an actress?"

"Um, no," Tiara answered.

"You ever thought about acting? You certainly have the look."

Tiara gave an inward sigh of relief. She hated to admit it, but she was feeling a little uncomfortable in this crowd. But this Roy person must have thought she fit right in.

"I've never really given it a thought," she finally answered. "I used to think about modeling, though."

"Modeling?" Roy cocked his head to the side and looked at her as if she had just sprouted a second head. "Oh, well, that's good. It's all good." He turned back to Rashad. "Jazzy made some crabmeat thingees. I've got to get them out of the oven. I'll be right back. But I think it's great you're thinking about putting this on film. We've got to talk later, okay?" With that he disappeared.

"What's he talking about?" Tiara asked as she and Rashad stood in line for refreshments.

"What do you mean?"

"About you putting something on film?" She sipped from the glass that Rashad handed her. Damn, it was some kind of fruit punch, not the wine she was anticipating.

"Oh, that." Rashad took a sip from his own glass. "My partner, Ed, and I are thinking about turning the play we just saw into a movie," he said nonchalantly.

"Huh? You make movies?" Tiara didn't bother to hide her surprise. "You didn't tell me you made movies."

"Just small ones for right now. Low-budget independent films." Rashad smiled. "Real low budget. And actually, I've only done one. But I've worked on a few others. I just helped out on one about drug dealers. And believe me, film work doesn't earn me any money. So like I said, driving a cab is what puts food on the table."

"Yeah, but still making movies . . . get out of here!" Tiara was trying to internalize everything she was hearing. "How'd you get into it?" Tiara looked up just then to see the blond man from earlier sauntering over to where they stood.

I'm getting on up outta here," he said when he reached them. "I'll give you call tomorrow."

"Ed Chambers, Tiara Bynum."

Ed nodded his head at Tiara, then turned back to Rashad.

"Let's talk tomorrow, and then if we decide to make a go for it, let's grab Freddy up this weekend. Okay?"

"Yeah, cool."

"You finished your drink? We need to be getting up outta here ourselves," Rashad said after Ed left. "Let me just go congratulate Freddy real quick and then let Roy know we're leaving."

"So tell me about this movie thing," Tiara asked when they were outside. "How'd you get into it?"

"I was a movie buff as a kid," Rashad shrugged, "and I always admired John Singleton, the Hughes brothers, and Spike Lee. I decided I wanted to do the same thing when I grew up."

Wow! A movie producer. Now that was impressive. Even if he was a broke movie producer. Wouldn't it be cool to marry a movie producer? They could live in Hollywood and shit and hang out with Halle Berry and Sanaa Latham. Maybe she should become an entertainment attorney rather than studying corporate law. Then she could help him with his movie deals. But naw, she didn't know much about Rashad, but from what she did she figured he wouldn't go for the Hollywood scene. He'd probably just want to spend his life making low-budget movies and driving a cab. And she wasn't about to marry some broke-ass cab driver whether he made movies on the side or not. But, yeah, she could go ahead and marry Lionel, live the life of a New York millionaire, and practice entertainment law in her spare time, just for the hell of it. And then she could help Rashad with his little old films, and he could eat his heart out because she was married to someone else. "But how did you, you know, learn how to make movies? I mean, you can't just read up on it and then do it."

"I'm still learning," Rashad laughed. "I'm a film major at NYU. A senior."

"You didn't tell me you were in school," Tiara said accusingly. "And how come you're just now telling me you make movies?"

"You didn't ask me." Rashad shrugged.

"That's not fair. I did ask you about your work," Tiara protested.

"No, you didn't. You asked me how long I had been driving a cab. I answered you, and then asked you a question in response, and you just took off from there."

"Took off from there? All I was doing was answering your question." Tiara was getting angry. No, he wasn't trying to get with her like that. "If you didn't want me to answer, why'd you ask?"

"Because I was interested in the answer, Tiara. But it's just that I was hoping for, well, a little back-and-forth, you know? That's how it usually works," Rashad said gently. "But don't get upset, it's not that big a deal."

"I didn't say it was a big deal. I'm just saying . . ." Tiara stopped and poked out her lips. "Now you're making me feel bad."

"Don't." Rashad reached over and rubbed her shoulder. "You're just being you."

"And what's that supposed to mean?"

"That you're kind of wrapped in yourself, sis. And I'm not even saying that's a bad thing," Rashad answered as they turned the corner onto Malcolm X Boulevard. "The way the world is now it's good for sisters to have high self-esteem. That way they won't let people take advantage of them. Too many cats out here trying to prey on young girls. Way too many."

"Well, I'm not going to let anyone take advantage of me," Tiara huffed.

"I know that's right. That's what I like about you."

"Really? Anything else you like about me?" Tiara asked coyly.

"Yeah, a lot. You're definitely an interesting person. And like you've already mentioned two or three times, you're pretty and you're smart."

Well, there it was. He was finally admitting he wanted her. Took him long enough. And since he was such a nice guy, she was going to let him down easy.

"Rashad, I guess it's only fair to let you know that I've already got a man," Tiara said slowly. "But I would like it if we could still be friends."

Rashad looked at her curiously. "Well, yeah, that's fine with me. I wasn't trying for anything else. Like I said, I think you're interesting and all, but I'm not trying to get with you."

Yeah, he was being real cool about it—pretending he didn't care and shit. But she could tell when a man was playing it off, and . . . but, oh shit! He didn't seem like he was playing it off. He was coming off real sincere. But he couldn't be!

Tiara stopped in the middle of the sidewalk and stamped her foot. "But you just said you liked me!"

"And I do," Rashad seemed puzzled by her reaction.

"But, then, you just said . . ."

Rashad cocked his head to the side and looked at her for a few seconds before saying anything. "Little sis," he began slowly, "a brother can like you without wanting to get with you. I think you're real cool, and all, but I wasn't looking to start a relationship with you. I'm happy . . . quite happy . . . to have you as a friend."

The lump in her throat was huge, and she struggled to make sure the tears that had sprung to her eyes wouldn't fall. "Yeah, th-that's all I'm saying," she stammered. "We should, you know, just be friends."

"On the real, sis. Okay?"

"Okay." Tiara managed a smile, though she kept her eyes averted.

"Cool. Let's go ahead and get you home."

10

Tiara sat in front of the vanity in her salmon-colored teddy bear nightgown, brush in her hand, staring in the mirror. She shouldn't have the blues. There was no reason for her to be in a funk at all. After all, she had Lionel, and he was twenty times better than Rashad. Why should she care if Rashad only wanted to be friends? It wasn't like she wanted to be his woman, anyway. Shit. She wasn't even sure she wanted to be his friend. Anyone who was stupid enough to pass up on a girl like her wasn't smart enough to have her. She didn't even know why she was thinking about him.

It didn't help that now her father was going to be hanging out with him every week. She might have to put a stop to that. It had really pissed her off when Rashad brought her home the night before and, sure enough, her father actually asked Rashad for the address of that stupid recreation center. And then the two of them sat down and her father started telling Rashad about the "glory days" of boxing. Muhammad Ali, George Foreman, Ken Norton, Joe Frazier, Ernie Shaver—all the hard-hitters, as her father called them. And of course, Aunt Charlie was there egging them on. What the hell was her agenda, anyway? There she was, all upset about how Rashad treated her, and no one even bothered to ask her what was wrong. Not that she would tell them, anyway . . . the whole thing was so embarrassing. But you'd think they'd at least ask. But no, they were too wrapped up in their own selves to even notice. She finally gave up after about fifteen minutes and went to bed. She didn't even know what time Rashad left.

"Tiara." Jo-Jo's voice startled her. She hadn't bothered to look over at her sister's bed when she woke up that morning, because Jo-Jo was usually up and out of the house by nine on Saturdays to go to basketball practice. She didn't even know the girl was home.

"Tiara," Jo-Jo said again.

"What?" Tiara said irritably, not wanting to be bothered with Jo-Jo or anyone else this morning.

"I need to ask you a serious question, and I need a serious answer, okay?"

Tiara turned and looked at her sister quizzically. Jo-Jo's elbow was propped on the pillow, and her expression was impossible to read.

"Go ahead," Tiara said cautiously.

"You can't tell anyone I asked you, though, okay?"

"Okay."

"Do you think I'm gay?"

Tiara's head jerked back in surprise. "Hell, no! Why?"

Jo-Jo shrugged her shoulders, then laid her head on the pillow and let out a sigh. "I was just wondering."

"Why? Do you think you're gay?"

"No!"

"So then why you ask me a stupid question like that?" Tiara demanded.

"No reason," Jo-Jo said quietly.

"Girl, stop acting like you ain't got no sense, or like you think I ain't got none," Tiara snapped. "You don't ask a question like that unless you have a reason."

Jo-Jo sighed. "Asia told me everyone says I'm gay."

"Asia? You mean Shakira's little sister? The little bitch doesn't know what she's talking about. She's just a troublemaker, just like her sister." Tiara went over and sat on the side of Jo-Jo's bed. "Don't pay that shit no mind."

"She's not lying. I heard some girls in school saying it, too," Jo-Jo said dismally.

"Oh, Jo-Jo, those girls are just jealous," Tiara said gently. "That's the only reason they buggin' like that."

Jo-Jo was silent for a few minutes, and Tiara thought she might have actually drifted back off to sleep. She started to get up and go to the bathroom when Jo-Jo finally spoke up.

"Tiara?"

"What?"

"How does someone know they're gay?"

"Well," Tiara hesitated, wondering how she should answer. Obviously, Jo-Jo was really bothered, and she didn't want to sound flip or anything. "Have you looked at a girl and wanted to kiss her?"

"No."

"Well, see, then you're not gay," Tiara said. "And anyway, whoever heard of a twelve-year-old lesbian? You're too young to be homosexual or heterosexual, or any kind of sexual. You're just a kid."

"What if I become a homosexual when I grow up? Then what?"

"What? You planning on becoming homosexual?"

"No."

"Then why are you worrying about it?" Tiara shook her head. She was going to make Shakira kick Asia's butt for putting all this shit in Jo-Jo's head.

Jo-Jo sighed. "You know they're probably only saying that because I like sports."

"Yeah, probably."

"Not all women basketball players are homosexuals, you know," Jo-Jo continued.

"That's right, they're not."

"Those girls are just stupid, right?"

"Right," Tiara nodded solemnly.

"I'm not going to pay them any mind." Jo-Jo shrugged her shoulders.

"Good."

"But I bet they wouldn't say that if I was as pretty as you and Mommy."

Tiara peered at her younger sister. Now where did that come from?

"You're pretty, too. It's just that I take after Mommy and her side of the family, and you take after Daddy's side of the family. But don't let anyone tell you you're not pretty."

"Thanks, Tiara." Jo-Jo pulled the blanket over her head and turned away.

"Hey, Jo-Jo. Tell me something." Tiara shook her sister.

"What?" Jo-Jo asked from under the covers.

"Is that why you didn't go to practice this morning? Because you're afraid people are going to think you're gay?"

Jo-Jo started chuckling. "Naw, practice was canceled because Coach had to go out of town. We're practicing tomorrow instead."

"Okay." Tiara got up from the bed, relieved. "Just checking." She walked over to her bed and grabbed the gold satin robe lying on it, then put it on and headed to the bathroom for a shower.

"And, Tiara . . ."

She turned to find her sister looking at her anxiously. "Now what?"

"Remember, don't tell anyone I asked you, okay."

"Shut up," Tiara said affectionately. "I said I wasn't telling, okay?"

"Okay."

Sheesh, Tiara thought as she stood over the sink and brushed her teeth, poor Jo-Jo—having people talk about her because she's a tomboy. *They're just jealous because they know she's good and will probably get a basketball scholarship. Boy, they're just jealous of everybody in this family.*

She showered, then blow-dried her hair, and was on the way back out to bedroom when she heard the key turn in the lock.

"Tiara!"

"Hi, Daddy!" Tiara headed to the living room to greet her father, but before she reached the room she heard another voice.

"Hey, Sweet Pea!"

Lionel? What's Lionel doing here? She rushed now, forgetting she was still wearing her robe. Her father was dropping his blue and white gym bag on the couch, and Lionel was standing in the middle of the room, hands in his pockets, and a large smile on his face.

She stood on her tiptoes, and gave her father a peck on the cheek, then turned to her boyfriend. "Hey, Lionel. I didn't know you were coming over. Why didn't you call?"

"I wasn't planning on coming over," Lionel smiled, "but as I was driving along Eighth Avenue, I happened to see your father waiting at a bus stop. So of course I offered him a ride, and ta da, here I am."

"And guess what?" Reggie strode over and put his arm around Lionel. The gesture looked as awkward as the expression on Lionel's face.

"Lionel told me that his parents invited me, you, and Jo-Jo to join them and him on a Caribbean cruise on his yacht for Christmas." Reggie beamed.

"Your folks have a yacht?" Tiara's face broke into a huge grin.

"Well, two actually. Dad has an Oracle BMW for racing, but we also have a hundred-and-twenty-footer that we use for family vacations. It sleeps twelve, and has two hot tubs and a couple of jet boats and everything, so it's great for a getaway."

"Oh, my God . . ." Tiara's mind was racing. She'd have to buy a new swimsuit for sunbathing on the deck. Something sexy enough to have Lionel's mouth watering, but not too sexy because she didn't want to give Lionel's parents the wrong impression. She always wanted to go snorkeling, and she could imagine herself swimming with dolphins. Jo-Jo with her crazy self would probably want to swim with the sharks. It would serve her right if her skinny ass got chewed up. And at night they could dock, and they could party all night at some of those Caribbean nightclubs and shit. When was the Sinbad festival held? Wasn't it during Christmas vacation? Even if it wasn't, she was sure there would be enough places to party, anyway. Yeah, she could do the shit out of a Caribbean cruise on a yacht.

"I'll have to get back to him on it, of course, make sure I can get the time off from the job," Reggie was saying. He slapped Lionel on the back, almost knocking the young man forward. "Make sure you give me your father's phone number so we can talk."

"No problem," Lionel said after he recovered. "So, anyway, I was wondering what you were doing today, Sweet Pea. I don't have any plans so I thought . . ."

"Oh, great," Tiara grinned. "You can take me to breakfast." This would be just what she needed. A full splendid day with Lionel to take her mind off the horrible evening she had with Rashad.

"Kinda late for breakfast, isn't it?" Reggie cut in. "It's almost eleven o'clock.

"Well, brunch then," Tiara said gaily.

"It would be my pleasure," Lionel said gallantly.

"Okay, just give me five minutes." Tiara turned to run back to the room.

"Hold on! Hold on!" Reggie put his hands in the air. "Tiara, I love you madly, girl, but I can't let you do my man like that."

"What?" Tiara stared at her father, wondering what he was talking about.

"We both know what, Princess," Reggie turned to Lionel, still shaking his head. "Son, I just can't let her do you this way."

Tiara eyes widened. He couldn't possibly be thinking about telling Lionel that she went out with Rashad, could he? She stepped closer to her father. "Daddy . . ." she said in a low voice.

"Daddy nothing." Reggie stepped back from her. "I love you, Princess, but as a man, it's my duty to pull this young man's coat about something. And I think you know what."

"Daddy, come on now!" Tiara was almost in a panic. He couldn't possibly do her like this. Not her own father.

"What?" Lionel looked back and forth between Tiara and Reggie.

"Lionel, I really like you so I'm going to dime out my daughter, as much as it hurts me." Reggie took a deep breath. "I can't let my daughter lie to you like this."

"Daddy!"

"Lionel," Reggie continued, "I've known Tiara all her life, and I think it's only right to tell you that girl ain't never in her life been able to get ready in five minutes."

Tiara let out an audible sigh of relief, but immediately played it off by pounding on her father's chest. "Daddy, why you going to go and tell him that?" She giggled and turned to Lionel. "Don't pay him any mind. Just give me a few minutes."

"A few minutes? Get real," Reggie laughed. "It takes an hour for her to get ready to go the corner store."

Lionel chucked. "I don't mind waiting."

"See! So there." Tiara playfully cut her eyes at her father.

"No, I'm serious. I'm going to take a quick nap, and Jo-Jo's still at basketball practice, so you don't want to be hanging out in the living room for an hour to wait for this girl," Reggie said. "Why don't you just come back in an hour to pick her up?"

"Yeah, that makes sense." Lionel said. "I'll be back around noon, then. Okay?"

"Okay. No big deal. That's fine," Tiara gave a quick shrug. She walked him to the front door and kissed him on the cheek. "And I promise I'll be ready."

"Okay, Daddy . . . enjoy your nap—and by the way, Jo-Jo's practice was canceled, so she's still in bed," she said airily as she headed to her room to get dressed.

"Not so fast."

"What's wrong?"

"We have to talk." Reggie waved his hand toward the sofa, signaling Tiara to sit down.

"About what?" Tiara asked anxiously. Her father's voice was serious, and he looked none too happy.

Reggie sat in the armchair. He looked at her, let out a big sigh, and shook his head as if he were disappointed in her.

"What did I do?" Tiara demanded.

"Princess, you're playing a dangerous game."

"What do you mean?"

"I think you know what I mean. You know exactly what I mean," Rashad said wearily. "You seem to have a good thing going on with Lionel, but then you go out with Rashad last night."

"But, daddy—" Tiara started.

Reggie held up his hand to shut her up, then continued. "And then you do shit all raggedy. First off, when Rashad and I were talking at the rec center this morning, he mentioned that he goes to NYU. Now tell me again, where's Lionel working on his business degree?"

"NYU," Tiara said reluctantly. "But, daddy . . . ."

"And then, when I run into Lionel, he asks me how was my mother's birthday party."

Tiara's face grew hot with embarrassment.

"Of course, I didn't know what the hell he was talking about,"

Reggie continued. "But something told me to play it off, so I just told him it was fine. So then he tells me that both his grandmother and my mother have the same name—Eula Lee. Well, my mother's name was Ruthie Ann, so now I'm really confused. But I keep on playing it off. And I just laughed at the coincidence. So he keeps on talking, and I'm able to kind of figure out that he invited you to have dinner with him and his father, but that you couldn't go because you had to go to your grandmother's birthday party." Reggie scooted to the edge of his chair and looked Tiara directly in the eyes. "Girl, what the hell is wrong with you? You have a great guy like Lionel, inviting you to meet his rich daddy, and you lie to go out with some broke-ass fellow who goes to his same school, and you use me in the lie, but don't tell me so I can cover for you? Have you lost your mind? And why, for the love of God, would you tell him your grandmother's name was some damned Eula Lee? You couldn't come up with a better name than that?"

"Um, that was actually Aunt Charlie who came up with that, Daddy," Tiara said in a low voice.

"Your Aunt Charlie?" Reggie furrowed his brow. "How did she get involved with this shit?"

"Well, she was there when Lionel called, and I was trying to come up with something to say," Tiara said sheepishly.

"You know? It figures Charlene would be right up in this shit. She used to play men like I played cards," Reggie grunted. "But, see, the difference was, she knew how. You'd better believe she would have every lie she told completely covered."

Tiara shrugged.

"See, Tiara, the way you're acting is not you. You never put yourself in a position where you had to juggle like this." Reggie sat back in the chair. "I mean you've played the field, and I've always encouraged you to do that, right?"

Tiara nodded.

"But there's a difference between playing the field and lying to one man to be with another." Reggie let out another sigh. "And why would you start now with a guy like Lionel? This is a man you should be thinking about making a future with. This is the kind of man I've always dreamed you'd end up with. A man who adores you, buys presents, has money, has a future . . . Princess, you know I'd never want to give you up to somebody, but at least if it was a man like Lionel, I could accept it. He's a man who has something to offer you. Someone who treats you as good as I do." Reggie paused and looked at Tiara again. "Now, of course, if you don't care for him, that's different. I don't want you to be with a man just because I want you to be with him."

"I do want to be with him, Daddy . . ."

"Then why the hell are you trying to fuck it up!" Reggie jumped up from the chair and paced the floor.

"I'm not trying to fuck it up, Daddy!"

Reggie whirled around. "What did you just say?"

"Mess it up, daddy," Tiara quickly corrected herself. "I'm not trying to mess it up. But see, that's what I've been trying to tell you. I don't even like Rashad. I just went out with him last night because . . . well . . . just because. But I told him last night when he was taking me home that I've already got a man, and that I couldn't get involved with him."

"You did?"

"Yes, Daddy. I swear."

Reggie was silent for a moment, seemingly contemplating this new information. "Okay. But I want you to know that I don't have anything against Rashad. He's a nice guy, and I even like him, but he's just not for you, Princess. He's a dreamer. Not grounded. When he told me he wanted to be a movie director, I told him I hoped he'd become the next Steven Spielberg. You know what he said? He doesn't want to do blockbuster movies, just films that make a difference in the community."

What a loser, Tiara thought. *I'm glad I'm over him.*

"Now, granted, I think that's really good of him to be so concerned about the community, but community concern doesn't pay the bills," Reggie continued. "He couldn't afford to treat you the way you deserve to be treated. He's a nice kid, though, just not for you." Reggie slowly walked back over to the armchair and sat down. "I'm glad you see that."

"Well, I'm not even sure he's all as nice as he makes himself out to be," Tiara said lightly. "I think he has you and Aunt Charlie fooled, but I don't know, maybe he's really nice. But like I said, it doesn't matter, because I'm going to marry Lionel. Later for Rashad."

"Whoa!" Reggie sat up abruptly. "Marry? He asked you to marry him? You guys have only known each other a little bit! Isn't this kind of quick?"

Tiara laughed and went over and knelt at her father's knee. "I didn't mean right away. I'm just saying that we really have a good thing going, and, you know, if things keep going the way they are, we'll probably wind up getting married. After I finish school of course."

Reggie nodded his head appreciatively, then leaned back. "Well, okay. And I don't want you to think that I'm trying to butt in your business, Princess. I just want the best for you, you know that, right?"

"I know, Daddy." Tiara stood up and kissed him on the cheek. "Now, let me go get dressed so I'll be ready when Lionel gets back."

"Okay, baby." Reggie gave her hand a quick squeeze.

"Tiara," he said, just as she was about to disappear into her bedroom.

"Yes?"

"Your Aunt Charlie seems to think that you really like Rashad. Is that true?"

Tiara shrugged. "I mean he's okay. Like you said, he's nice. But he's just not for me."

"And you told him that?"

Tiara nodded.

"And he just accepted it?"

"Well, yeah. He didn't make a big deal about it." Tiara paused. "I mean, he was a little upset, I guess. Why? Was he acting depressed or something this morning when you saw him?"

Reggie shrugged. "No, he seemed fine."

Damn, Tiara thought, as she closed the bedroom door behind her. *Damn, damn, damn.*

II

D ang. Who the hell's blowing up your cell phone like that?"
Tiara grumbled. It was freezing outside, but Lionel had the heater in
the car blasting. She could have asked him to turn it down, but it gave
her an excuse to be in a foul mood, and since she was in a foul mood,
she was happy to keep it as an excuse. Another excuse was that they
had been in the car only fifteen minutes, and he had already received
four calls. All from his friend, Tommy, according to Lionel. Tiara had
met Tommy a couple of times, and he was a true pain in the ass.
Skinny, whiny, and always borrowing fifty or sixty bucks from Lionel.
She couldn't stand him, and she really couldn't stand him now since
he was preventing her from getting her grub on with all these inces-
sant calls.

None of the calls lasted more than two minutes, but since Lionel's
headset was broken, he had to keep pulling over to answer the call because of the New York law prohibiting people from using a hand-held
phone while driving.

"I told you I'd call you back when I can talk," Lionel growled into the telephone. Tiara watched his jaw tighten as he listened to the person on the other end.

"Okay, I'll be there in about ten minutes." He turned off the telephone and placed it on the console, then stared out the car window, jaw still tight.

"Well, what's going on?" Tiara finally asked.

"Nothing."

"How you gonna say nothing when you're sitting there like you're catatonic or something?" Tiara snapped.

"Look, babe," Lionel turned to her. "Why don't I drive you back to your apartment and I'll pick you up this evening and take you out to a nice dinner. I really gotta take care of some business right now."

Tiara's mouth dropped, and she put her hand on her hip. "Are you crazy? Have you lost your fucking mind?"

"Come on, Sweet Pea—"

"Sweet Pea my ass! What you think I'm stupid or some shit?" Tiara leaned over and waved her finger in his face. "You promise to take me out to eat, then you gonna change your mind after I get dressed and come out my house and shit? Why? I bet that wasn't even Tommy calling you all them times. You got some girl sweating you or something?"

"Come on, Tiara, you know I ain't messing around." Lionel sighed.

"You better not be, because I don't play that shit." Tiara tossed her head and then ran her fingers through her hair. "If you don't want me you just let me know and I'm out."

Lionel pulled back out into traffic. "I'm taking you home, and I'll call you later."

"What? You ain't heard a word I said, or something," Tiara almost hissed. "Who the fuck you think you're playing with, boy? If I get out of this car and go in my building, you'd better believe I ain't never gonna get back in. I promise you that!"

"God damn, Tiara!" Lionel gritted his teeth. "Why are you making such a big fucking deal about this?"

"'Cause I don't like the idea of you dumping me to go shack up with some bitch. And don't tell me that shit about it being Tommy calling you," Tiara almost shrieked.

"It was Tommy!"

"Fine, if it was Tommy, then let me answer the phone next time it rings!"

"It's not going to ring again."

Riiing.

Still driving, Lionel reached for the telephone lying on the console, but Tiara snatched it first.

"Who the fuck is this?" She leaned back toward the passenger side window to avoid Lionel's desperate grabs for the phone.

"Who the fuck is this?" came back a gruff masculine voice.

"Tommy, why can't you get a life, and leave me and my man alone." Tiara sucked her teeth. "Didn't he say he'd call you back when he got a chance? Why don't you stop calling?"

"Girl, shut up and put Lionel on the phone," the man answered.

"The fuck you going to tell me to shut up. I want you to listen real close to what I'm about to say—" *Click.* Tiara turned off the telephone and handed it to Lionel. "You better tell your boys to watch their damn mouths."

Lionel pulled the car over, and punched a couple of buttons on the telephone. "Damn," he exclaimed when he saw the number of the person who had called. "Why you do that shit!"

Tiara shrugged her indifference. "He'll call back if it's important."

Lionel closed his eyes and shook his head. "He'll call back if it's important," he said under his breath. "Do you believe this shit?" He opened his eyes and turned the key in the ignition to take off again. "Tiara, you just don't know how to act. I don't appreciate—" The phone rang again, and he put it to his ear immediately.

"Yeah, man," he said. He listened for a few seconds, then glanced at Tiara, who sat with her arms crossed, glaring at him. "Yeah, I got it covered," he continued into the phone. "I said I got it covered," he repeated. He looked at his watch. "I can be there in ten minutes." He ignored the punch Tiara landed on his shoulder. "Peace out," he said, then turned off the phone and sat quietly for a few seconds.

"Look," he finally turned to face Tiara. "We're going to go eat, but first I have to make a quick stop, okay?"

"So, what is it you got covered?"

"Huh?"

"You just told Tommy that you had it covered. What's 'it'?"

"Girl! I got to tell you everything?" He peeled off.

"First of all, that wasn't Tommy you hung up on. And I don't appreciate you acting stupid in front of my friends. I told you that shit before," Lionel said quietly. "Second of all, it's none of your damn business what I got covered."

Tiara rolled her eyes and looked out the window. He was getting on her last nerve. She thought about jumping out of the car so he could chase her down, but it was too cold outside. And besides, he obviously really wanted to get rid of her anyway, so he just might not chase her. The thought pissed her off even more. "And why you got the heat blasting, anyway? It feels like we got front row seats in Hell."

"No problem." Lionel obligingly turned the heat down. "But now listen. Like I said, I've got to make a stop, and I'm not going to be more than five minutes. And I just want you to wait in the car."

Twelve minutes later they pulled up on a corner on Amsterdam Avenue, not far from her school. Lionel turned off the engine and jumped out, beeping the remote once to lock the doors. Tiara banged on the windows, but he gave no indication that he heard as he strode to the entrance of a storefront. The windows were soap frosted, and there was an outline of missing letters on the dingy white sign above the door that indicated it was once the location of Sandy's Shrimp Shack.

Tiara watched as Lionel raised a gloved fist to pound on the door, but it opened before he could make contact, and he disappeared inside.

Damn, I can't even play music while I wait since he took the fucking keys, Tiara thought grimly. To top it off, the car that had been roasting hot just a few minutes before was getting chilly quick. She couldn't get out since the locks were electronic, and there was no music, so what was she going to do while she waited? Damn that Lionel. She tried to jerk open the glove compartment, but it was locked, and she got a broken fingernail for her effort. *Shit. I'm going to make him pay for a full set of tips,* she thought angrily. She pulled a file from her Coach purse and began angrily sawing her ragged nail. *And if he thinks I'm going to just stay in here and wait on him like some kind of a hostage he has another think coming.* After she rounded her nail, she began to look around for something she could use to crash through the thick windows. Finding nothing suitable for the job she leaned hard against her seat, crossed her arms, and fumed. *Men ain't shit. Here's Lionel locking me up, and Rashad ain't barely willing to look me up.* Her thoughts surprised her. Now why the hell was she even thinking about Rashad? He certainly wasn't thinking about her. He didn't even have enough class to act like he was bummed out when he saw her father that morning. But then again, why should he act bummed out? It wasn't like his heart was aching for her like hers was aching for him.

Shit, I might as well admit, I'm crazy about that man. There's something about him. I don't know what. But he's always so calm, and so kind. A really deep brother. I don't think he cares about how smart someone is, or how much money they have, or even how they look. It's like he looks into a person and sees who they really are. I wonder what he really sees when he looks at me. Who does he think I really am?

She shifted uncomfortably in her seat. Who was she? Good looking, smart, full of lofty goals, and the envy of almost every woman she knew.

But that's all the superficial stuff. I mean, how would I really define who I am? It would be so cool to be able to see myself in the mirror of his eyes.

"Damn," she said out loud. "Now he's got me thinking all philosophical and poetic." She shook her head vigorously. She had to stop thinking about him. If he didn't want her, then she'd be damned if she was going to waste her time wanting him. Especially since she had a man that wanted the hell out of her. A man with money, good looks, style, and sense enough to want a good thing. Namely her.

She sighed and once again leaned back, at the same time fingering the soft leather of the seats. *Here I am, treating Lionel like shit, and why? Because he isn't Rashad? I'd better get a grip.*

Her deliberations were interrupted when she heard a double beep, indicating the doors had been unlocked. She looked up to see Lionel approaching the car. She smiled, not caring that he couldn't see her through the tinted windows. *I better act like I know, and make him realize that I really do want him instead of treating him like a piece of shit just because he lets me.*

Lionel jumped in the car, inserted the key in the ignition, and revved the engine to take off. He paused when Tiara gently put her hand on his arm.

"You know I love you, right?" Tiara leaned over and up, and kissed him softly on the cheek. "And I'm sorry if I piss you off sometimes. I don't mean to."

Lionel turned to her, a puzzled but pleased look on his face. But before he could say anything, there was a rapid knock on his car window.

"Hold up, you forgot your cell." Lionel lowered the window to accept the phone from a black leather sleeve and a huge rough brown hand.

"Thanks, man," Lionel mumbled as he quickly rolled the window back up. Tiara watched through the tinted glass as the giant of a man crossed in front of the parked car and headed back to the storefront, stopping briefly to take a last puff of a cigarette before flipping the butt on the sidewalk.

"Who's that?" She tapped Lionel's arm, her eyes following the man's progress to the storefront, where he demanded entrance with a few bangs of his fist. Something about him was familiar, but she couldn't place him. She was sure he wasn't one of the few friends to whom Lionel had introduced her, but she knew she had seen him somewhere before. She rolled down her window hoping to get a better view of his face.

"No one." Lionel pulled out, then braked hard, throwing Tiara back in her seat. Her purse flew into the dashboard, its contents spilling out onto the car floor. A purple Dodge Neon that had almost hit him now had him wedged in, and the driver was leaning on the horn in a fury.

"Will you get the fuck out the way?" Lionel yelled, sticking his head out the window.

"I beg your pardon?" A gray-haired woman rolled down her window. "You were the one pulling out in traffic without looking, you know." She turned to her companion, an even older looking woman who it seemed could barely see over the steering wheel. "Can you believe it, Lizzie? He almost caused us to hit him, and then he's going to curse at us."

"Will you PLEASE get the fuck out the way!" Lionel shouted.

"Hmmph!" the woman said before rolling up her window. The Neon slowly backed up to get clear of the Porsche, then drove off.

"Damn, Lionel. What's wrong with you?" Tiara's heart was still beating fast as she bent over and started stuffing items back into her purse.

"Nothing. I'm just trying to get out of here," Lionel mumbled. Tiara noticed perspiration beading on his forehead, even though it was still cold in the car. She also noticed his furtive glance at the store. She turned to see if the man was still there, but he was gone.

"Who was that guy, anyway?" She turned back to Lionel.

"I told you, no one," Lionel snapped as he took off up Amsterdam Avenue. "I don't even know him. He was just there while I was talking to Tommy. He must be Tommy's boy. All right?" He turned right on 181st Street and got on the Cross Bronx Expressway.

"Well, what did Tommy want that was so important, anyway?" Tiara demanded.

"He just needed to borrow a couple of dollars to buy his mother a birthday present." Lionel seemed to relax a little bit. "He only asked for twenty dollars so it was no big deal."

"We came all the way uptown to give that asshole twenty dollars?" Tiara sucked her teeth. "You should have told him to eat shit and get a job."

Lionel chuckled. "I told you it's no big deal, and it's not like it was really out of our way."

"We're not going down to the Village?"

"Nope."

"Where are we going?"

"My mother told me about this great little Greek restaurant in New Haven I've been dying to try. I figure today's as good a day as any."

"New Haven, Connecticut?" Tiara had lived in Harlem all her life, but had never been to Connecticut, which was only an hour or so away. As far as she was concerned, Connecticut was the haven of rich white folks.

"Got a problem with that?" Lionel grinned.

"Well, no, not at all." Tiara leaned back in her seat, reached over and took Lionel's hand. *Yeah, this is the life I want. This is the life I deserve.*

. . .

Tiara yawned and looked at her watch. Six thirty already. She wrapped the jade satin sheet around her and headed to the living room where she found Lionel sitting on the black leather couch wearing only his green silk pajama bottoms, a pair of stereo headsets on his head and the television remote in his hand. How someone could listen to hip-hop and watch college football at the same time was beyond her, but that was Lionel's thing. She walked in between him and the seventy-inch Mitsubishi television, her bare toes gripping and releasing the plush white carpet as she gave a sexy stretch, letting the sheet slide down her body a few inches.

"Hey, Sweet Pea." He slid the headphones off as she settled next to him and put his arm around her. She nestled her head into his shoulder and started twirling his curly chest hair through her fingers. "You finally decided to get your lazy butt up, huh? Hungry?"

"No, I'm still trying to digest that big lunch."

"Don't even hand me that shit." Lionel grinned. "You were doing some serious aerobic exercise in the bed a little bit ago. You've done worked all those calories off."

"Oh, be quiet." Tiara gave him a playful nip on his shoulder.

"Mmmm, girl." Lionel cupped her face in his hands. "Now you know I'm going to have to bite you back, right?"

Tiara smiled and lay back on the couch, letting the sheet fall from her nude body. "Do what you got to do, Count Dracula."

Riiing.

"You going to get that?" Tiara said in a husky voice as Lionel leaned over and started kissing and nibbling her throat.

"No."

"It might be somebody important." Tiara flicked her tongue over Lionel's chin. "Tommy might need to borrow another twenty dollars."

"Fuck Tommy." Lionel was breathing hard now, as his hands slid down her body.

Tiara leaned up and kissed him hard on the lips so that he wouldn't notice her reaching for the telephone which was on the black marble end table by the couch. She brought the receiver to her ear. "Hello, Evans residence, may I help you?" She tried to suppress a giggle as Lionel's eyes flew open.

"Hello," she said again when there was no answer on the other end of the phone.

"Hello, yes, this is Lionel's mother," a cultured female voice finally spoke. "Is he there?"

Tiara's eyes widened. "Yes, he is," she said in the most refined tone she could muster. "Hold on one moment, please?" She put her hand over the receiver. "Your mother," she mouthed to Lionel.

Lionel mouthed back an expansive groan, then took the phone. "Hey, Mom."

Tiara scrambled up from the couch, eluding Lionel's grasp. She ignored his pleading look that silently relayed that he intended to get off the telephone quickly to finish what they had started. As ridiculous as it seemed, she felt as if they had just gotten busted by his mother. What if she figured out what they were doing when she called? What a helluva first impression! The mood was gone as far as she was concerned. She headed to the bathroom and quickly washed up, then headed to the bedroom to retrieve her clothes. Lionel was still talking on the phone when she walked back in the living room.

"I don't know, I'll have to ask her," he was saying. When he looked up and saw her, he added. "Here, you can ask her yourself." To her shock, he handed her the telephone. Oh God, she thought, what if she asks what they had been doing?

"Hello, Mrs. Evans, how are you?"

"Oh, I'm doing fine, dear," Mrs. Evans answered sweetly. "I was just asking Lionel if you would be joining us for Thanksgiving."

"Well, I would love to," Tiara answered, then added quickly. "That is, if it's not too much trouble."

"No trouble at all. And I'm looking forward to meeting you. Lionel has told us all about you and your family," Mrs. Evans answered gaily. "I have to run, but let me tell my son a quick good-bye. It was nice talking to you."

Tiara handed the telephone back to Lionel. *Wow, I'm going to go to Washington, D.C., to have Thanksgiving with a family of millionaires. Is this wild or what? Just wait until I tell Daddy.* She sat on the couch next to Lionel while he finished talking to his mother. *And just think, none of this would have happened if it weren't for that asshole getting mad and threatening me because I wouldn't give him a play. Damn, things have really—* Tiara's train of thought was interrupted by a flash of clarity. That asshole. That guy that had knocked on Lionel's car window this afternoon. It was the same guy, wasn't it? But how . . . ?

Lionel hung up the telephone and grabbed for her. "So you're finally going to meet my family, Sweet Pea. My folks are going to love you. Especially my moms."

"Lionel!" She struggled out of his arms and scooted back on the couch to put some distance between them. "Who was that guy this afternoon?"

"What guy?" Lionel's expression suddenly went blank.

"The guy who brought your phone." Tiara squinted her eyes as she looked at him.

"I told you I don't know him. He's some friend of Tommy's."

"Don't you bullshit me!" Tiara jumped up from the couch and stood in front of the still seated Lionel waving her finger in his face. "I ain't playing with you, boy!"

"Stop acting crazy, Tiara." Lionel got up from the couch. "Here I'm trying to talk to you about you coming home with me for Thanksgiving, and you want to talk about Tommy and his friends." He tried to pull her into his arms. "Now come on, let's figure out what you're going to wear when you meet my family."

"First off . . ." Tiara pushed him back, then put her hand back in his face. "I ain't never needed a man to pick out my clothes before, and I don't need one to help me now. And second off, I know that guy was the one that was bothering me the day we met."

"Come on, Tiara, stop acting crazy!"

"Crazy, my ass. I don't know what kind of game you're trying to play, but you ain't running it on me!" Tiara stormed to the hallway closet, snatched her jacket off the hanger, then slammed the closet door so hard the whole apartment shook.

"Look, I'm not even going to offer to drive you home, because you need to cool off." Lionel headed to the bedroom. "I'll call you a cab."

"Oh, no, you're not going to call me a cab," Tiara screamed after him. "I ain't get here by cab, and I ain't leaving by cab. You're taking me home, and you're going to hear my mouth the whole way!"

"I'm not taking you anywhere if you keep screaming like that, damn it!" Lionel stormed back in the living room.

"Well, I'm going to keep on screaming, and I'm going to scream even louder. SO WHAT ARE YOU GOING TO DO ABOUT IT? NOTHING, RIGHT? THAT'S WHAT I THOUGHT YOU WERE GOING TO DO!"

"Tiara, stop!" Lionel said. "I can't take all this racket!"

"THEN MAKE ME STOP!"

Lionel looked at her and sighed, then slowly turned and walked to the couch and sat down. "Look," he said, "if I tell you the truth, would you please shut the hell up?"

"Maybe." Tiara crossed her arms and patted her foot on the carpet. "Depends on what you say."

"Okay." Lionel looked at her thoughtfully. "Okay, I'll tell you the truth. Come here." He reached his arm to her.

"No. You talk there, I'll stand here."

"If you don't come sit next to me, I ain't telling you shit," Lionel snapped. "So you can stand there and shout yourself hoarse for all I care."

Tiara glared at him. She didn't want to admit it, but her throat was already beginning to get a little sore. She walked over and plopped on the couch, her arms still crossed.

"All right, I'm here. Now start talking."

Lionel looked at her and shook his head. "You're a fucking trip, you know?"

"Oh, I'm the trip?" Tiara started raising her voice again. "I'm the fucking trip?"

"All right, all right, calm down," Lionel said hurriedly. "I shouldn't have said that."

"You sure shouldn't the fuck have said that," Tiara snapped.

Lionel looked at her intently, and then sighed. "All right, I'm going to come clean. That guy is a friend of mine. His name is Al. And I put him up to messing with you so I could have an excuse to meet you."

"You did what?" Tiara asked in quiet fury. "You put my life at risk because you wanted to meet me?"

"Oh come on, stop it. Your life wasn't at risk. I just told him to bother you a little so I could come to the rescue. He wasn't going to really hit you." Lionel snorted. "I don't know why you always have to be dramatic."

"Oh, yeah, I'm the one being dramatic." Tiara cut her eyes at Lionel. "You get some thug to threaten me just so you can get your rap on, and I'm the one being dramatic? You've got some nerve!"

"Yeah, well, I'm sorry. But at least I'm being honest now," Lionel grumbled. "I don't know why you're still making such a big deal about it."

"Lionel, please. I'm just finding all this shit out. I think I have the right to be upset!" Tiara huffed. Damn, he must have been checking her out for a while, waiting for his chance. Trying to figure out how to make his move. He was like obsessed or something. Ain't this some shit? She knew she was irresistible, but come on. "So? What? Like how long were you stalking me?"

"Stalking you?"

"Yeah. How long had you been following me around before you got your boy to mess with me so you could finally meet me?"

"Girl, what the fuck I look like stalking someone? That was the first time I'd ever seen you."

"Whaaaat?"

"Yeah. Me and Al were driving up Amsterdam Avenue and I spotted you, and you know, you were looking good. And, well, we weren't going anywhere in particular, so I thought it'd be fun to try some shit like that to see what would happen," Lionel shrugged.

"Oh, no, you didn't say that." Tiara put her hand in the air and shook her head from side to side. "Oh, no, you are not even trying to tell me that."

"What?"

"You mean, you went through all that shit just on a whim?" Tiara got up from the couch slowly. "You know what? You're a fucking sicko. I'm out of here."

"Now you're going back into your dramatics." Lionel sighed. "You've known me a month now. Do I seem like a sicko to you?"

"You didn't until now," Tiara retorted.

"Tiara, come on. I admit I was wrong in the beginning, but you've got to admit in the long run it was a good thing." Lionel disappeared into the bedroom but continued talking. "We got something special going on, girl, you know that. And if I didn't pull that little trick, we might never have met each other." He came back into the living room. "And if we never met each other, I would never be able to give you this." He pressed something into her hand. She gasped when she realized what it was. A diamond solitaire ring in a white gold setting, ringed by tiny rubies.

"Oh my God!" She held it up for closer inspection. "How many carats is it?"

"Only one and a half," Lionel grinned. "But look, this is not an engagement ring, okay?"

"I didn't say it was," Tiara said, her eyes never leaving the ring. It was so beautiful. The lights from the overhead lamp seemed to dance in each cut of the diamond.

"All right, I just want to make sure you understand that." Lionel took the ring from Tiara and gently slipped it on the pinkie of her right hand. "'Cause when I buy your engagement ring, it's going to be a helluva lot bigger than that. Okay?" He kissed her lightly on the lips.

"Okay." Tiara said softly. *Not* if *he buys me an engagement ring, but* when. *Yeah, I got it like that.*

12

Damn, I'm really slipping. Tiara slid her chemistry quiz out of her purple spiral notebook and looked at it again, as if this time the score would be different. But the red circled sixty-five was still there. The bus stopped short just then, and the exam paper slipped out of her hand and onto the floor. The bus was packed, and before she could retrieve the paper, someone stepped on it, leaving a soggy dirty footprint. She considered leaving it on the bus floor, but bent over and picked it up, because, after all, she did need to go over it again to see what the hell she was doing wrong. She looked out the bus window just in time to see that the next stop was 116th Street and Malcolm X Boulevard—her stop.

I've got to stop spending so much time with Lionel. I'm going to blow my GPA, she thought as she walked toward the building. She briefly wondered if Lionel's grades had gone down because of the time they spent together. They never really talked about school when they were together, she realized for the first time. He'd never said anything about having to stay up and cram for a test, but then again neither had she. But she would sure be cramming this weekend for the big chemistry test on Monday. She had four days to get it together. *Aunt Charlie's just going to have to be mad tonight, because I don't have time to sit and play games or watch a video after dinner, even if it is Thursday Family Night. I'll just explain to Daddy I gotta get some studying done, and let him duke it out with her.*

It was only 2:00 P.M., but the sky was dark gray, and the brisk damp air seemed to suggest snow, which was ludicrous since it was early in the season. The whole world was going crazy. A sixty-five on a chemistry quiz and snow in November.

She glanced over at a crowd of excited high-school girls gathering on the corner of 115th Street. They must be crazy, she noted indifferently. It was too cold to be fighting. She was skirting around the group when someone reached out and pulled her arm. It was Shakira's sister, Asia.

"Tiara," she shouted.

"Don't be pulling on me." Tiara jerked her arm away.

"They getting ready to jump your sister," Asia said urgently.

"What! Who?" Tiara whirled around and ran back toward the crowd, pushing her way into the middle. Sure enough there was Jo-Jo, her arms crossed, her head cocked toward the sky. In front of her were three girls, all of whom looked like they were about seventeen. One of them, a tall girl with platinum-blond-dyed dreadlocks pulled back into a ponytail and Vaseline smeared all over her face was waving her hand in Jo-Jo's face.

"You big doofus bitch!" she was screaming. "You so bad pushing someone who's smaller than you, huh? Why don't you push me, you fucking homo bitch. You gonna hit my sister, why don't you try hitting someone your own size."

Tiara tensed to leap in between the girl and Jo-Jo, but to her surprise, Shakira was there first.

"Naw, naw." Shakira slapped the girl's hand away. "You ain't gonna be coming up here in the Foster's with that shit. Y'all better carry your stank asses back over to 117th Street before you get them kicked."

"And who's going to kick them?" challenged a second girl with short red hair plastered to her scalp.

"Me, bitch!" Tiara stepped up next to Shakira, snatching her earrings out of her ears as she talked. "You wanna beef with my sister you gonna have to go through me!" The crowd gave an appreciative "Whooo!" at the sight of a new combatant.

Tiara fingered the diamond ring Lionel had given her the weekend before. She thought about the bloody imprint it was going to leave when she smashed the girl's face, but reconsidered and slipped it off her finger and into her pocket. No sense in risking the rock coming out of the setting. Her eyes never leaving her foe, Tiara slipped off her shoulder bag and handed it to Jo-Jo, then balled up her fists.

"Bitch, I'll kick your ass and your sister's ass," the girl taunted.

"I know you ain't thinking we going to let you bitches jump our girl," the redheaded girl added as she balled her own fists.

"Y'all the ones coming up here try to jump a kid, bitch!" Shakira snarled.

"That lesbian bitch is bigger than me," the dreadlocked girl screeched. "And she ain't had no business fucking with my little sister."

"She hit me first," Jo-Jo said calmly. Tiara ignored her.

"Call her a lesbian again and I'll knock your ass all the way from here to Brooklyn, you slut," Tiara shouted.

"And I'll help her!" Niecie was at Tiara's side now. "This is our fucking territory. Don't be coming up to Foster thinking you gonna start some shit with one of our girls. We don't play that shit."

"Bitch, we'll kick all of your asses," the first girl screamed, though she was starting to retreat.

"Bring it the fuck on, then." Tiara assumed a perfect boxer's stance—her left hand balled in a fist slightly above chest level, waving the girl to come closer with her right.

"Hit her, Tiara. Punch the shit out of her. Kick her ass," someone in the crowd yelled.

"Come on, come on, break it up." Two uniformed police officers stepped in between the girls. Tiara suddenly noticed a police car parked haphazardly on the sidewalk with the lights flashing. She hadn't even heard it pull up.

"They started it," Niecie was screaming. "These grown-ass bitches coming up here to fuck with a junior high school kid."

"Fuck you, bitch! Watch me stomp your stank ass into the ground," the girl with the blond dreadlocks screamed back.

"Oh yeah, you're real fucking bad now that the five-oh is up in here," Shakira taunted back. "I noticed your ass was backing up a minute ago."

"I said break it up." The taller of the police officers, a white man with a grizzly red beard and a potbelly, gave the girl a slight push. "Don't make me bring you in."

"What's going on?" Tiara looked up to see a wide-eyed and breathless Aunt Charlie. Her pocketbook was slipping off of her shoulder, and her car keys were in her trembling hand. Her eyes darted from the police officers to Tiara and Shakira, and then to Jo-Jo who stood in back of them. She turned slightly and looked the 117th Streets girls up and down, a sneer on her lips as she correctly identified them as the enemy.

"Nothing, Aunt Charlie." Tiara straightened her shoulders and adjusted the collar of her jacket. "We got it handled."

"You ain't got shit handled," the girl spat at Tiara. The girl then looked Charlene up and down in return. "And I don't know what you're looking at, you old Frankenstein bitch!"

Tiara gasped. Children would make fun of her aunt behind her back, and sometimes Tiara had even joined in, but never, ever had she heard anyone—man, woman, or child—insult Charlene to her face. She couldn't even imagine her aunt's reaction, and she didn't want to look and see. Tiara lunged forward and landed a haymaker to the girl's jaw. The girl fell back into the arms of one of her companions, aided by Jo-Jo's hard blow to the middle of her chest.

"Don't you be talking about my aunt!" Jo-Jo screamed, pulling her arm back for another swing. But before she could deliver it, the grizzly red-bearded officer stepped behind her, jerked her arms together behind her back, and handcuffed her.

"Come on," he said gruffly, pushing her toward the police car.

"Let her go!" Tiara jumped between them and the police car. "She ain't do nothing."

"Move out the way or you're coming, too." The police officer pushed her to the side. His partner calmly walked over to his side.

"Then you're going to have to take me," Tiara hissed. Out of the corner of her eye she saw Shakira, Niecie, and a few of her other friends grabbing up the dreadlocked girl by her collar, while Aunt Charlie leaned over her talking rapidly, her finger jabbing the air close to the girl's face.

"Cuff her," the first officer said to his partner.

"Miss, calm down." The second officer, a tall thirty-ish dark-skinned man with a bushy mustache, placed his arm on Tiara's shoulder. "Your sister's going to be okay," he said in a gentle voice.

"Then let her go!" Tiara shook off the officer's arm. "She didn't do anything!"

"Hold on." Charlene was suddenly standing next to Tiara. "We all just need to calm down for a minute." She held her hands up in front of her.

"But Aunt Charlie, they're going to arrest Jo-Jo," Tiara shouted. "Look!" She pointed to the officer, whose hand was on top of her sister's head, guiding it down into the back seat of the patrol car. Tears were streaming down Jo-Jo's face, and her body shook with sobs. "They're taking her away." Tiara tried to lunge toward them, but Charlene held her back.

"Sweetie, I've got this handled. Just go stand over there with your friends," Charlene said soothingly. She turned to the mustached officer. "Officer Scott," she said, reading the name on his silver badge. "Can we just talk for a minute? I really think we can clear this all up."

"Ma'am, I was just telling your niece that her sister's going to be okay." Officer Scott stepped closer to Charlene and lowered his voice. "We'll just probably take her into the precinct for a couple of minutes, and if the other girl doesn't come down to press charges we'll just let her go."

"But look, those girls left." Charlene pointed in the direction of the dwindling crowd. "So you know they're not going to press charges."

"It doesn't matter. She hit the girl right in front of us, and was getting ready to hit her again." The grizzled officer had walked up to Charlene and Officer Scott. "We're not giving her a walk."

"She didn't hit her, I did," Tiara piped up. Charlene gave her a warning look.

"She only hit her because the girl had shoved me," Charlene addressed Officer Scott. "I know it was wrong, but you know how young people are. She was only trying to protect me."

"I was right there and I didn't see you get shoved," the grizzly officer growled.

"Well, I did, Jack. The girl almost knocked her down," Officer Scott said. Tiara's eyes widened, but Charlene seemed to be taking the handsome officer's lie in stride. "The girl was still wrong, but I think we can cut her some slack."

"Let me talk to you over here for a minute." The grizzled officer motioned his partner toward the patrol car.

"Officer Scott," Charlene touched the policeman lightly on the arm, and spoke in a husky voice. "My niece is only twelve. Look at the poor baby." She waved toward the back seat of the police car where Jo-Jo was crying uncontrollably. "She's scared to death. Can you let her get out and at least stand next to us while the two of you talk? I promise she's not going to break for it or anything." Charlene gave a throaty laugh.

Tiara couldn't believe it. Was Aunt Charlie actually flirting with this guy? And even more amazing, was it working? The police officer was certainly grinning from ear to ear. And he had just told a barefaced lie for her. The left side of her face remained almost expressionless, but Aunt Charlie was working the shit out of the right side, smiling so sweet, batting her eyes, and doing a little wrinkle of the nose. As messed up as the whole situation was, Tiara actually had to suppress a giggle. *Go, Aunt Charlie.*

"That big-ass girl isn't fourteen years old. She's trying to shit us." The grizzled officer snapped.

"I beg your pardon," Charlene said pointedly.

"Jack, watch your mouth," Officer Scott snapped. He walked over to the car and bent down to speak to Jo-Jo. "How old are you?"

"Fourteen," Jo-Jo wailed.

"Jo-Jo!" Aunt Charlie said sharply.

"Twelve," Jo-Jo sniffed, and looked at her aunt apologetically.

"Come on, honey." Officer Scott helped Jo-Jo out of the car, turned her around, and unlocked the handcuffs.

Jo-Jo rubbed her wrists as if trying to soothe the dark red rings the cuffs had left. Tiara rushed to her side, and helped her rub.

"How tall are you?" Officer Scott asked.

"Five-five," Tiara said brusquely.

"He was talking to Jo-Jo," Charlene laughed and shot an amused look toward Officer Scott.

"Five feet nine," Jo-Jo said sullenly.

"You play basketball?"

"Yeah."

"What position?"

"Forward."

"You play for a team?"

"Yeah."

"Jo-Jo, stop giving the officer one-word answers," Charlene interrupted the questioning. "Show you have some breeding."

"Yes, Aunt Charlie," Jo-Jo answered, still sullen.

"It's okay," Officer Scott said kindly. "I have a niece her age myself." He turned back to Jo-Jo. "So, what team do you play for?"

"The Hawkettes."

"Over at St. George's center? Albert Hall's your coach?"

Jo-Jo nodded.

"He's a good friend of mine." Officer Scott fingered the edge of his mustache. "I'm going to make sure he looks out for you and makes sure you don't get in any more trouble, okay?"

"I can go home then?" Jo-Jo said hopefully.

The grizzled officer grunted and walked over to the patrol car, slamming the door as he got in the driver's seat.

"Yeah, you can go home." Officer Scott ignored his partner's displeasure. "But I mean what I said. I'm going to be calling Coach Hall to make sure you're flying right. When's your next game?"

"Saturday."

"Well, if I'm off I might even stop by and check you out."

"Oh, that would be so nice." Charlene put her arm around Jo-Jo's waist. "Thank you so much for being so understanding," she said to Officer Scott. "I hope this isn't going to cause a problem between you and your partner."

The officer tilted his cap back on his head and smiled, his eyes twinkling as he did so. "Don't give it a second thought. He needs to be reminded who's the senior partner every now and then."

"Senior partner? No!" Charlene smiled up at him, twirling a lock of her auburn hair. "I hope you don't mind my commenting, but you don't look a day over twenty-five." *Oh, damn, Aunt Charlie's laying it on thick,* Tiara thought.

"Actually, I'm thirty-eight," Officer Scott said.

Okay, he's seven years younger than she is. Bet she's not going to comment about that. Tiara grinned at her aunt, but Aunt Charlie paid her no attention. *Come to think of it, Aunt Charlie could probably pass for a lot younger. Especially right now with that "come hither" look on her face.*

"Do you mind if I talk to you privately for a minute, Mrs. . . . um . . ."

"Miss Bynum. Charlene Bynum." Charlene flashed a sexy smile. "Please call me Charlene."

"My pleasure, Charlene. Please call me James."

"Is he trying to rap to Aunt Charlie?" Jo-Jo whispered as the police officer and Charlene walked a few feet away from them.

"It sure as hell looks like it." Tiara shook her head in a combination of disbelief and amusement. *Ain't this some shit? I ain't mad at her, though. I hope she does start getting some. Maybe she'll stop acting like she lives at our house.* And they did look good together, she noted as she looked back at them over her shoulder. He was tall, about six-four, with a dark bronze complexion, and though he was wearing the heavy police uniform coat, the broadness of his shoulders was apparent. Aunt Charlie, like Jo-Jo and Reggie, was tall—five-foot-ten—and slender. Her shoulder-length auburn hair flowed airily in the chilly breeze as she smiled up at the officer, who was smiling back down at her. Yeah, they looked real good standing there smiling as they talked. Real good.

"Damn, y'all shoulda heard your aunt threatening them 117th Street bitches." Shakira handed Tiara her shoulder bag. "She told them if they didn't split right that second she was going to wait until the police left, then kick their ass, and then go to their houses and kick their mother's ass, too. So then they were still talking shit, and she told them that she was going to tell the police that they hit her, and make sure their asses got hauled off to jail right along with Jo-Jo, and then they'd get searched and spend the night in jail."

"Yeah," Niecie added. "I think the bitch that was doing all the wolfing musta been holding something, because she wanted to get the hell up outta here when your aunt said that. She probably had some drugs or something. 'Cause if she had a gun she woulda pulled it and shot your ass when you slid her."

"You think she had a gun?" Jo-Jo's mouth dropped open.

"Girl, you ain't listen to what she said? She just said it couldn'ta been a gun. Pay attention," Shakira snapped.

Tiara looked at Shakira but didn't say anything about her tone with Jo-Jo. After all, just a few minutes before she had been willing to step up for Jo-Jo, but still . . . she better not get carried away.

"Come on. Let's get in the apartment. I'm freezing." Tiara started rubbing her hands together.

"Yeah, but we were going to kick those bitches' ass, weren't we?" Shakira put her hand out, and Tiara grinned and gave her a pound. "They think we were going to let them come up on our block and mess with one of our girls, huh?" Shakira continued as they walked toward Tiara's building. "You hear me when I told them they'd better carry their stank asses back to 117th Street? I almost slid her right then. You see when I slapped her hands out of Jo-Jo's face? The bitch was so bad, but she ain't do shit then."

"Yeah," Niecie chimed in. "Did you hear me when I told her that we don't play that shit over here in the Foster? I was ready to kick all their asses. They better be glad the police rolled up. We'd still be beating their asses up and down the street, right? They'd have to pick their teeth up out the gutter and shit. I was going to snatch them locks right out that bitch's head. She woulda been bald by the time I got through with her."

"Naw, I was going to take care of the bitch with the locks. Her ass was mine. Y'all were going to go after them other bitches," Tiara said confidently. "I had that Medusa bitch covered. You see how I hit her?

Bam!" Tiara punched the air. "I hurt my fist on that girl's jaw. I was ready for my follow-up, but then Jo-Jo was on her ass." She looked at her sister appreciatively. "You were getting ready to fuck that girl up."

"Yeah, well, you know," Jo-Jo grinned and shrugged her shoulders like a boxing champion shrugging off her robe in the ring. "I wasn't going to let 'em talk about Aunt Charlie and not do anything."

"Shit, girl, I didn't even know you could fight," Shakira said. "Why come you let them get all up in your face like that?"

"Oh, she can fight," Tiara chortled. "Believe me, she can fight. She works out with my dad, boxing and shit."

"So why you let them get with you like that?" Shakira demanded again.

"I wasn't going to waste my breath arguing with them." Jo-Jo shrugged. "I just decided I was going to wait until one of them put their hands on me, and then I was going to kick all their asses."

"Stop cursing." Tiara hit Jo-Jo on the back of the head.

"You were cursing," Jo-Jo said accusingly.

"Shut up."

"You shut up."

"Well, I'm outta here," Shakira said. "Come on, Niecie. We're gonna hafta haul ass if we're going to get my weave at the Korean store before they close."

"Aunt Charlie," Jo-Jo said as their aunt joined them on the stoop. "Tell Tiara to leave me alone. She's hitting on me."

"Tiara, leave your sister alone," Charlene said in a light sing-song voice. She pulled open the front door to the building and waved the girls in. "Come on, sweeties. Let's get out of the cold."

Tiara and Jo-Jo looked at each other, both grinning with amazement.

"Aunt Charlie and a police officer up in the tree. K, I, S, S, I, N, G." Jo-Jo chanted as she entered the building.

"Aunt Charlie, you can tell me." Tiara put her arms around her aunt's shoulders. "What did you guys have to talk about privately? Did he ask you out?"

"None of your business."

"Oh, see, but it's okay for you to be all up in my business when it comes to men, huh?" Tiara pouted.

"That's different. I'm your aunt." Charlene unlocked the front door and walked into the living room, Tiara and Jo-Jo trailing behind her. "And since your mother isn't around, it's my duty to get all up in your business."

"Is that right?" Tiara hung her coat in the hallway closet then reached for her aunt's. Jo-Jo had already flung her jacket on the couch and was seated sideways on the armchair, her feet hanging over the side. Tiara placed her school bag next to the sofa, then reached over and pulled out the soiled chemistry exam and sighed.

"Yeah, that's right." Charlene went to the stereo and started flipping through the large stack of CDs, finally settling on Whitney Houston's *Bodyguard* album. As the strains of "I Will Always Love You" filled the room, she disappeared into the kitchen, emerging a minute later clinking a glass of ice which she promptly filled with Johnny Walker Black from the bottom shelf of the entertainment center.

"Ooh, Aunt Charlie's playing love songs," Jo-Jo crooned from the arm chair.

"Now, Jo-Jo, you know it's not nice to tease your aunt about her boyfriends." Tiara absentmindedly threw the chemistry quiz on the coffee table and grinned at Charlene. "So did you give him a kiss good-bye?"

"Be quiet, girl," Charlene huffed, though unable to suppress her smile.

Tiara sat on the couch and looked at her aunt slowly swaying to the music. She was positively glowing. Even the drooping left side of her face seemed brighter. "Well, I hope you got his, too. And not just his cell number. If he didn't give you his home number, he's probably married."

Charlene turned and looked at Tiara for a moment, then chuckled and took a swig from her glass. "So now you're going to give me advice on men, huh?"

"Well, I know a little something-something on the subject, you know. You seen how many guys I've had trying to get with me."

"Please." Charlene took another sip. "I had five times the men chasing me when I was your age than you'll ever have in your life."

"Ooh, she told you," Jo-Jo teased.

"Well, excuse me," Tiara said with a smile.

"Yeah, excuse you." Charlene started swaying her shoulders to the music again. "Ask your father. I had so many men I used to have to do eeny-meeny-miny-mo to figure out which one I would go out with each night. I could go out two weeks straight without dating the same guy twice."

"Damn," was all Tiara could say.

"And when me and my girls would go to a bar by ourselves, I'd have so many men buying me drinks I'd give them away to my friends. In fact—now remember this was in the seventies—there were a couple of clubs, especially this one, The Pit, that used to be up on 125th and Madison, where the guys didn't even offer fly girls like me a drink. They would just come over and hand me a bill filled with coke."

"Ooh, Aunt Charlie! You used to sniff coke?" Jo-Jo asked.

"Aw hell no. But some of the girls I used to hang with were coke-heads." Charlene shook her head vigorously. "So I'd take the bill, pre-tend I was dipping some, but then when I brought the straw up to my nose, I'd put my hand over my face so they couldn't see me actually spill the coke into another bill I had on my lap. I would do that all night, and by the time the night was over I'd have this bulging bill of cocaine that I'd give to my friends so they could party."

"And the guys never figured it out?" Tiara asked incredulously.

"Who cares? If they did they didn't say anything. They didn't want to blow their chance with me. Let them throw even a little bit of attitude and I'd do like that song, 'Burn Rubber.' I'd burn rubber on a brother in a New York minute, girl. I just had so many to choose from, and believe me they all had money. Much money. I remember one time I told this guy I wanted to get a really good piña colada, and he flew me to Puerto Rico that same evening—first class."

"Get out of here." This was a side of her aunt that Tiara had never seen. And she had to admit she was fascinated. She knew from old pictures she'd seen that Aunt Charlie was beautiful, but she never figured her to be so wild.

"Oh yeah, I had a good time when I was your age. Enough fun to last a lifetime." Charlene stopped then, and slowly fingered her left cheek. She took a sip of her drink, her mood suddenly somber.

Tiara felt an unexpected pang in her heart. She hadn't known her aunt before the accident, and had never considered how it must have changed her life. But to go from being the most desired woman in New York City to tainted goods that no man would ever want . . . God, that must be horrible. Tiara shuddered involuntarily. No wonder Aunt Charlie was so mean and nasty all the time.

"You know, I don't want you to think that men don't ask me out anymore because of my . . ." Aunt Charlie dropped her hand from her face, "because of the accident. I still get approached."

"So how come you don't go out with any of them, Aunt Charlie?" Jo-Jo asked innocently.

The question seemed to take Aunt Charlie by surprise. "What makes you think I don't?"

"Well, 'cause you're over here all the time."

Tiara had to hold her breath to keep from busting out in laughter. Aunt Charlie, however, seemed to take the question seriously.

"I just haven't," she finally said with a shrug.

"So, why are you going out with the police guy?" Tiara demanded.

"I didn't say I was."

"You didn't say you weren't either."

"I don't know. Maybe I just developed a taste for men in uniform. And . . . uh . . . he just seems nice." Charlene smiled dreamily.

"Nice and ten years younger then you," Tiara taunted.

"So what? I never minded going out with men ten years older than me, I ain't worrying about going out with one ten years younger," Charlene grinned.

"Go ahead, Aunt Charlie," Jo-Jo hooted.

"Uh huh, so you did give him your number?" Tiara teased.

"Yeah, I did." Charlene grinned and swirled her watered-down drink.

"Honeys! I'm home!" Reggie suddenly appeared in the room. He threw his keys on the coffee table and threw his coat over Jo-Jo's head. She giggled as she struggled out from under it.

"Hey, what you cooking tonight?" he turned to Charlene. "I'm starving. I had to make an extra run today, so I didn't have time to grab lunch."

"Oh shoot! Dinner! I completely forgot!" Charlene's hand flew to her mouth.

"Aunt Charlie's got a boyfriend, Daddy!" Jo-Jo said with a grin.

"Huh?" Reggie looked from Jo-Jo to Charlene.

"And Jo-Jo was handcuffed and thrown in the back of a police car, Daddy." Tiara started giggling.

"What?" Reggie's mouth flew open.

"And Tiara failed her chemistry test." Charlene snatched the quiz paper from the coffee table and waved it in the air, at which point all three Bynum women burst into hysterical laughter.

13

Damn, Reg, where the hell are you going all suited up?"

Tiara emerged from her bedroom, just in time to see her aunt—whom she hadn't even heard enter the apartment—giving Reggie a stiff appraisal. To her surprise she saw he was indeed dressed to kill, at least for a man his age who still couldn't accept that Hugo Boss had replaced Pierre Cardin at least a decade before. He did a quick runway turn for Charlene, showing off the perfect fit of his fully lined Cardin wool charcoal-gray pinstripe suit, white silk shirt, and light-gray silk tie flecked with burgundy. Then he took his hand and did a slow slide over his short curly brown hair.

"Am I sharp or what?" he grinned at Charlene.

"You got a hot date, Daddy?" Tiara plopped down on the couch and looked at her watch. Seven fifteen. Lionel should have been there a half hour ago.

"Nope. A friend of mine is having a get-together for his birthday." Reggie reached into the closet for his black wool overcoat. "Over at Perks."

"Red Oscar's? That's right, you did mention it a couple of weeks ago." Charlene sat down on the armchair and casually crossed her legs. "Tiara, honey, I need those jade earrings I loaned you last week."

"Hmm, and where are you going?" Tiara surveyed her aunt. A pale green silk fitted jacquard blouse topped a mid-calf emerald green suede skirt, with dark green brushed suede boots. Her auburn hair was brushed up in a loose bun, with a few curly tendrils hanging softly around her face.

"Out," Charlene said simply.

"Ahem." Tiara sat up and cleared her throat. "And may I ask, out with whom?"

"No, you may not." Charlene cut her eyes at the girl. "Now, go get those earrings."

Tiara disappeared into her bedroom and returned a few minutes later with the earrings in her hand. "So, is Jimmy picking you up here?"

"Who's Jimmy?" Reggie asked.

"The police guy that was rapping to Aunt Charlie yesterday," Tiara teased. "That man moves fast, doesn't he? They just met yesterday and he's asked you out already."

"His name isn't Jimmy. It's James," Charlene said as she hooked the earrings in place.

"Well, you know, with him being just a kid and all . . . ," Tiara grinned.

"A kid?" Reggie furrowed his brow.

"Tiara, what are you bored or something?" Charlene cut her eyes at her niece again. "You just feel like starting some shit with me because you ain't got nothing else to do? Are you looking for some drama, little girl? Because in about half a minute I'm going to jump out of this chair and truly deliver."

"Dang, I was only making a joke." Tiara rolled her eyes and sat back down on the couch. *Lionel better hurry up. Here it is Friday night, Jo-Jo's at her friend's house, Daddy's going to hang out with his friends, and even Aunt Charlie's got a date, and I'm sitting around waiting on Lionel. That boy better act like he knows.*

"So, how old is this guy, Charlene?" Reggie asked, a little too casually.

"He's thirty-eight, Reggie. Why? You got a problem with that?" Charlene jumped up and headed for the entertainment center. She reached for the bottle of Johnny Walker Black, then paused, and grabbed her lamb-collared green suede coat that she had neatly folded over the back of the armchair.

"Don't be so touchy, Charlene. I was just making conversation," Reggie admonished. He rummaged through the pocket of his everyday gray bomber jacket and pulled out a set of keys, which he dropped in the black wool coat he was wearing. "So when do I get to meet this guy? Is he picking you up here?"

"Why should he pick me up here? Do I live here?" Charlene snapped.

Tiara grinned and started to say something smart, but the warning look Reggie gave her shut her up.

"Come on now, Charlene. I'm on my way out to have a good time. You're going out to have a good time . . ."

"I'm going out, too," Tiara cut in.

Reggie continued, ignoring his daughter. " . . . Let's not argue or anything. I'm glad to see you all gussied up." He put his hand on his hip in an effeminate manner. "And did I tell you, Miss Thang, that you are doing that skirt to death. You are looking fierce." He snapped his fingers.

A slow smile brightened on Charlene's face. "You think so?"

"Oh, I know so, honey," Reggie continued in his falsetto. "Don't you be hurting that young boy now."

"Oh, shut up." Charlene grinned as she walked over and gave Reggie a light slap on the shoulder. "I'm going to meet James uptown at the Flash Inn for some Italian food. You want me to give you a lift?"

"Yeah, thanks."

Tiara looked at her watch again. Shit, she thought. Lionel's going on an hour late now. I'll be damned if I'm going to be sitting up here in the apartment waiting on him all night. "Aunt Charlie, can you give me a lift to the Sugar Shack on 139th Street? It's right on your way."

"No," Charlene said abruptly.

"Oh, come on, Aunt Charlie. You know I was only playing with you," Tiara pleaded.

"Your problem is you don't know when to stop playing," Charlene said as she grabbed her keys off the coffee table. "Hurry up and grab your coat. I ain't got all night."

"Why don't you come in real quick and wish Red Oscar a happy birthday?"

"You know how tight the parking is up here, Reg. And I'm not double-parking with the police precinct right down the street there."

"Look. That white car is pulling out." Reggie pointed to a spot almost directly in front of Perk's, on 122nd and Manhattan Avenue. Charlene obligingly pulled over.

"I'm going to stay in the car," Tiara said sullenly as her father and aunt undid their seat belts. She hated it when she had to wait on people to take her where she wanted to go. She started to tell her aunt not to take too long when her cell phone rang.

"Yeah," she said, answering it.

"Hey, Baby. I just called your place and you weren't in." Lionel's voice came over the other end.

"You had me sitting waiting on you almost an hour. What did you expect?" Tiara rolled her eyes. "Where are you right now?"

"I'm on 125th and Fredrick Douglass. Where are you?"

"I'm only about three blocks away. I was going to get my Aunt

Charlie to drop me off at the Sugar Shack, but why don't you just swing by and pick me up since you're so close?"

"Okay, where?"

"In front of Perk's."

"Tell him to meet you inside. You might as well come in for a minute and meet my friends," Reggie interrupted her.

Tiara sighed. What the hell, she thought. Lionel's only a few minutes away, so she wouldn't have to stay long. "Lionel. Meet me inside, okay?" She snapped the phone shut.

"I gotta leave as soon as Lionel gets here," she warned as they entered the dimly lit club.

"No problem. I just want the world to see me with the two most beautiful women in the world on my arms," Reggie said heartedly.

"Where's the party?" Charlene asked as she took in the twenty-something crowd around the bar on the first floor.

"They rented the private room upstairs." Reggie steered Charlene and Tiara to the stairway. "Come on."

Charlene pulled away. "Hold on," she said. "Let me run to the little girl's room for a minute to freshen up. I'll meet you up there."

A large red and yellow "Happy Birthday, Ya Old Red Dog" banner was the first thing Tiara noticed when she and Reggie entered the small room. Cigar smoke hung heavy in the dimly lit room. From speakers set high on the wall, Tiara could hear the strains of a doo-wop song. About thirty people, mostly men in expensive suits, most of whom seemed eligible for Social Security retirement checks, sat around the sprinkling of small round tables covered with red cloth. The few women that were there were heavily made up, heavily perfumed, and favored heavily dyed blond hair, sequined dresses, and fur coats that hung over the backs of their chairs. A large sheet covered a long white table in the middle of the room. Six or seven people stood by the table, laughing and holding drinks. The center of attraction seemed to be the man who had introduced himself at Shakira's apartment months before.

"Hey, Red, you old dog!" Her father called out as he waved and headed in the man's direction, pulling her along. Tiara could see Red's mouth drop open, as a hush suddenly fell in the room, followed by loud whispering. *What the hell . . .* , she thought, but her father didn't seem to notice as he pulled Red into a warm embrace. "Happy birthday, old man," he said. In response, Red tried to push Reggie out of the room.

"Man, come out here and let me talk to you a minute," he said gruffly when the solidly built Reggie resisted the shoving.

"Man, what's wrong?" Reggie said as he finally turned to follow Red.

"I just gotta talk to you a minute, man. I tried to call you but you'd already left the house. Come on."

Tiara noticed people turning their heads to avoid her father's eyes, then whispering to each other. *What the hell is wrong with these folks? We look ten times better than them.*

"Tiara, you stay here while I talk to Red," Reggie said when they reached the door.

"Naw, naw, she can come out here, too," Red insisted.

"Man, if you need to talk to me privately, then you need to talk to me privately," Reggie said irritably. He turned to her again. "Stay right here, baby. I'll be right back."

Tiara stood by the door for a minute, then shrugged and sat at a nearby empty table. She looked at her watch. *Lionel should be here any minute now, or he better be if he knows what's good for him. Shit, at this point I wish Aunt Charlie would hurry her ass up. This is fucked-up sitting up here with all these old folks, and me not knowing anyone.*

She scanned the room, hoping to at least see Shakira's father, Mr. Richard, so she could at least have someone to smile at. She suddenly noticed a petite dark-skinned woman standing by the birthday cake. She wore short curly hair, à la Halle Berry. Her long ivory satin evening dress was fitted at her tiny waist with a slit to the mid-thigh on one side. Her matching ivory satin shoes had gold trim at the toes, and a gold-trimmed shawl hung loosely over her smooth shoulders. The woman, Tiara couldn't help but notice, was simply stunning.

She looked about thirty, but her poise suggested she was probably older, maybe in her late forties. *Now see, that's how I'm going to look when I get old.* They were even about the same height and had the same coloring. She suddenly realized the woman was staring at her as hard as she was staring at her. Embarrassed, Tiara turned her head, and looked at her watch again, wishing that either her father would reappear or Lionel would come rescue her from the awkward situation.

"Excuse me." Tiara turned to see the woman standing over her. "What's your name?"

Tiara blinked wildly. For some reason this all seemed like a dream. If ever she were to imagine a fairy godmother, this woman would be it with her poise, sophistication, and beauty. But why was she over here asking her name? Was she a lesbian or something?

"Why?" She had wanted to sound haughty, but she was barely able to croak the question out. Her throat, for some reason, was suddenly dry.

The woman seemed unperturbed by Tiara's question, and her nervousness. "Because you look like someone I know," she answered. The woman suddenly looked up at a couple of women who had casually wandered over and planted themselves within discreet listening distance. "What the fuck are you bitches looking at?" she snarled, then laughed as the women scurried away. Tiara giggled nervously along with her. She didn't know who this woman was, but she certainly liked her style.

"I'm Tiara Bynum. Reggie's daughter," she extended her hand to the woman, who simply gave it a quick squeeze.

"Well, Tiara Bynum, you are certainly a truly beautiful young lady." The woman had a wistful smile on her face, and Tiara wasn't sure, but it seemed her eyes were misting. The woman suddenly sniffed and turned and walked away a few steps, then suddenly turned on her heel and headed back to Tiara's table. She pulled out a chair and sat down, placing her gold satin clutch purse on the table.

"Tiara." There was an urgency in her voice that made Tiara uncomfortable. "Do you know who I am?"

"Um, no . . ." Tiara looked closely at the woman, trying to place her. There was something familiar about her, but she couldn't imagine having met this beautiful woman and not remembering her.

"Tiara!" Reggie's voice suddenly boomed from the door. Tiara looked up to see her father staring stonily at her, his hazel eyes tightened into a squint, the muscles in his face taut. "Get your stuff and come on."

The room suddenly fell silent again. The woman, who was sitting facing Tiara and away from Reggie, lowered her eyes to the table and started chewing her bottom lip.

"I said *now*." Reggie stomped over and grabbed Tiara by the arm, pulling her out of the chair so quickly she had to scramble to keep from stumbling.

"Daddy, I'm coming," Tiara said quickly. "You didn't give me a—"

"God damn it, Reggie. Give the girl a chance to get up on her own, you controlling bastard." The woman glared at Reggie, her breathing becoming deep and fast, as she slowly put her hands on the table and pushed herself out of her chair.

"I ain't say shit to you, don't say shit to me," Reggie shot back, keeping the volume in his voice to conversational level, as did the woman. "And don't say shit else to my daughter."

"Fuck you, you pussy bitch," the woman hissed, one hand on her hip, the other clutching her purse. "You ain't shit, and never was shit."

"Hey, yo . . . don' be talking to my father like—" Tiara started, but her father cut her off.

"Look, I'm going to pretend like you're the lady you never were, and ignore your ignorant ass." Reggie's voice was still controlled, but his shoulders were squared back, his chest heaving, his fists clenching and unclenching.

"You asshole, I didn't do anything but say hello to the girl." The woman stepped closer to Reggie, seemingly unafraid. "What, you think I was trying to steal her away from you or something?"

"Bitch, you couldn't steal her away from me if you tried. You made your decision twelve years ago." Reggie's voice was still low, but the fury was evident. "Don't be trying to squirm your way back into my family. We sure as hell don't want you. I wouldn't take you back if you got on your hands and knees and begged."

Take her back? When was he with her? Tiara looked at the woman again and gasped. Could it be? But she looked so different . . .

"Take *me* back? Bitch, are you out of your mind? You think I want your broke ass?" The woman dropped her head back and gave a hearty laugh. "I got a man. A good man who knows how to take care of a woman. I got a man who can give me anything I want, no questions asked. Not some big jerk picking up garbage in the street."

Reggie's eyes widened, and his breathing became heavier. "Sharon, if you don't get the fuck out of my face, I swear . . . I ain't never laid a hand on a woman in my life . . . but I will stomp your funky ass into the ground."

Sharon! Tiara felt her knees begin to buckle, and she fell back against the wall, feeling for a chair and sitting down to prevent herself from sinking to the floor. It was her. It was her mother. Her mother. After all these years, her mother was right here in front of her. And she hadn't even recognized her. Tears streamed down Tiara's face, and her sobs were so heavy she could barely breathe. If anyone asked why she was crying she wouldn't have been able to explain, but it didn't matter because no one was paying her any attention. They were too busy watching her parents ready to come to blows.

"Hey, hey." A shrunken-looking man in a custom-tailored suit of golden olive heather wool sharkskin with wide lapels and tapered pants and a gold fedora, who appeared to be in his seventies, stepped up from the crowd that had gathered around the arguing couple. "I let you get your say, boy, but I ain't gonna let you threaten my woman."

This time it was Reggie's turn to laugh. "Oh shit. This is your 'good man'? He looks like if you blow on him he'll keel over and die."

"Yeah, well then blow, motherfucker," the older man sneered. He fumbled to unbutton his jacket. But Red was suddenly in front of him, pushing him back.

"Okay, this shit don't make no sense. I don't want no shooting up in here. Reggie, just get on up outta here," Red said as he continued to push the struggling man back.

"That ancient-ass motherfucker ain't gonna shoot nobody," Reggie hollered. "Let him pull out a gun and watch me make him eat that shit. Let the motherfucker go."

"There's not going to be any shooting anywhere." Charlene had pushed her way into the room and was at her brother's side, pulling him by the arm. "Come on, you don't need this shit. Let's get out of here."

"I ain't going no fucking where." Reggie roughly pushed her away. "Let go of that motherfucker, Red. He ain't got the guts to shoot me. He knows this bitch ain't worth shooting nobody over. That old motherfucker would probably have a heart attack trying to pull the trigger anyway."

Charlene grabbed the sobbing Tiara by the shoulders and pulled her up from the chair. "Reggie, you're right. That bitch ain't worth this shit. And we both know you could stomp the shit outta that man. But not in front of Tiara. She doesn't need to see all this shit. Come on, Reggie, look at Tiara. You got her crying."

"Oh look at Aunt Charlie suddenly becoming Mommy Charlie. You still ain't got a man, bitch?" Sharon jumped in front of Charlene. "Let me guess, you ain't got no man and no children, and so you trying to come in and claim mine?"

To Tiara's surprise, Charlene remained calm. "I'm not trying to claim your child, Sharon. I'm just trying to calm her down. Look at her. She's about to have a breakdown."

Reggie blinked his eye and shook his head at the words, as if to clear his thoughts. He looked at Tiara, then grabbed her up in his huge arms.

"Oh, baby, I'm sorry. Don't cry. I'm sorry, baby." He started rocking her back and forth as she sobbed into his chest.

"Come on, Reggie. Let's get your little girl outta here," Charlene said gently, pulling Reggie by the arm, leading him and Tiara toward the door.

"But I want to talk to my mother." Tiara pulled away from Reggie.

"Don't worry, sweetie. I'm going to get you guys settled in the car and then I'll go back in and get her telephone number so you can call her later and hook up," Charlene said soothingly. "But we gotta get out of here now so things can calm down. Everyone's too upset right now to talk."

"You promise?" Tiara sniffed as she lay her head back on Reggie's chest.

"I promise," Charlene said. She ushered both Reggie and Tiara into the back seat of her Camry and hopped in the front seat. She turned the heat on and found some smooth jazz on the car radio. "You guys okay?" she asked into the rearview mirror. Tiara's head was on Reggie's shoulder. She was still crying, but silently, as Reggie stroked her hair.

"Yeah," Reggie answered for both of them.

"Okay. I'm going to be right back."

"Man, Charlene, don't go back in there." Reggie sucked his teeth. "Just take us home, please."

"I'll only be a minute, I promise," Charlene said hurriedly. "Just let me talk to Sharon for a minute for Tiara's sake."

"Tiara doesn't need that bitch!"

"Daddy!" Tiara whimpered.

"Don't worry, I'll be right back." Charlene left the key in the ignition so the heat and music would stay on as she hopped out of the car.

"Daddy?"

"Yeah?"

"I thought you said you didn't know where she was? You told me she had left the city and you didn't know where she went."

"I didn't, Baby."

"Then why is she here tonight?" Tiara whimpered, nuzzling her head into her father's shoulder.

Reggie sighed. "I don't know. Red said she came down from Detroit with that guy. He said he didn't know she had hooked up with the guy, or he wouldn't have invited him. And when she walked in, Red tried to call me and give me a heads-up, but we had already left."

Tiara was silent.

"Tiara?"

"Yeah?"

"I'm sorry you had to see all that, Baby. I didn't mean to lose my temper like that." His voice was breaking. "I didn't mean to upset you."

"I know, Daddy. I know," Tiara said gently.

"Tiara? . . . Are you ashamed of me?"

"What?" Tiara jerked her head up to look at her father. His face was suddenly haggard, and his eyes were watery and red. He looked old—old and defeated. And the sight of him like that made her want to cry again. But she held back her own tears, knowing that it would be too much for him to deal with.

"Are you ashamed of me?" Reggie repeated, pushing her head back into his shoulder. "I mean, you know, that I'm a sanitation worker. A garbage man."

"Daddy, I could never be ashamed of you."

"Because you know I've always tried to give you girls everything you wanted." Reggie continued on as if he didn't hear her. "We don't have a lot of money, but I've never told you no when you asked me for something, have I? I've been a good father, haven't I?"

Tiara choked back her tears. "You're the best father in the world. All the girls I know are jealous of the way you treat me."

"They are?"

"Yeah."

He patted her head. "I love you, Baby."

"I love you, too."

She suddenly looked out of the window. "Hold up." She sat up. "That's Lionel's car across the street."

"Where?"

"Right there." Tiara pointed to the black Porsche that was parked in front of a fire hydrant and had a ticket on the windshield to prove it.

"You think he's in the club?" Reggie asked.

"I'm going to go see." Tiara unlocked the door and prepared to get out, but Reggie held her arm.

"No, you stay here. I'll go see."

"No, you shouldn't go back in there—"

They both turned at the sudden knocking on the window.

"Hey! Y'all better get in there quick. They've called the cops on your aunt," Lionel shouted.

Reggie and Tiara jumped out of the car and flew into the club.

"And you know what else, you stank-ass funky slut bitch? You ain't shit. You abandoned your husband and your two daughters to run after some old man with some money. And you know that motherfucker's so ancient he couldn't get it up if you blew him like Bazooka bubble gum. You just want him for his money," Aunt Charlene was being held by two men who were trying to pull her back toward the front door. "Don't you ever think you're going to get up in my brother's face and I ain't gonna do shit. I'll beat your ass so bad your mama won't claim you. I ain't never liked your ass, you low-class, slutty-ass gold-digger bitch. And you ain't never had no class. I'm the one that taught you how to dress. You ain't even know how to use a knife and fork before you hooked up with my brother, you low-class bitch."

"Come on, Charlene. You done knocked out one of that poor girl's teeth already," said one of the men holding her.

"Only one? Well, that means I got thirty-one more to work on," Charlene hollered. "Let me go so I can kick that bitch's ass."

"Come on, Charlene." Reggie took over from the men, who gladly let go of her. "Let's get out of here."

"Not until I finish kicking her ass." Charlene struggled against her brother.

"Oh, shut up, you old ugly hag." Sharon held a bloody handkerchief to her mouth. The bodice of her gown was speckled with blood, and one of her earlobes was split, as if someone had removed her earring the hard way. Her escort, the shrunken man in the sharkskin suit, came up behind her and put a silver mink coat over her shoulders.

"Yeah, I got your old ugly hag right here, bitch," Charlene spat. "You can kiss this old ugly hag's black ass."

Sharon suddenly spotted Tiara and walked up to her, carefully avoiding walking too close to Charlene. "Here," she thrust a paper napkin at Tiara. "This is my number. Call me anytime you want." She put her arms through the sleeves of her mink and stomped off toward the back door of the club.

"Huh?" Tiara's eyes darted from her mother to her boyfriend, but before she could ask the obvious question, Charlene was shouting again.

"You sure you don't need to give me your number, 'cause I got your number, you gold-digging, two-timing, dick-sucking slutty-ass bitch!" she hollered at the woman's back, still straining to break free.

"Charlene, come on, the girl's gone. She went out the back door already. And the police are on the way." Reggie grabbed his sister by the waist and hauled her up and out of the door. "Here you make me calm down and you come back here and start acting the fool? What the hell's the matter with you?"

"I didn't want you kicking her ass because I didn't want Tiara traumatized by the sight of her father kicking her mother's ass," Charlene said huffily when he finally released her outside. "She ain't going to have any nightmares about her aunt beating the shit out of her, though."

"Charlene, you're a trip." Reggie shook his head and led his sister to the car, Tiara and Lionel trailing behind them.

"You okay?" he asked Charlene as they were standing outside the car.

"Yeah, I'm okay."

"Then get in the car. I'm telling you they called the police."

Charlene suddenly realized her car was running.

"Y'all left my keys in the car? Someone coulda stole it. What's wrong with you?"

"Aunt Charlie! Lionel came and told us you were in there fighting," Tiara shouted at her aunt. "I thought you were just going to get her telephone number. Why'd you have to go and hit my mother?"

"Your mother?" Lionel asked. "That was your mother?"

"Yeah." Reggie stepped forward.

"And, Tiara, I didn't go inside to hit her. Things just got out of hand," Charlene said as she tried to get control of her breath. "And you got her telephone number, didn't you? That's what counts."

"But you hit her!" Tiara stomped her foot on the pavement.

"Can we please get out of here? The police are on the way!" Reggie stepped in between the two women. "We can talk about it when we get to the house."

"Reggie, please," Charlene snapped. "If the police were on the way they'da been here ten minutes ago. They're right down the street." She pointed toward 121st Street.

"Either way, get in the car and let's go home." Reggie jumped in the front passenger seat and slammed his door. Charlene walked in front of the car to get to the driver's side door. "You coming or what?" she asked Tiara as she climbed in the car.

Tiara shook her head, then knocked on her father's window. "Daddy, I'm going to ride with Lionel," she said when he rolled the window down. "I'll meet you and Aunt Charlie at the apartment."

"So, you really kicked her ass, huh?" Reggie grinned at Charlene as he rolled the window back up.

"*Like it was my job,*" Charlene grinned back as she turned the ignition. "Like it was my job."

14

hy didn't you come to the game? I was high scorer, and they voted me MVP!" Tiara rolled over and groaned at the sound of Jo-Jo's voice, then sat up in the bed, rubbing her eyes before glancing at the clock. Two o'clock. How could she have slept that long? Then the events of the night flooded into her head and she groaned again, not because of her slight hangover this time, but because of the memories.

What a fucking night, she thought as she lay back down and pulled the blanket over her head. *After twelve years, I finally see my mom, and I don't even recognize her. And then for Daddy to actually threaten to hit her in front of everybody, and for Aunt Charlie to actually do it. Jesus Christ.* But she couldn't even take her mother's side. If she were Aunt Charlie she probably would have done the same thing. After all, her mom had said some pretty shitty things. *Why'd she have to go and call Daddy all those names in front of everybody like that, and curse him out and shit? She walked out on him, he didn't walk out on her. He was the one who stuck around and took care of us while she was out chasing the almighty dollar. And then she actually made fun of his job in front of all those people, calling him a garbage-collecting jerk. God, that shit was embarrassing. But damn, did Aunt Charlie actually have to knock out one of her teeth? And damn it all, why did all of it have to happen right in front of Lionel? He must think we're a bunch of low-class hooligans and shit.* What a great impression they must have all made. It was the most embarrassing night of her life. She hadn't wanted to go back to the apartment and see her father all depressed and hear Aunt Charlie all drunk and calling her mom all kinds of bitches, because she knew that's exactly what would be going on. So she and Lionel had gone from one club to another, and thanks to her phony ID she was able to order one drink after another, trying to come to grips with what had happened at Perks, and the unexpected, disastrous meeting with her mother.

She was surprised when she stumbled in the house at 3 A.M. to find her father already gone to bed—she had figured that he and Aunt Charlie would be up all night talking about the incident, but that was good, because she didn't want to talk about it with them. She hadn't even talked to Lionel about it, and thank God he didn't bring it up. Though to be honest, she didn't even know what he had talked about last night, if anything. She had completely tuned him out. She was still trying to figure out how she felt, and why, and what she was going to do next. The stereo was on low, playing Aunt Charlie's theme song, "Burn Rubber," which proved that Aunt Charlie had indeed been there, and probably had gotten so drunk on her Johnny Walker Black that she left without remembering to turn the music off. Tiara had stumbled over to turn off the stereo, then rushed to the bathroom and threw up. She then crawled off to bed, fully clothed.

"Tiara, get up." Jo-Jo started shaking her. "Hurry up and get dressed. Daddy's taking us all out to lunch to celebrate my MVP."

"What do you mean he's taking 'us all' out to lunch?" Tiara mumbled from underneath the blanket. "Who's us all?"

"Me, you, Rashad, Aunt Charlie, and Mr. James," Jo-Jo said as she straightened up. "You seen my New York Knicks sweatshirt?"

"What's Rashad doing here?" Tiara quickly sat up, then grabbed her head and groaned as the pounding in her skull reminded her how much she had drunk the night before. She slipped her feet into her slippers and slowly walked over to see if she looked as bad as she felt. Yep, she did. Like pure hell. She had gone to bed without removing her makeup, and the smudged mascara and eyeliner had left rings around her red—but not quite bloodshot—eyes, making her look like a raccoon. She grabbed an Oil of Olay beauty wipe and started rubbing. As bad as she felt physically and emotionally, she wasn't going to miss a chance to see Rashad. And she wanted to make sure she looked good when she did. After all, they hadn't seen each other in weeks. And he probably did want to see her. Why else would he be there? He probably could care less that Jo-Jo had won some MVP or whatever it was that the family was supposed to be celebrating.

"He came over from the gym with Daddy to see me play." Jo-Jo started pulling out drawers from the bureau. "I could have sworn I saw that darn sweatshirt yesterday, but I can't find it now."

"So, is Rashad actually here now?" Tiara asked as she rummaged around in her nightstand drawer, looking for the Visine she kept there to erase tell-tale signs when she smoked weed.

"He drove over here with us, but he didn't come up and said he'd meet us up here in a half-hour because he had to run an errand," Jo-Jo said as she started rummaging through the closet. "You sure you ain't seen my sweatshirt?"

"How long ago was that?"

"How long ago was what?"

Tiara sucked her teeth. "When did you guys get in the apartment?"

"I don't know, about ten minutes ago. Come on, Tiara, you sure you ain't seen my sweatshirt?"

"Didn't I already tell you no!" Tiara slammed the drawer shut. She tilted her head back and dripped two drops of the Visine in each eye, then grabbed a tissue and wiped the excess liquid from her face.

"No, you didn't. And I asked you three times already." Jo-Jo slammed the closet door shut in response. "I'll see you when you drag your butt in the shower so we can leave. And hurry up!"

"Wait!" Tiara couldn't let Jo-Jo leave before getting more information.

"What?" Jo-Jo stood near the door, arms crossed, tapping one of her sneakered feet.

"Where's Daddy taking us?"

"I don't know. He said, but I don't remember."

"Who all did you say was going besides Rashad?"

"Yeah, figures you'd remember that I said Rashad," Jo-Jo said in a teasing voice.

"Shut up and tell me who all is going," Tiara snapped.

"No. I ain't telling you nothing," Jo-Jo shot back. "You don't know how to talk to people. And you ain't even congratulated me!" She tucked her crossed arms even closer to her body.

Tiara rolled her eyes and sighed. "Congratulations, Jo-Jo."

"Thank you very much," Jo-Jo grinned. "Now, see, that didn't hurt at all, did it?"

"Don't push it," Tiara snapped. "Now who else did you say was going to lunch?"

"Aunt Charlie and Mr. James."

"Mr. James?" Tiara's brow furrowed. Didn't that guy, Red Oscar, introduce himself as Red Oscar James when she first met him at Shakira's house? Why the hell would he be going to lunch with them?

"Yeah, you know. That cop that likes Aunt Charlie."

"Oh! Officer Scott! Yeah, that's right, his first name is James." Tiara breathed a sigh of relief. "How did you guys hook up with him?"

"He came to see me play, just like he said he would." Jo-Jo grabbed an imaginary pass in the air, dribbled the imaginary ball, and made a perfect imaginary three-point shot. "I had my own cheering squad in the stands."

"Cool." Tiara turned to the mirror and grabbed another beauty wipe and began rubbing it over her cheeks. *Man, at least that makes me feel a little better. I was feeling bad that Aunt Charlie blew her date last night because of the fucking drama. I mean, shit, she ain't been out with a man in years. And that's probably why Daddy really wants to take everyone out to lunch. He probably wants to get the 411 on the dude. Cool, 'cause I wanna find out a little something about him, too. I better hurry up, because if I know Aunt Charlie, she's going to try and convince everyone to just go ahead and leave me if I take too long. And I don't want to miss out on this.*

Tiara put on her robe and headed to the shower. It'll be good to see Rashad again, she thought. She was going to see if she could pull him off to the side, or maybe convince him to go somewhere else after lunch so they could be alone. She wanted to talk to someone about the whole mess the night before, and she suddenly realized that he was the only person she could really open up to about the subject. He wouldn't judge her, or tell her that she was being silly, or hostile or anything. He would just listen, and not judge. He was cool like that. And who knows, it might actually bring them closer.

It took another forty-five minutes before Tiara finally appeared in the living room, dressed in a pair of Express blue jeans, a royal blue turtleneck sweater and a silver pendant with matching silver earrings. For once, no one made a comment about her taking forever to get dressed. James was sitting in the armchair, a Knicks ball cap on his head, and Aunt Charlie was perched on the arm of the chair, just beaming. Jo-Jo—her imaginary basketball in hand—was in the middle of the room giving them an instant replay of the last seconds of her basketball victory, and her father, who was sitting on the couch in a green-and-white Adidas sweat suit and white Adidas sneakers, was providing the play-by-play action.

"Bynum steals the ball! What a play! But there's only two seconds on the game clock—there's no way she's going to be able to move the ball down court in time to score! But wait! Bynum pulls up at half court and takes a shot! Oh my God! Can you believe it? She makes the shot at the buzzer! Pure net! Three points, folks! The crowd is on its feet as the Hawkettes win the game, forty-seven, forty-six!"

Jo-Jo raised her hands over her head and did a little jig.

"And the crowd goes wild!" Reggie rushed from the sofa and grabbed Jo-Jo in a bear hug.

On cue, Aunt Charlie and James exploded into cheers and applause.

"Looks like I missed a heckuva game." Tiara walked over and gave her father a kiss on the cheek, and Jo-Jo a quick pat on the back. "So, what's this I hear about us all going out to lunch? Where are we going?"

"Amy Ruth's, right up the street," her father answered.

"I thought you needed reservations days in advance to get in there." Tiara frowned. Amy Ruth's was only two blocks away, which meant they would be walking. Dang.

"It's not usually too crowded on Saturday. And besides, my man here has the hook-up." Her father strode over to James and gave him a high five. "We have a table for six waiting on us."

"Come on, then, everyone grab your coats so we don't lose our table. It's almost three-thirty now," Reggie said as he slipped into his gray bomber jacket.

"What about—"

Tiara was interrupted by three knocks on the door.

"We were just getting ready to leave without you," Reggie said as he opened the door. Rashad stood there, in his usual green army jacket and brown combat boots, a large grin on his face, and a bouquet of red roses in his hand. *Oh, God, he looks good,* Tiara thought as her face relaxed into a smile. *And he actually brought me flowers!* She walked toward the door to greet him.

"Hey, Tiara, long time no see," Rashad greeted her warmly, even giving her a quick kiss on the cheek. The brisk winter chill on his face felt soothing on Tiara's cheek, and she closed her eyes to inhale his musk. *This just feels so right, she thought. I know he's got to realize it, too.* She opened her eyes and smiled up at him, and that's when she noticed Alice standing shyly in the doorway.

"I ran into Alice on my way back from the florist," Rashad said as he followed Tiara's eyes.

"Hi, everybody." Alice gave a slight wave of her hand. "How you doing, Tiara?"

"Fine," Tiara all but snapped at the girl.

Rashad walked over to Jo-Jo and placed the roses in her arms. "It's not much, but it's the least I could do for the Queen of the Basketball Court."

"Oh, my God, no one's ever given me flowers before!" Jo-Jo looked excitedly from her aunt to her father. "Look, I got flowers."

"Well, then I am privileged to be the first to so honor you." Rashad gave her a deep bow. "But I'm sure it's only the first of many. It's not often that the world produces a young woman so talented and beautiful at the same time. I bet you'll have all the boys around here going crazy over you in no time."

Jo-Jo dissolved into a fit of teenage giggles and blushes.

"Of course," Charlene piped up as James helped her on with her coat. "She's a Bynum woman."

"And Bynum women are certainly true beauties," James said in his deep voice, prompting a slow blush to creep onto Charlene's face.

It was all too much for Tiara. Jo-Jo was getting flowers that should have been hers. Aunt Charlie was being flattered by a handsome suitor, and Alice was standing there, looking all innocent, when she obviously was trying to horn in on her time with Rashad. *I've always been so nice to that pig, and she's going to do me like this? See if I butt in the next time Shakira or somebody tries to dog her out.*

Her father must have sensed her rising ire, because he came and put his arm around his oldest daughter. "You're looking sharp today. I've always said that blue was your color."

"Didn't you say we need to be getting out of here?" Tiara said sullenly.

"Oh, listen, is it okay if Alice joins us?" Rashad turned to Reggie. "I'll be glad to pick up her tab."

"We only have reservations for six," Tiara said quickly.

"No problem, I'll call and change the reservation." James reached in his coat pocket, pulled out a cell phone, and started punching buttons.

"You shouldn't have to do that." Tiara let out a snort. "If we . . ."

"Tiara, aren't those my earrings you're wearing?" Charlene squinted her green eyes at her niece. "I don't remember you asking to borrow them."

Tiara whirled and looked at her aunt. "You know darn well these aren't your earrings, Aunt Charlie. You gonna start tripping on me, too?"

"That's it!" Charlene stomped off toward the girls' bedroom. "Get in here now. I want to talk to you, young lady."

Tiara turned to her father. "Daddy, why do we have to—"

"I said get in here now, Tiara!" Charlene said through gritted teeth. "Don't make me drag you in here, okay."

"Charlene, what the hell is wrong with you?" Reggie looked at his sister quizzically.

"Reggie, would you just stay out of this? I'll talk to you about all this later," Charlene said quickly. "Now, Tiara, get in here before I have to really call you out in front of everyone."

Tiara crossed her arms in front of her as she followed her aunt into the bedroom, then slammed the door hard behind her. "I ain't take none of your stank jewelry. This is my shit." She leaned against the door, breathing hard. If her aunt wanted to fight, she was going to go toe-to-toe with her. Why did she have to go embarrass her in front of everyone like that anyway? It's not like things weren't fucked up already.

To her surprise, though, Charlene walked over and gently tugged her arm, motioning that she wanted her to sit on the bed. "Come here, Sweetie . . . let's talk."

"About what?" Tiara said without budging.

"About what you're going through right now. I saw the look on your face when Rashad walked in. And I saw the look on your face when you saw Alice, too. Let's talk." She put both her hands on Tiara's shoulders and tried to look her niece in the eye, but Tiara turned away.

"There ain't nothing to talk about. If he wants to go out with that fat frumpy bitch, that's on him. I got a man. I don't want him." Tiara blinked hard, trying to prevent the tears she felt forming in her eyes from showing.

"I know you don't, baby." Charlene led the now willing Tiara to the bed, and they both sat down.

"I'm too good for him anyway," Tiara said sullenly.

"Well, I'm not going to say that," Charlene said softly as she rubbed Tiara's back.

"You trying to say he's too good for me." Tiara turned and faced her aunt angrily.

"No, I'm not trying to say that either." Charlene said quickly. "You're a beautiful young woman, Tiara. You know that. There are plenty of guys who'd give their right arm to be with you."

"Then why doesn't Rashad like me?" Tiara tried to sniff back her tears. "Why would he choose Alice over me? I look a hundred times better than her."

"Well, first of all, we don't know if he chose Alice over you. It might just be that they're friends, right? And second, honey, looks aren't everything. A lot of men—men with substance—look for something beyond that. They look for what's inside a person. James is like that." Charlene touched the left side of her face, and even through her own frustration, Tiara noticed that the gesture didn't bring about the usual bitterness in her aunt's voice.

"We're not talking about you and James, Aunt Charlie." Tiara grimaced. "We're talking about Rashad and me!"

"Yeah, I know, Sweetie." Charlene smiled. "It's just that I think Rashad is the same way."

"So you're trying to say there's nothing attractive inside of me?" Tiara wanted the question to sound sarcastic, but to her dismay it sounded as pathetic as she felt at the moment. She didn't bother to wipe the tears that slowly rolled down her cheeks, nor did she turn away as she waited anxiously for her aunt's answer.

Charlene grabbed Tiara into a hug. "No, baby, I don't think that at all. I do think that you and Rashad just aren't a good fit, though, and he realizes that even if you don't. That's all. And I'm sorry because I really like him, but it's just like that sometimes. It's just like that."

"Yeah, it's just like that." Tiara sighed and reached over her aunt and grabbed a tissue from the tissue box on the nightstand. "Don't worry," she said as she wiped her face. "I'm all right."

"Are you sure?" Charlene said gently.

"Yep, I'm sure." Tiara blew her nose noisily.

"Tiara, honey, it might be that Rashad really does like you, but doesn't even want to admit it himself." Charlene started rubbing Tiara's back again. "He might just be struggling with it because, like I just said, he just doesn't see it as a fit."

"I don't care what he's struggling with," Tiara sniffed. "Like I just said, I already got a man."

"Okay, so here's what we'll do." Charlene grabbed another tissue and started dabbing at Tiara's eyes. "I'll go out there and say that we argued, but that you set me straight, and proved those are your earrings, but you were so mad at me that you don't want to go out to lunch anymore."

"Why would I do that?"

"Come on, Tiara. Do you really want to go out with Rashad and Alice?"

Tiara sniffed. "Well, you said yourself that they might only be friends, right?"

"Well, yes, but . . ."

"So I'm fine with that. And even if he does like her, I'm fine with that, too. Just because things didn't work out between me and Rashad doesn't mean I have to hole up in my room and cry all day. And don't worry, Aunt Charlie, I promise I won't throw myself at him or anything, or try and make Alice look bad." Tiara straightened her shoulders. "I'll be out in a minute, okay? I just want to fix my face."

Charlene sighed and stood up. "Well, okay, if you say so. But if you change your mind just give me a signal, and I'll start an argument with you so you can stomp out."

"Aunt Charlie?" Tiara said just before her aunt reached the bedroom door.

"Yes?"

"Make sure you let them know that you were wrong and that these are my earrings. And make a big deal about apologizing to me over and over in front of them, too."

Charlene shook her head and smiled as she headed out the door. "Anything you want, Your Royal Highness," she said over her shoulder.

"Thanks." Tiara sniffed as she sat down in front of her vanity and looked at the damage done to her eye makeup. Time to make herself look beautiful again—because showtime was about to begin.

15

"Did I tell you the food was great here, or what?" James sat back in his chair. Tiara could have sworn he was going to loosen the belt on his pants, but thankfully he did not. But after eating a half slab of barbecued ribs, macaroni and cheese, greens, and corn bread—then topping it off with bread pudding and two cups of coffee—Tiara figured he had to have put on an extra ten pounds. Even her father, who ate more than anyone she knew, had commented. James took the teasing with good nature.

"I don't know how you can eat like that today considering the giant-size meal you had last night." Charlene tapped James lightly on the shoulder. "You should have seen him go," she addressed Reggie. "He had antipasto to start off, along with fried calamari as an appetizer, a huge plate of pasta and a whole loaf of garlic bread, and then had the nerve to order cheesecake for dessert."

"Oh, so you guys did hook up last night after all?" Tiara looked at her aunt quizzically.

"Uh huh. I dropped your father off at the building and kept on going," Charlene answered. "I wasn't going to let that drama spoil my evening."

"What drama?" Jo-Jo asked.

"Nothing," Reggie said quickly. "I'll tell you about it later."

Oh man, how is he going to tell Jo-Jo about what happened? I should probably talk to her and let her know. I'll do it when I get home tonight.

"But you went up to the apartment for a minute last night, right?" Tiara asked Charlene.

"No, why?"

"Your song was still playing on the stereo when I got in. That 'Burn Rubber on Me' song."

"Well, I wasn't there to put it on." Charlene turned to Reggie, her eyebrows raised. "I thought you hated that song."

"Man, you know you're not going to be able to get in your uniform on Monday. Remind me to never offer to buy you a meal again," Reggie addressed James, ignoring his sister's questioning look.

"Don't worry, I'll work it off tomorrow on the racquetball court." James grinned as he patted his bulging stomach.

"You play racquetball?" Jo-Jo asked as she pushed back her dish of chocolate ice cream. "I've always wanted to learn how to play."

"You can have your aunt teach you," James said jovially.

"Aunt Charlie doesn't play racquetball," Tiara giggled.

"She will tomorrow. I'm teaching her." James gave Charlene's hand a quick squeeze. So cute it was sickening, Tiara thought. They had even held hands during the two-block walk to the restaurant. *I mean, I'm happy for Aunt Charlie and all, but dang. Did she have to act so damn happy? Doesn't she even care about my feelings? She knows what I'm going through.*

The walk had been hell for Tiara, although she felt she pulled it off pretty well. Her father, Jo-Jo, and Rashad kept going on and on about the game, leaving her to make small talk with Alice. She thought she had done a pretty damn good job, too—asking her about school, and how her mother was doing and all, as if she really cared. All she cared about was what kind of relationship Rashad had with the girl—was it just friendly or were they an item—but there was no way she was going to ask. When they got to the restaurant, she was careful to watch any interaction between Alice and Rashad, but although Rashad was sweet and attentive to Alice she still wasn't sure. He was so damn nice and attentive to everyone. He pulled out the chairs for both Alice and Tiara, and would have done so for Charlene if James hadn't beaten him to the punch. Charlene and James were seated next to each other at the round table, Tiara was on Charlene's other side, Alice was next to her, then Rashad, then Jo-Jo and Reggie. When they were all seated and had ordered, Reggie dominated most of the conversation, talking about how proud he was of his two daughters. Tiara smiled and nodded at all the right cues, but she really wished he didn't have such a booming voice. She wanted to make sure she heard any conversation between Rashad and Alice.

"So, James, good thing your idiot partner didn't arrest Jo-Jo the other day, huh?" Reggie was saying. "Good looking out, man. I appreciate what you did."

"It was nothing." James shrugged his shoulders. "Sometimes things get a little out of hand out here, but that doesn't mean we need to be hauling people in all the time. You've got to learn how to handle situations. Sometimes it's just about letting people's tempers die down."

"Ooh, yeah, I heard about what happened," Alice addressed Tiara. "I'm sorry I wasn't there to help out."

"Don't worry about it." Tiara gave the girl a sweet smile. "You know my girl Shakira was there, and you know she had my back." Alice leaned back, but not before Tiara caught the crushed look on her face. *Good. I know how she hates Shakira.*

"What happened? Jo-Jo almost got arrested?" Rashad looked from Jo-Jo to Reggie.

"Yeah, it was all pretty stupid, really," Tiara offered. "Some girls from around the way were going to jump Jo-Jo, and it just all got a little crazy. Jo-Jo punched one of the girls, and this stupid cop threw her in the back of the police car and was going to take her in." No need to embarrass Aunt Charlene and mention why Jo-Jo hit the girl, Tiara thought.

"Why did the girls want to jump you?" Rashad asked Jo-Jo as he spooned some honey from the small earthenware jar on the table into his herbal tea.

Jo-Jo shrugged her shoulders. "I got into an argument with one of their sisters at my school, and I accidentally pushed her." She looked at her father and added, "And it really was an accident." She turned back to Rashad. "She and a bunch of her friends were teasing me about being a tomboy."

Rashad grunted and shook his head. "I'm sure you know they're just jealous of you."

"You think so?" Jo-Jo said disinterestedly.

"Yeah, of course. Look at you, you look like a runway model. All tall and slim, and you have such an innocent attitude you don't even realize how good-looking you are. But you'd better believe all the girls know," Rashad chuckled.

"Ya think?" Jo-Jo said slowly.

"Oh yeah, definitely," Charlene piped in.

"Well, then how come none of the boys at school think I'm cute?" Jo-Jo demanded.

"I'm sure they do," Rashad smiled. "But you're taller than most of the boys in your class, right?"

Jo-Jo gave a reluctant nod of her head.

"Well, right now they might be a little intimidated. But in another year or so they're going to catch up in height, and then watch out," Rashad chuckled again.

"You really think so?" Jo-Jo grinned.

"Definitely." Rashad nodded his head. "They're going to be on you like white on rice."

"I've always wished I was tall and thin," Alice said quietly.

"Why?" Rashad turned to her.

"Or even short and thin, like Tiara."

"Five-five isn't short," Tiara snapped. She would have said more if her aunt hadn't shot her a warning look.

"No, I don't mean to say you're short or anything. I'm sorry," Alice said quickly.

"Girl, you look fine just the way you are." Rashad gave Alice a friendly nudge on her arm. "Different people have different body types. It doesn't mean one is preferable to another."

Rashad had this thing about him. He just seemed to know the right thing to say to the right person at the right time, Tiara thought. Like telling Jo-Jo that soon boys would be all over her. It's like he knew she was insecure about her sexuality. And now with Alice. He didn't tell her that she was beautiful or anything—even she might have a hard time swallowing that. But just telling her that different people have different body types . . . wow. That had to make her feel good. But dang, he was handing out all these compliments but he'd hardly said a word to her since they left the apartment. Was he trying to punish her for not wanting Alice to go along with them?

"That's true," Tiara said. It was time for her to regain her gracious face. "It's important to be comfortable with the skin you're in."

"Exactly," Rashad said approvingly.

Dang. He could have said something about what a profound statement I made. To hell with him then. Tiara grunted out loud.

"You say something, Princess?"

"Just clearing my throat, Daddy."

"Hey, isn't that Lionel?" Jo-Jo said suddenly.

Tiara smiled, but didn't look up until Lionel leaned over and kissed her on the cheek.

"Hey, Baby," she said as she nuzzled her cheek against Lionel's hand resting on her shoulder. She glanced at Rashad from the corner of her eye to make sure he was watching. He was. In fact, the look of shock on his face was just delicious.

"How are you doing, Mr. Bynum? Miss Bynum?" Lionel nodded politely at Reggie and Charlene. "What's up, Jo-Jo? I heard you kicked some serious butt on the court this morning."

"Hey, how's it going, Lionel?" Reggie tilted his seat back and reached over to slide a chair from a nearby table over next to him. He motioned Lionel over.

"Oh, let the lovebirds sit next to each other. Lionel, move that chair over by Tiara," Charlene said, giving her niece a little nudge under the table.

Good, Tiara thought as she lightly tapped Charlene's knee in acknowledgment before sliding her chair over to make room for Lionel between them. *Aunt Charlie knows what's up, and she's going to play along. 'Bout time she showed some support!*

"Lionel, let me introduce you. This is James Scott," she waved toward James. "This is a good friend of mine, Alice Garrison." She paused, trying to hide a smile that was trying to break through as she readied her next introduction. "And this," she waved toward Rashad, "is Rashad Harrison." She smiled now, and placed her hand over Lionel's hand on the table. "Guys, this is my boyfriend, Lionel Evans."

"Yeah, I know Lionel." Rashad was staring down at his tea, swishing around the leaves at the bottom of the cup.

"You do?" Tiara's smile widened into a grin. She had almost forgotten that the two of them went to the same school. Good, that meant Rashad probably knew that Lionel had a banging car. Lionel, for his part, squinted his eyes and studied Rashad's face, but no recognition registered on his face.

"Well, we've never actually met. I've seen him around campus, though, and maybe a few other places." Rashad lifted his head and looked Lionel in the eye. "What's up, man?"

"You go to NYU? Cool," Lionel nodded. "What year?"

"Senior," Rashad answered.

"What's your major?"

"Film."

"Cool. NYU's the best school in the country for film," Lionel said as he leaned back in his chair and draped his arm around Tiara's shoulder. "Me, I'm a business major."

Tiara leaned her head into Lionel's shoulder and smiled at Rashad, enjoying his obvious displeasure. *Oh yeah . . . if he didn't want to admit to himself he wants me, he has to now. Yeah, I got it like that.* She glanced over at Charlene, trying to catch her eye to get a congratulatory wink or smile, but her aunt was busy watching—with furrowed brow—the interaction between Lionel and Rashad.

"Business, huh? Now you know," Rashad said slowly as he too leaned back in his chair and studied Lionel. "That doesn't surprise me."

"What do you mean?" Lionel asked.

"Nothing, brotherman. Just, you know, you seem to be all about business." Rashad picked up his teaspoon and started tapping it softly against the table. "You *are* all about business, right?"

"Depends on what you mean by that, brotherman." Lionel's voice dropped and his face hardened. He removed his arm from around Tiara's shoulder and placed his hands against the edge of the table as if to ready to push his chair back.

"Hey, hey, hey!" Reggie suddenly said urgently. James also sat at attention, looking back and forth between Lionel and Rashad as he put his arm out in front of Charlene protectively.

"I don't know what's going on, but I suggest you two cool out," Reggie continued.

Rashad leaned back into his chair and shrugged, but Tiara could see a small vein in his forehead working overtime. She turned to look at Lionel who still sat tensely, staring at Rashad as if to see what he was going to say—or do—next. *Dang, I know they aren't getting ready to fight over me.*

"Hey, you ready?" Lionel said to her suddenly. "You wanted to catch that matinee downtown, didn't you?"

"Um, sure," she said quickly. "Daddy, do you mind if we go ahead and leave right . . ."

Her attention returned to Rashad as he suddenly got up from the table. "Look, I'm going to have to go ahead and split myself," he said, grabbing his army coat from the back of his chair and quickly putting it on. "I guess I'll see you next Saturday," he said to Reggie before sticking his hands in his pockets and walking toward the exit. "I hope everyone has a nice day," he said over his shoulder. Tiara's mouth dropped open. She looked around the table at everyone else, but they were all staring at Rashad's back in clear shock, also.

James leaned over toward Charlene. "What the hell was that all about?" he asked.

She shrugged her shoulders and shook her head, still staring at the departing Rashad. "You know? I think—" she stopped as Rashad slapped his forehead just before reaching the door, whirled around, and slowly walked back to the table.

"I'm sorry, Alice, my head is just somewhere else," he said tapping the girl lightly on the shoulder. "I really do have to leave, though. If you're finished I'd be glad to walk you home, or you can sit and talk for a while and walk home with the Bynums. It's totally up to you."

"I'm ready to leave." Alice pushed back her seat and got up. "I guess I'll see everyone later," she said sheepishly.

"Oh. I didn't know that was your woman." The smirk on Lionel's face was unmistakable as he looked from Alice to Rashad. "She, uh, has a pretty face. Bet she has a really nice personality, too."

Alice's face turned crimson, and she looked from Rashad down to the floor where her eyes stayed. Tiara audibly gasped before she could catch herself. She had wanted to hurt Rashad—and even Alice—but not like that.

"Naw man, I'm not fortunate enough to have such a quality woman like Alice in my life right now," Rashad said without missing a beat. He smiled down at Alice, and then hugged her around the shoulders. "She has a pretty face, a nice personality, and she's all around a beautiful woman. And I'm just glad to even be her friend."

"Aw, isn't that sweet?" Lionel chuckled.

"Yeah, it is sweet," Reggie said gruffly. "Lionel, let me see you in the back here for a minute." He nodded his head toward the restrooms.

"All right, it was good seeing you all." Rashad gave another wave, and then he and Alice disappeared out of the restaurant.

"Oh, well, that was really nice." Charlene looked at Lionel and snorted as she threw her napkin on the table. "Congratulations, my esteem for you has just shot up three points. Here I was thinking you had the maturity of a six-year-old, but you handled that like a very capable fourth-grader."

"What?" Lionel's mouth dropped open. "I only asked if that was his woman. What's wrong with that?"

"That was just plain mean," Jo-Jo said with downcast eyes and in a low voice as she quietly drummed her fingers on the table.

"He was only joking," Tiara said quietly, to no one in particular.

"He should try to refine his sense of humor," James said dryly.

"You should try and mind your business," Tiara snapped. "Weren't nobody talking to you. This is family business."

"Tiara!" Charlene and Reggie shouted simultaneously.

"Oooh," Jo-Jo said expectantly.

"Apologize to James right now," Reggie growled. "You know better than to talk to people like that." He motioned the waiter for the check. "Let's get up on out of here."

"Yeah, we're going to have to leave if we're going to make that movie, Charlene," James said as he looked at his watch.

"Ooh, what movie y'all going to go see?" Jo-Jo asked.

"Tiara, I didn't hear your apology." Charlene's eyes were squeezed into tiny slits.

"Sorry," Tiara murmured.

"That new Chris Rock film. You can come if your father and aunt don't mind," James said as he removed his wallet from his pocket. "Let me give you a little something toward that, man," he said to Reggie.

"Naw, man. I got this handled," Reggie said as he picked up the check the waiter placed on the table.

"Daddy, can I go to the movie with Aunt Charlie and Mr. James?"

"Why don't you let me get that? It's the least I can do since I seem to have managed to piss everyone off." Lionel reached over to take the check from Reggie, but Reggie jerked his hand back.

"I said, I've got this handled!" He glowered at Lionel.

"Sorry, I didn't mean anything by it." Lionel drew his hand back as if it had been burnt.

"Daddy, he was only trying to be nice," Tiara snapped.

"Daddy, can I go to the movies with Aunt Charlie and Mr. James?" Jo-Jo asked again.

"You'd better check your attitude, Tiara," Charlene said sharply. "And your boyfriend better learn that he can't go around insulting people and then think he can buy his way back into everyone's good graces."

"Aunt Charlie." Jo-Jo tapped her aunt on the shoulder. "If Daddy says it's okay, can I go to the movies with you and Mr. James?"

"He wasn't trying to buy his way into anyone's good graces, he was just trying to be nice." Tiara slapped the table with her hand to accentuate each word. "But then you wouldn't . . ."

"Tiara, shut up. And Jo-Jo, you shut up, too." Reggie sighed and reached around the back of his chair and grabbed his jacket. "A man can't even hear himself think with all this crap going on."

"But, Daddy, I just want to know if I can . . ."

Charlene put her hand over Jo-Jo's. "Hush, girl. You can go, okay?"

"Lionel, you ready?" Tiara stood up abruptly.

"Girl, sit your ass down!" Reggie almost shouted.

"Daddy, dang." Tiara dropped back down into her seat. "Why you gotta talk to me like that?"

"'Cause I'm tired of all this crap," Reggie shot back. "You've had an attitude since we walked out the house. If you didn't want to come, I don't remember anyone begging for your presence."

He turned to Lionel. "And I don't know if you and Rashad have some kind of history or what, but he was my guest at this table, and I don't appreciate the way you talked to him, and I sure don't appreciate you trying to embarrass that girl, Alice, like that. You'd better grow up."

"Why you gotta take Rashad's side?" Tiara slid her chair back again. "He started it. You didn't say anything to him about the way he was talking to Lionel."

"I'm not taking anyone's side." Reggie was obviously trying to keep his voice under control, but the volume was rising. "Lionel was wrong to make that crack about Alice and you know it."

"I didn't make a crack. I just asked if she was his woman," Lionel cut in.

"Don't sit there and try to make me and everybody at this table seem stupid." The bass in Reggie's voice was loud and clear as he addressed Lionel. "We all know what you meant, and so did poor Alice. I would think you were brought up better than that. And I wouldn't be calling you out like this if you had gotten up like a man and come to the back with me like I asked."

"Daddy you're just acting like this because Rashad doesn't like Lionel, and now you don't either. Just because you go boxing with him every week and he sucks up to you and makes like he's such a nice guy doesn't mean he's part of the family, you know." Tiara was shouting now, and people at other tables were staring, but she didn't care.

"I'm acting like this because if Rashad and Lionel wanted to get into it, then they should have just handled it like men," Reggie shouted back. "Rashad was on his way out the door, and if Lionel wanted to get with him he should have followed him out. But no, he's got to try and insult that girl who didn't do anything to anyone. He should have been a man and handled his business with Rashad and left Alice out of it. That's what a man would do."

Lionel jumped up. "Come on, Tiara. I think it's time for us to get out of here." He took Tiara's hand and tried to pull her up from her chair.

"Get your funky hand off of my child." Reggie's voice was now a growl, and the intensity in his eyes clearly conveyed his mood. "Don't you ever try to pull my daughter away when I'm talking to her, you understand?"

Lionel sat back down with a thud, but said nothing.

"Now, see, why you gotta talk to Lionel like that?" Tiara protested loudly.

"I thought I told you to shut up a couple of minutes ago." Reggie turned back to her.

"That's right, Reggie. And don't forget . . ." Charlene leaned forward eagerly.

"Charlene, stay out of it. Reggie can take care of it," James said gently.

"But I was just . . ."

"Let the man handle his business." James stood up and pulled Charlene's chair out without her assistance. "Come on and handle your own business, lady. We got a movie to catch."

"But, I was just . . ." Charlene said as she got up.

"Stop butting and start walking." James kissed her full on the mouth, causing Charlene to blush and James to chuckle. "Come on, Jo-Jo. Let's roll."

Tiara sat at the table, her arms crossed and her mouth drawn into a pout, after Charlene, James, and Jo-Jo left. She waited until Reggie paid the bill and received his change before saying sullenly, "Is it okay if we leave now? We've got to catch a show."

"I don't care what you do. I'm going uptown to catch up with some of my friends from work." Reggie stood up and put on his jacket.

"You want us to give you a ride back home?" Lionel asked as he also stood.

Reggie snorted and walked out the door.

"Okay. I guess that means no," Lionel said as he helped Tiara on with her coat. "Can't say I wasn't trying to be polite."

16

Damn, your dad was really tripping. Why did he have to act so fucked-up because of some little remark? Shit, I said I was only kidding." Lionel slammed the car door and settled into the driver's seat. He put the key in the ignition and switched on the stereo, but didn't start the car.

Tiara sat in the seat, her arms crossed, pouting. She turned to Lionel.

"Don't be talking about my father like that, Lionel." She rolled her eyes and turned to look out the window.

"Yeah, well," Lionel shrugged. "I'm sorry, 'cause I wasn't trying talk about your dad, but I just can't believe he broke like that. Not just on me, but on you, too. Telling you to shut up and shit like you're some kind of kid or something."

Tiara sighed and re-crossed her arms. "I can't believe Daddy talked to me like that in front of everyone. And I didn't even do anything wrong. You're right. He acts like I'm eight years old instead of almost nineteen. It's that damn Rashad's fault. Daddy acts like he likes him more than me."

"You shouldn't let him talk to you like that. My parents would never talk to me like that. They know I'm their son, but they also respect the fact that I'm a man," Lionel said as he pushed the buttons on the car stereo until he found a song that he liked.

"Well, I didn't hear you saying anything about the way Daddy talked to you." Tiara rolled her eyes.

"Because I respect you too much to get with him like that."

"Yeah," Tiara said unconvincingly.

"And anyway, it's your fault that your father treats you like that. You act like a little girl, so he treats you like one." Lionel leaned over and kissed Tiara on the cheek, then brushed his hand over her hair. "You need to move out. Let him see you can make it on your own without him."

Tiara sucked her teeth. "Move out, huh? I'm not going to get a job just so I can pay rent. You've got to be crazy. I'm in school, remember."

"You wouldn't have to get a job," Lionel said softly. "And you wouldn't have to pay rent."

Tiara moved Lionel's hand away and cocked her head to look at him. *He can't be ready to say what I think he's going to say, could he?*

"You can just move in with me. My place is big enough." Lionel cupped her face in his hands. "And I think it would be wonderful to finally be able to wake up in the morning and find you in the bed next to me."

"Lionel, I can't do that." Tiara lowered her eyes.

"Why not, Baby?" Lionel kissed her on the forehead, then her nose, then on her lips, parting them slightly with his tongue. "You know I love you. And I know you love me, right?"

"You know I love you, Lionel."

"Then prove it. Come on, Baby, let's do this." Lionel tried to pull Tiara into his arms, but the gearshift blocked the move. "We can go get your stuff right now. Or just leave it all, and I can buy you new stuff. A whole new wardrobe. You'd like that, wouldn't you?"

Oh wow, a whole new wardrobe? That would be so cool. I can get those Manolo Blahnik crocodile shoes I saw on Sex and the City. *Daddy would freak if I told him I wanted a nine-hundred-dollar pair of shoes, but I bet Lionel would buy them for me. And I can get that black Coach leather zip-up jacket. That only cost six hundred dollars.* Tiara shook her head to bring herself back to reality. No, she couldn't do it. No way. Forget the shoes and jacket. Daddy would kill her.

"We don't have to do it today, Lionel. Let me think about it a little bit," she said, pushing away from him. "There's no big rush."

"Man." Lionel's lip turned up into a grimace. "What's there to talk about. Your father just showed he doesn't respect you. You don't care about that?"

"He was just angry."

"Just because he's angry he doesn't have to dog you out like that, Tiara. Come on now."

"Baby," Tiara said softly, taking his hand into hers. "I just want some time to think about it, is all. I didn't say no, remember?"

Lionel sighed, pulled his hand away, and turned on the ignition. "Okay. But I hope you make the right decision. You've got to let that man know that you're a grown woman now, Tiara."

"Yeah, I know." Tiara looked out the tinted windows as Lionel screeched away from the curb. Maybe she should go ahead and move in with Lionel. It would be nice to be on her own. Well, kinda be on her own. After all, she wouldn't be living alone, she'd be with Lionel. But she wouldn't have to answer to him about staying out too late. And she wouldn't have to worry about hiding her birth control, or her marijuana. But at the same time, she had always imagined moving from her father's apartment into her own place. Playing the role of career-girl for a while before marrying a rich handsome man and living the life of a jet-set couple. But here her rich handsome man was asking her to move in now. She wished she had someone to talk to about this. But it wasn't like she could talk to her father, and she certainly wasn't going to confide in Aunt Charlie, especially after the way her aunt had turned on her in the restaurant. Her thoughts turned to her mother. *Maybe she'll know what I should do. It would be nice to have some motherly advice.* She opened her clutch bag and rummaged around for a minute looking for the piece of paper with her mother's telephone number. Damn, it wasn't there. She must have put it in the pocket of the jacket she wore the night before. Suddenly, having her mother's telephone number with her was the most important thing in the world.

"Lionel, can we swing by my house? I forgot something."

"I really don't feel like seeing your father right now," Lionel said sullenly. "Whatever it is, can it wait?"

"Daddy went uptown to see friends, remember?" Tiara stroked Lionel's hand. "Please? It will only take a minute."

"Yeah, all right. We already blew the show anyway," Lionel said reluctantly as he turned the car around. "And anyway, I do have to go to the bathroom."

"Tiara? That you?"

"Yeah, Daddy." *What the hell is he doing here?* She turned to look at Lionel and shrugged in answer to the question in his eyes.

"Good, I need to talk to you."

"I thought you went to see some friends, Daddy," Tiara said as she walked into the living room, Lionel trailing behind her. The first thing she noticed was the agitated look on Reggie's face. He was standing in the middle of the room, his forehead beaded with sweat and his chest heaving. The second thing she noticed was Rashad standing off to the side of the room, his hands in his pockets, looking like he'd rather be anywhere else on earth than in that apartment at that moment.

"What's he doing here?" Reggie pointed to Lionel.

"He's with me. What's he doing here?" She pointed to Rashad.

"He's here because he wanted to tell me that your no-good motherfucking boyfriend is a fucking drug dealer, is what he's doing here." Reggie rushed toward Lionel, but Tiara jumped in front of him before he could reach the younger man.

"What are you talking about?" She tried, unsuccessfully, to push him back. Lionel retreated a few steps and put his hands, palms up, in front of him.

"Mr. Bynum, I don't know what's going on, but that dude is lying," he said in a panicked voice.

"You're the fucking liar, you sorry son of a bitch." Reggie pushed Tiara to the side and again lunged toward Lionel, but this time Rashad jumped in front of him.

"It's okay, Mr. Bynum. You just gotta calm down, man," he said soothingly.

"I'm not going to calm down until that motherfucker gets outta my house!" Reggie roared. He whirled around and looked at Tiara. "Don't you ever bring him up here in this house again, you hear. Don't you ever go near him again!"

"Daddy, please," Tiara pleaded. "He's not a drug dealer. Rashad's just lying on him because he's jealous."

"Mr. Bynum, let me at least say something. At least hear me out." Lionel's back was against the wall. "Give me a chance to defend myself."

"Okay." Reggie backed away a few steps and crossed his arms over his chest. "What you got to say?"

Lionel took a deep breath. "First of all, I don't sell drugs, I don't hang out with people who sell drugs. And I don't even do drugs. Do I, Tiara?"

"Nope." Tiara shook her head frantically. "He sure doesn't."

"And that man," Lionel pointed to Rashad, "doesn't even know me. I've never seen him before in my life, and he doesn't know anything about me. Just like Tiara said, he's probably just jealous because he likes Tiara. You saw how he started in on me as soon as I walked into the restaurant today."

"I started in on you, man, because I don't like what you do," Rashad said calmly. "And I told Mr. Bynum because I know he wouldn't want his family around scum like you."

"He's lying, Daddy." Tiara tugged on Reggie's arms urgently, but he didn't budge. "He's just jealous because I chose Lionel over him."

Rashad screwed his face up and shook his head as if in disbelief at what he'd just heard. "Tiara, I only want the best for you, sis. I'm not trying to push up on you, I'm just trying to look out for you. And I know you probably didn't know what he's been doing."

"He's not doing anything, you liar!" Tiara shouted at him.

"Mr. Bynum, why would I sell drugs? I've got money. My dad's rich. He buys me anything I want, and on top of that, he gives me a fat allowance." Lionel's words came out in a rush. "I don't need to sell drugs. I don't even need a job. You know that."

"That's right, Daddy!" Tiara piped in. "I told you Rashad was making it up. He just wants you to make me stop seeing Lionel. That's why he's over here telling you all these lies."

"Tiara, listen to me. It's not a lie. I have no reason to lie. And if I weren't positive, I wouldn't have said anything," Rashad said. "I know what I'm talking about. Remember me telling you and your father about my godbrother, Alvin? Well, your boyfriend is down with him. Yeah, I've seen Lionel on campus a few times, but I've seen him more often with Alvin. And Alvin's told me about him. Your boyfriend is the one who puts up the money for Alvin to buy his product, and your boyfriend gets the first cut of the profits. Tiara, these scum have little kids working for them."

"Man, you're crazy. I don't even know anyone named Alvin," Lionel shouted.

"You're a liar!" Rashad shouted back. "Alvin lives right in my building and I've seen you over there. And he told me himself that you were his bankroll."

"Daddy!" Tiara whirled around to face her father. "I've met all of Lionel's friends, and he doesn't know anyone named Alvin. Rashad's just lying because he's jealous."

"Girl, open up your goddamn eyes," Reggie shouted. "I don't care how much money his damn father's got, Lionel ain't shit. And in fact, it's worse that he's doing this shit when he doesn't even need the money. What's he coming down here to the ghetto and playing the Nicky Barnes role for the thrill of it?"

"Tiara, get real. How could I ever be jealous of a crack dealer!" Rashad snorted.

"All right, that's enough. I'm not going to just stand here and get insulted like this." Lionel grabbed Tiara's arm. "Come on."

Reggie took two steps forward and landed a haymaker square in the middle of Lionel's face, which sent him barreling back into the entertainment center, causing the stereo and sports trophies inside to crash to the floor. "Motherfucking crack-dealing punk! You trying to pull on my daughter when I'm talking to her? Didn't I tell you about that shit?"

"Daddy!" Tiara ran to Lionel and tried to help him up. Blood was spurting from his nose and upper lip and onto the floor, and he appeared dazed, his arms wobbling in the air.

"Leave that punk be!" Reggie roared as he advanced toward him again.

"Mr. Bynum, stop. You've got to calm down." Rashad jumped in front of him.

"I don't have to do a damn thing! But don't worry, I ain't gonna hit the sissy motherfucker again. Bitch can't even take a punch."

"Daddy, you're acting crazy! Lionel's not a drug dealer, and now you've messed up his face." Tiara ran into the kitchen and grabbed a dish towel, then ran back to the living room and pressed it against

Lionel's nose. "Oh, my God, Lionel, we're going to have to get you to a hospital. Come on, Baby, just lean on me."

"Let him drive himself to the goddamned hospital."

"Daddy, he can't drive himself like this. I'm going to have to take him in a cab."

"Tiara, you're not going any damned where with a drug dealer," Reggie snorted. "Get in your room, and I'll talk to you later."

"Daddy, please!"

"Daddy, please, nothing. Go to your room now!"

Lionel leaned against the wall groaning. "Shit, I think my nose is broken." He removed the towel from his face and touched his nose, then winced. "Oh, God," he moaned.

"Tiara, I thought I told you to go to your goddamn room!"

"But, Daddy!" Tiara looked from her infuriated father to her groaning boyfriend. "I've got to get him to the hospital."

"You have to do what I tell you, is what you have to do! Now, stop trying me and get in your room like I said!"

"Daddy, you can't tell me what to do. I'm a grown woman." Tiara stomped her foot on the floor. "If I don't want to go to my room, I'm not going."

"Look, as long as you live in my house, you'll do what I goddamn tell you to do!"

"Fine. As of right now, I don't live here anymore," Tiara spat.

"Oh, man, this is going too far . . ." Rashad started.

"What the hell are you talking about?" Reggie reached over and tried to grab Tiara by the arm.

"Get off of me!" Tiara snatched her arm away. "I'm leaving, and you can't stop me!"

"Oh, yeah? Watch me!" Reggie grabbed at Tiara again, but she darted backward out of the way.

"What you going to do, Daddy?" she shouted. "You going to hit me, too? You're going to break my nose, too?" Tiara flung one of

Lionel's arms around her shoulders and started walking him toward the door.

"What are you talking about? I've never laid a hand on you in my life," Reggie sputtered.

"Yeah, well look at what you did to Lionel," Tiara said turning back to her father. "And I'm tired of you telling me what to do like I'm some baby. I'm a grown woman and you can't stand that."

"If you're a grown woman, stop acting like a two-year-old. You're so fucking fascinated by that man's goddamned money you don't care that he's a drug pusher?"

"Yeah, well, Daddy, I don't remember you being so upset about Lionel having money. What did you tell me? 'This is the kind of man I've always dreamed you'd end up with. A man who adores you, buys presents, has money, has a future.' You do remember saying that, don't you, Daddy?"

"God damn it. You know I ain't know he was a fucking drug pusher when I said all that."

"Man, I keep telling you I don't sell drugs," Lionel groaned.

"Shut the fuck up before I clock you again!" Reggie roared at him.

Tiara said nothing as she opened the door, Lionel leaning heavily on her.

"Fine! Leave, see if I give a shit," was the last thing she heard as the door closed shut behind her.

17

H ello?"

Tiara hung up the telephone at the sound of her father's voice. *Damn, why couldn't Jo-Jo answer the phone?* It had been four days since she'd left and moved in with Lionel, and so far the living was good. Very good.

Lionel was still in pain after the trip to the hospital and a restless night's sleep, so he wasn't able to take her shopping, but he had given her his Bloomingdale's credit card, and called the store telling them to expect her. She conservatively bought only enough clothes to last her a week, thinking that by that time Lionel would be well enough to take her to do real shopping, but the bill still came up to $3,500, including the $900 Italian red leather jacket and matching $300 red leather mini-skirt. She didn't expect Lionel to bitch about the bill, but she was especially pleased when he didn't even ask about it. She could see living with a millionaire was going to be really cool. Well, the son of a millionaire, anyway. Must be nice to have a father who gave you everything you wanted.

"Who was that?" Lionel called from the living room.

"Who was what?" Tiara walked in to find Lionel lounging on the couch watching *106 and Park* on BET while sipping a Heineken through a plastic straw. The sash to his gray print silk robe was loose, revealing matching boxer shorts and his six-pack stomach and burly chest. From the neck down, he looked fine. But there was a large bandage over his nose to cover the packing done at the hospital, his left eye was black, and his stitched lip was so swollen it looked deformed.

"Who were you talking to on the hallway phone just now?" Lionel sounded as if he was talking through a funnel, thanks to the bandage. He had eased up on the Tylenol with codeine, but his words were still slightly slurred, so he was a little difficult to understand.

"No one. I was trying to get Jo-Jo, but my father picked up the phone so I hung up." Tiara sighed and went over and gently sat down next to Lionel on the couch. Even that movement made him wince.

"Damn, girl. Go sit on the love seat or something. Can't you see I'm wounded and in pain?"

"Sorry, baby." Tiara eased off the couch and moved over to the loveseat. "Anyway," she continued, "I think I might have to wait until Daddy goes to work tomorrow and go back over to the apartment and leave a note for Jo-Jo."

"What do you have to talk to Jo-Jo about that's so important, anyway?"

"Nothing. I just want to talk to her." Tiara shrugged. "I just don't want her to be all upset and everything. And I want to tell her my side of the story." *And I gotta tell her about Mommy. I know they didn't tell her. And I want her to get me Mommy's telephone number.* Tiara sighed. *I really want to talk to my mom. I bet she'd understand. She's probably the only one who would.* She looked at Lionel as he took another sip of Heineken and flicked the television remote. *Shit, I know he's in pain, but why does he have to be so wrapped in himself? He doesn't even seem to care about how I'm feeling.*

"So you're missing your family, huh?" Lionel said as if reading her mind.

"No, just Jo-Jo." Tiara sighed.

"Good. 'Cause I know you haven't forgiven your father for that crap he pulled. Broke my fucking nose. Someone ought to teach him a lesson. I would have kicked his ass, but I didn't want to upset you."

Tiara snorted. "Yeah right."

"What do you mean by that? I know you don't think I'm scared of your father?" Lionel raised up slightly on his elbow and looked at Tiara. "The only reason I didn't kick his ass was because I didn't want you to get all pissed off."

"Please, my daddy would stomp you into a mud hole." Tiara giggled.

"Oh, you think that old man could really beat me?"

"Not a doubt in my mind."

"And why's that? You don't think I'm good with my hands? Just because I didn't hit an old man doesn't mean I'm a punk."

"No offense, baby. But my father can throw down. He used to be a boxing champ back in the day. I once saw him thug it out with two men for insulting my Aunt Charlie, and kick both of their asses."

"Is that right?" Lionel took another sip of his beer.

"Yeah, that's right."

"You know, you act like you think it's cool that your father hit me. What's up with that?" Lionel said slowly.

"Please. I'm not saying anything like that. I'm just saying he's not a pushover." Tiara shrugged. She looked at Lionel, wheezing and looking pitiful. She couldn't resist the laugh that bubbled up from her chest. "And he sure did push up on your ass."

"Oh now, you think this shit is funny?" Lionel's mouth dropped open. "You think it's funny?"

"Naw, naw, I'm only joking, baby." Tiara tried to control her giggles as she went over and knelt by the couch near Lionel. She touched the good side of his face lightly.

"You joke too fucking much." Lionel knocked her hand away.

"Damn, Lionel." Tiara stood up. "I said I was only joking."

"And I said you joke too fucking much. Get the fuck away from me!"

"Well, fuck you then!" Tiara stomped into the bedroom and slammed the door behind her. She grabbed her economics book from the nightstand and plopped on the bed, flipping pages furiously. To hell with Lionel. She knew she was only kidding around. Acting like he couldn't take a joke, all of a sudden. And if she wasn't going to put up with her father talking to her like she was a kid, she sure as hell wasn't going to let Lionel talk to her any kind of way. If he wasn't all banged up like that she would have really let him have it. He'd better be glad she had a big heart. But she wasn't going to put up with this shit long. It wasn't like she didn't have anywhere to go. *I mean push to shove, I can always go back home. As soon as Daddy calms down.* She closed the book and softly fingered the cover as if reading the title in Braille, wondering how her father was doing, and what he was thinking. *He's probably all broken up. Aunt Charlie's probably over there comforting him day and night, and cursing her out at the same time.* No, if Aunt Charlie tried to curse her out, Daddy would stop her. Even if he was mad at her and everything. After all he was still her father. *But you would think he would have tried to contact me by now. What's up with that? I mean, he has Lionel's phone number, and I know he knows I'm over here. And shit, he knows it's me that keeps calling and hanging up. You would think he'd do a star sixty-nine and call me back and ask me to come home. Not that I would if he did ask.* She threw the book across the room. *But why the fuck isn't he asking?*

She sat up on the bed and reached for the telephone on the nightstand, but changed her mind and retrieved her cell phone from her pocketbook. This is just pure hell. I gotta talk to someone. She brought Shakira's telephone number up from the cell phone memory and called her sometime friend, but got no answer. Her mother was probably on the telephone, and not clicking over to the call waiting. Shit, Shakira needs to get a damn cell phone, she sighed as she hung up. She picked it up again quickly and dialed her home number.

"Hello?"

"Jo-Jo!" Tiara's heart jumped. "It's about time you answered the damn telephone!"

"Ooh, Tiara, where are you? Daddy is pissed!" Jo-Jo's high-pitched voice came over the line.

"I don't care. Is he home?"

"Naw. I wouldn't have been able to answer the phone if he was here. He yells 'I got it' as soon as it rings. Where are you, anyway?"

"Over at Lionel's."

"You living there now?"

"Is that what Daddy told you?"

"No. He just said you moved out."

"He didn't say why?"

"No. When Aunt Charlie and Mr. James dropped me off the other night he was going off and saying that Lionel wasn't shit. And then when we asked him where you were he got even more pissed and sent me to our room. Don't you hate that?"

"Yeah, I do." Tiara sighed.

"So what happened? Why's he so pissed? Why aren't you coming home?"

"It's a long story . . ."

"Aw man, Tiara. You going to give me that long story stuff, too?" Jo-Jo sucked her teeth. "Ya'll better stop treating me like a baby, you know. I'm a teenager, remember?"

"Hey, Jo-Jo. Did Daddy tell you what happened Friday night?"

"No. What?"

"We saw Mommy."

"Mommy, who?"

"Our mother, stupid!"

"Get outta here!" Jo-Jo's voice grew so excited Tiara could almost see her jumping up and down. "Where? What was she doing? How did she look?"

"We saw her at some party Daddy was going to."

"Oh, man! How did she look?"

"Guess what? I didn't even recognize her. Her hair is all short and stuff."

"It was? Oooh, hold on! Let me go get her picture from your dresser."

"What? Jo-Jo . . ." Tiara sighed as she heard the receiver clunk onto the coffee table and Jo-Jo running into the bedroom.

"Okay. Go ahead." Jo-Jo was back on the phone in less than a minute.

"Why did you have to get the picture?"

"So I can look at her while you talk," Jo-Jo said matter-of-factly. "So go ahead."

"Anyway, I was saying that I didn't recognize her because she cut her hair."

"Is she still pretty?"

"Yeah, she's beautiful."

"Did you talk to her?"

"Yeah, but not a lot . . ."

"Did she ask about me?"

The question made Tiara pause. Now that she thought about it, her mother never did ask about Jo-Jo. That was strange. It was like she'd forgotten she existed. Maybe because she never really knew her youngest daughter? After all, Jo-Jo was an infant when she left. But how could you not ask about your own daughter?

"Tiara? What did she ask about me?"

"Well, she asked how you were doing and everything. And she wanted to know how you were doing in school," Tiara said carefully.

"She did? Oh, man. Oh, man. Oh, man. What did you tell her? Is she going to come see me?"

"Well, we didn't talk long because then she and Daddy started arguing," Tiara said quickly. "And guess what? Then she and Aunt Charlie got into a big fight and Aunt Charlie knocked out one of her teeth."

"What?" Jo-Jo's tone changed from excitement to horror. "Why'd she do that? Oh God. Now she's never going to come see me."

"Jo-Jo, calm down . . ."

"Hold on, someone's coming in the house." Tiara realized that Jo-Jo had taken the telephone from her ear. "Aunt Charlie," Tiara heard Jo-Jo say. "You hit my mother?" Tiara could hear Aunt Charlie speaking, but couldn't make out her words. "Tiara told me you hit our mother the other night. Why'd you do that?"

The next thing Tiara heard was Charlene's angry voice. "What the hell do you think you're doing?"

"Aunt Charlie, get Jo-Jo out of the room and I'll explain why I said that," Tiara said quickly.

"Hold on." The voices in the room became muffled, as if Charlene had put her hand over the telephone, but Tiara could tell that Charlene and Jo-Jo were arguing furiously. That was something Jo-Jo had never done with her aunt.

"Okay, she's gone. Now what's going on?" Charlene demanded after a few minutes.

"Aunt Charlie. I was telling her about us seeing Mommy Friday night, and she asked if Mommy asked about her. And I couldn't tell her the truth, so I said she started asking about her, but then you and Daddy and her started arguing. I had to give her some excuse."

"So you had to make me the Wicked Witch of the West? Thanks a bunch."

"Oh man, Aunt Charlie . . ." Tiara's eyes started watering. She'd never in her life gone this long without talking to Jo-Jo and Aunt Charlie, and she didn't mean for it to wind up like this. She was just trying to do the right thing. "I didn't mean to . . ." She tried to stifle the unwelcome sobs in her voice.

"Hush, child. I'm only playing," Aunt Charlie said gently. "I understand. You were just trying to spare your sister's feelings. Good girl."

"Yep. That's all I was trying to do." Tiara sniffed.

"And that's a good thing. I'll straighten it out on this end."

"Okay."

"And how are you doing, girl? You ready to come home? You know your daddy really misses you. We all do."

Tiara closed her eyes and let out a grateful sigh. God, it felt so good to hear that.

"Tiara?"

"Yeah?"

"Are you staying at Lionel's?"

"If I say yeah, are you and Daddy going to come over and try and drag me out of here or something?" Tiara said suspiciously.

"Please. As much a kick as I *know* you'd get out of that, it's not about to happen." Charlene snorted.

"Well, then, why do you need to know?"

"Just because, Tiara. You're my niece, and I love you. And Reggie told me what Rashad told him about Lionel."

"Rashad's lying!"

"Are you sure?" Charlene said cautiously.

"Yes! He's just jealous because he can't have me so he's trying to turn Daddy against Lionel. Don't let him convince you, too, Aunt Charlie."

Charlene sighed over the telephone. "Okay, I'm keeping an open mind, but I want you to, also. You be careful. And bring your little ass home. You don't need to be living with any man, drug dealer or not. You're too young for that shit."

"I'm a grown woman," Tiara huffed.

"You're a grown young woman," Charlene reminded her. "And check the attitude because I'm not coming at you like that. I hate that my brother's upset, but I hate that you're upset, too. I think the whole situation should have been handled differently. You two are going to have to work this shit out. He's actually been crying, Tiara. Sobbing his heart out. Did you know that?"

"No." Tiara's eyes began to water again.

"Well he has. And you do miss him, don't you?"

"Yeah," Tiara said softly.

"Then let's get you two together in a civil atmosphere and try to work everything out. Tomorrow's Thursday, so you know I'm going to come over and cook for Family Night. Why don't you come over then?"

"Well . . ."

"And, Baby, leave Lionel there and come on over alone. The two of you won't really be able to hash things out if he's around. Fair enough?"

"Fair enough. If I come I won't bring Lionel. But I'm not promising I'm going to come."

"I'll make baked macaroni and cheese," Charlene said in a teasing voice.

"Well, dang, in that case, I'll be there," Tiara laughed out loud.

"Okay, baby, I'll see you then."

"Hold on, don't hang up. I want to speak to Jo-Jo for another couple of minutes."

"Tiara, would you do me a favor and wait until tomorrow? She's all upset now about what you told her, and if she gets back on the telephone with you she's going to force you to tell her more, and then I'm going to have to get on the phone with you to find out what you told her and how I'm supposed to cover. I'm going to go take her out for a burger and a movie or something so we can talk. So why don't you wait and get with her tomorrow, okay?"

"Okay," Tiara said reluctantly.

"And I'll see you tomorrow night. About seven?"

"Sounds good."

"Okay, Sweetie . . . I love you."

"Aunt Charlie? I really love you." Tiara hung up so her aunt couldn't hear her cry.

Damn. I must have fallen asleep. Tiara glanced at the large gold-rimmed mirror clock on the wall across from the bed. Nine o'clock already? She stretched. *I wonder if Lionel ordered any food. I'm starved.* She suddenly realized there were voices coming from the living room. One was Lionel's, but she couldn't place the other. She quietly walked into the room and saw the guy from bus stop, the one that Lionel had put up to harass her. What was his name again? Oh yeah, Al, Lionel had told her. She leaned against the wall and listened to them, aware that they were oblivious to her presence.

"So, yo, man, you got this covered, right? I don't want no mess-ups on this shit." Lionel was sitting on the couch stroking his chin.

"Yeah, I got you, man." Al, who was standing close to the door with his coat on, shrugged his huge shoulders and yawned. "Let me go uptown and take care of this so I can get some shut-eye. I'm sleepy as all shit."

"You going to take anyone with you?"

"Naw man, I can handle this by myself."

"Handle what?" Tiara asked.

Lionel jumped slightly at the sound of her voice, but Al just turned and gave her an appreciative up and down look, as if she were standing in front of him naked.

"My business, baby." He licked his lips. "Some monkey business. 'Cause you know I'm a big gorilla."

"Yeah, whatever." Tiara lips curled as she glared back at him. Big fucking asshole. She walked over and gingerly sat next to Lionel on the couch. "Why'd you let me sleep so long?"

"Weren't no reason to wake you up." Lionel patted her on the arm. "Why don't you go ahead in the bedroom so I can finish talking to my man here for a minute."

"Damn! First my father tries to banish me to the bedroom, and now you going to try and do the same thing?" Tiara rolled her eyes while bobbing her head. "I don't think so. You want to talk privately, you get the fuck up and go in the bedroom. I ain't going no fucking where."

Al crossed his arms over his chest and laughed, but Lionel didn't seem amused. "All right then. Al, come on man. Let me talk to you in the bedroom for a minute." Lionel leaned on the arm of the couch as he stood up.

"Shit man, you better learn to put your bitch in check. I'd knock a woman's teeth out if she came out her mouth like that to me."

"You going to let him call me a bitch?" Tiara stood up suddenly and tried to walk toward the man, but Lionel caught her by the arm.

"He ain't mean nothing by it. He was only joking," he said wearily. "Alvin, tell her you're sorry."

"Yeah, man, I'm sorry." The man shook his head and chuckled. "Anyway," he turned toward the door. "I'm going to go handle that now. And I got it. Hurt him, but not too bad. Peace out."

"Yeah, man. Keep your cell phone on and call me when you're through to let me know how it went." Lionel walked over and locked the door after the man left, then came back and stood in front of Tiara. "Why'd you have to embarrass me like that in front of my friend, Tiara?"

Alvin? Did Lionel just call that man Alvin a minute ago? Why was that name ringing an alarm bell in her head? Alvin. Didn't Rashad say his godbrother's name was Alvin? The godbrother he said was selling dope for Lionel. Tiara's eyes widened as she looked up at her boyfriend.

"What kind of *business* do you have Alvin taking care of for you?" she asked slowly.

"What are you talking about?" Lionel backed up a couple of paces.

"He said he was leaving here to handle some business, and I'm asking you what kind of business." Tiara got up from the couch slowly. "Drug business, right? Rashad wasn't lying, was he?"

The slap caught her completely off guard, and was so hard she flew against the wall. Before she could gather her senses, Lionel was pulling her up by the collar and choking her as he slapped her again and again. "Didn't I tell you not to embarrass me in front of my friends, you no-good ghetto bitch? You think you're so fucking bad you can talk to me any kind of way in front of my friends? You think just because I'm not from Harlem I'm some kind of punk?"

She wanted to reach out to punch him in the face, but he had her pinned to the wall, her arms behind her back. He finally loosened his grip around her throat, but before she could move, he reared back and landed a devastating punch to her right cheek. "Stupid bitch! You trying to make me look like a pussy in front of my friends?" he shouted.

She screamed and fell on all fours to the floor, only to almost be lifted back to her feet by the upward kick Lionel delivered to her stomach.

"Yeah, you thought it was so fucking funny that your dad hit me, huh? How come you're not laughing now?"

"Lionel, stop. Please stop!" she screamed through her tears. "Lionel, I'm sorry. Oh God, I'm sorry."

"That's just what you are. A sorry bitch. I tried to do right by you and your family treated me like shit. My father could buy your family ten times over, you know that? But I didn't look down on you. I should have, you fucking project ho." He reached down and grabbed Tiara by her hair, dragging her back to her feet. She brought her arms in front of her face, expecting another barrage of slaps or punches, but instead he grunted and dragged her to the bedroom, where he held her by one arm while he rummaged through a nightstand drawer, finally coming up with a pair of handcuffs. He placed one cuff around her left wrist, then snapped the other around the radiator pipe.

"You ain't so bad now, are you, Tiara?" Lionel sat down on the bed and looked at her as she cowered in the corner. He gave a half chuckle, but suddenly brought his hands up to his face. "Oh God, I don't believe this. Why did you have to go and make me do this, Tiara? Why'd you have to go and make me hit you? This shit is crazy."

"What?" Tiara croaked through her tears. "I didn't do anything but . . ."

"But run your goddamned mouth like you always do." Lionel removed his hands and glared at her again. "You and your fucking father, too, thinking he can talk to me any kind of way. A boxing champ, huh? Let's see what the champ looks like when Al gets through with him."

Lionel suddenly jumped up and picked up his cell phone from the top of his bureau. He punched in a number. "Yo, Al, change in plans. Swing back by and pick me up," he said. He started putting on a pair of pants that had been lying over the back of a chair.

"I want to be there when the ol' man gets his due," was the last thing Tiara heard before she passed out.

18

She wasn't sure how long she had been unconscious. Maybe an hour? Maybe two? She struggled to open her eyes beyond a slit, but found it impossible. She tried to moisten her swollen lips with her tongue, but found she had no saliva. She struggled to sit up, but the short chain on the handcuff barely allowed movement. Her head was pounding, and her chest hurt with her every breath. She wanted to give up and drift back into her dark daze, but something within her refused. She had to free herself.

She tried again to sit up, inching toward the wall and bracing herself against it as she slowly straightened each leg in front of her. The movements had drained her little remaining strength, so she rested for a moment as she tried to gather her wits. Okay, what to do now? Through the slits of her eyes she located the clock on the wall. Nine forty-five. In the morning? She painfully turned her head toward the window. No, it was dark outside. But she had originally wakened from her nap at nine. Had all this happened within forty minutes? That meant that Lionel was either still in the house or had just left. *Oh, God, he's going over to my house. They're going to beat up Daddy. They might even kill him. And if Jo-Jo is there they're probably going to hurt her, too. I've got to warn him.* She yanked as hard as she could on the handcuff but it wouldn't give. She looked around the room, trying to see if there was anything she could reach with her uncuffed hand that she could use to free herself. Nothing. But there was her cell phone on the carpet. It must have fallen off the bed when Lionel sat down, she thought. She stretched out as far as she could, trying to ignore the pain that shot through her entire body, but the cell phone was still at least three feet away from her. She settled back against the wall and sobbed softly. *Oh God, what am I going to do? How can this be happening to me? I haven't done anything to deserve all this. Oh God, Lionel is crazy. He's probably going to kill Daddy and come back and kill me and then throw our bodies in the river so no one will ever know what happened to us.* She yanked her handcuffed arm again. *I've got to get free.* She twisted her body to face the radiator pipe, braced her legs against the wall next to it and pushed with all her might, hoping to pull the pipe from its foundation. It didn't even budge. She turned again to the cell phone. There had to be some way to reach it. She lay flat on her back and stretched her legs out until the cell phone was just half an inch from her right foot, but it was a long half inch. She stretched even further, fully extending her bare foot. A thrill surged at the touch of her toe to the phone. Stretching even further, she managed to catch the phone's antenna between her toes and slowly drew it to her. Thank God. Her pain suddenly seemed to disappear as she scrambled back to a sitting position. *I've got to warn Daddy to get out the house.* She punched her home number into the telephone. Three rings. *Oh, Daddy, please hurry up and pick up the phone.* Just before the sixth ring, which would have sent the call into voice mail, the phone was picked up. She heard loud music blaring in the background but no one said anything on the other end. "Hello," she said frantically. "Anyone there? Daddy? Someone say something. This is an emergency!"

A man's heavily slurred voice finally answered her. "Who's this?"

"Daddy?" Was she too late? Had Lionel and his friend already been there and beat him up?

"Who the hell is this?" The man slurred in response over the music she now recognized as "Burn Rubber." "What the hell you want?" The man let out a loud belch.

Oh, my God, he's drunk! "Daddy, this is Tiara!" she shouted into the telephone.

"Tiara?" the man said slowly. "Hold on." The music blared louder. "Tiara!" She heard the man calling out. "Tiara, come answer the phone." Reggie got back on the phone a second later. "Tiara ain't here."

"No, Daddy, it's me. It's Tiara," she said frantically.

"Tiara ain't here," Reggie said again, oblivious to her words. "She left me. She burnt rubber on me." He started laughing hysterically. "Tiara burnt rubber on me, just like her goddamned mother." Tiara could hear his laughter turn into large sobs. "Oh, God, my baby left me," he was saying over and over.

"Daddy! Daddy! Listen to me. You've got to get out of there!" Tiara was shouting. She heard the phone drop onto the hard tile floor as the music played on. She continued to shout over the phone, but he never picked the receiver back up.

What the hell am I going to do now? she wondered dismally as she finally hung up. She dialed him back, but the call went into voice mail, so the telephone must have been off the hook. Jo-Jo couldn't be there, because he wouldn't be drinking if she were. In fact, she must be staying over at a friend's house, or maybe at Aunt Charlie's, because her father wouldn't be drinking like that if he knew Jo-Jo'd come back and see him all drunk. She called Aunt Charlie's house but got no answer. She tried her aunt's cell phone, but again got no answer. That's right, Aunt Charlie said she was going to take Jo-Jo to the movies. She tried Shakira's house, but as usual she got a busy signal. What to do? Who should she call now?

"Hello? Nine one one? You've got to send a police officer over to my house. Someone over to my father's house. Someone's getting ready to attack him."

"Okay, calm down," a soothing voice came back. "What's your name?"

"Tiara Bynum. But you've got to send someone over to 97 West 114th Street, apartment 1G, right away!"

"Do you live at that address?"

"Yes."

"Are you there now?"

"NO! But my father is there and he's drunk and someone's going over there to kill him."

"What's your father's name?"

"Reginald Bynum. But what difference does it make? You've got to send someone over there now!" She screamed into the telephone.

"I'm going to send a unit over, ma'am, but first I need some more information," the irritatingly calm police dispatcher answered. "Who's on their way to attack your father."

"My boyfriend. Lionel Evans."

"Your boyfriend? Is this a domestic dispute?"

"No, it's not a domestic dispute. My boyfriend's crazy, and he beat me up, and now he and his friend are on their way to kill my father. PLEASE get someone over there RIGHT AWAY!"

"All right, I'll dispatch a unit over there right away. Now . . ."

Tiara hung up before the dispatcher could say anything else. *Maybe now the bitch will get some police over to the house instead of keeping me on the phone with bullshit.*

That jerk didn't seem like he was taking me seriously. What if he doesn't send the police over there? Or what if he takes his time sending them out? This is all my fault. She started crying again. *Why didn't I just listen to Daddy? Now he might get hurt up because of me. Oh God, please. If you get the police over to the house before Lionel gets there I promise I'll go to church every Sunday. I'll devote my life to the church. I'll do anything. Just please, let my Daddy be okay.*

She tried to calm herself down, and began going through the phone book on her telephone. Alice's number came up first since it began with 'A.' Tiara hit the call button.

"Hello."

"Alice, thank God you're there!"

"Tiara? Is that you? Are you okay?"

Tiara started crying uncontrollably, trying to talk between her sobs. "You've got to come get me. I'm at 423 Varick Street, apartment 13. Lionel beat me up and he's going to go kill my father."

"What? Tiara, you've got to calm down. I can't understand you!" Alice was saying frantically. "Where are you?"

"I'm at Lionel's house." Tiara tried to control her sobs. "He beat me up and has me handcuffed to a radiator. And now he's on his way to my house to beat up Daddy!"

"Oh, my God. Did you call the police?"

"Yeah. But I don't know if they're going to get there in time. You've got to get over there and make sure he's okay."

"But didn't you just say you wanted me to come get you? What about you?"

"Don't worry about me! Just take care of my father!" Tiara screamed into the phone.

"Okay. I'll get back to you as soon as I find out what's going on."

Tiara hung up, leaned her throbbing head back against the wall, closed her eyes, and cried.

Bam!

Forgetting that she was handcuffed, Tiara tried unsuccessfully to scramble to her feet. What was that noise? Did someone just kick down the door?

"Tiara!"

"I'm in here!" she screamed. It was a man's voice. It had to be the police. Alice must have sent them. But what about her father? Was he okay?

"I'm in here!" she screamed again. "In the back. In the bedroom."

Her mouth dropped open as Rashad ran breathlessly into the bedroom. How the hell did he get here? How did he know what was going on?

"Jesus Christ, are you okay?" He rushed over to her and cupped her face in his hands. He kissed her gently on top of her head, then examined the handcuffs. "Do you know where the keys are?" he asked gently.

She averted her eyes and shook her head.

"Okay, no problem. We'll get you free." Rashad stood up and looked around the room.

"How . . . how did you get here?" Tiara said haltingly.

"Alice called my dispatcher and they patched her through. Thank God I had just dropped a fare near here." He investigated the walk-in closet. "Damn, there's only wooden hangers in here."

"What about my father?"

"I don't know. Alice was on her way over there when she called. As soon as I get you free we'll call and then head over there." He emerged from the closet with a wire hanger and started unbending it into a straight wire as he walked back over to the radiator. He stopped when he saw Tiara trying to pat her hair into place.

She looked up at him, and tried a little smile. "I hate that you have to see me like this. I must look a mess."

"What?" Rashad stepped back, his eyes narrowing, his upper lip curling into a sneer.

"What's wrong?" Tiara flinched at the coldness in Rashad's eyes.

"You're sitting there, all bloody, handcuffed to a radiator, and you're worried about the way you look?" He glared at her while tapping the wire hanger against his leg.

"What? I was just . . ."

"What the fuck is wrong with you, girl?" he spat. "Is it always all about you?" He shook his head and shot her a look of disgust that made her cringe. She had never seen him really angry before, never heard him curse.

"Heh," he let out a mean chuckle. "But I guess this time it *is* all about you, isn't it? You like to start shit to make yourself look important, and you really started some shit now, huh? You got yourself hooked up with a drug pusher. You got the shit beat out of you. You got your goddamned boyfriend intent on killing your father. Yeah, girl, it's all about you. All this shit is all about you. I hope you're enjoying the attention." He knelt beside her and grabbed her wrist roughly, trying to insert the wire into the handcuff.

"But it isn't my fault," Tiara whimpered. "I mean, I didn't know Lionel was going to go crazy. And I didn't know he was a drug dealer. I thought you were . . ."

"Lying?" Rashad snapped the handcuff open, and then straightened up, although Tiara remained on the floor, rubbing her bruised wrist. "Oh yeah, that's right. You thought I was lying because I was jealous. You thought I secretly yearned for you and I was so eaten up by jealousy that I would actually slander a man's reputation in hopes that you'd dump him and choose me." He snorted. "Do you know how insulting that is to me, Tiara? Please let me know if I've *ever* done or said anything that would make you think that I'm anything but a man of honor, because I certainly don't think I have. I try to do right by people. I'm not perfect, nobody is, but I do my damn best to be principled. But your mind is so perverse, so decayed by your own vanity, that you actually think that I would stoop so low as to lie in the *desperate* hope that I might be able to get with you. Your mind is so warped that you actually twist reality to make it fit your belief that the entire world revolves around you. You're pathetic."

Tiara's eyes were dry as she listened to him, but her head was spinning, and her chest felt as if he had just delivered a hard blow to her ribs. *So this is what Rashad really thinks of me? This is how he sees me? How could he be so wrong about me? He is wrong. Isn't he?* She got up slowly and reached for her cellular phone as if in a daze.

"Come on, you can call Alice from the cab." Rashad walked out the door ahead of her.

"You still can't get through to the apartment?"

Tiara shook her head as she returned the cell phone to her lap, then gingerly wiped the tears from her swollen eyes.

"Okay, don't worry. I know everything's okay." Rashad patted Tiara gently on the shoulder with one hand as he steered his cab onto the FDR Drive with the other. "We'll be there in less than fifteen minutes, okay?"

Tiara nodded numbly. What if it wasn't in time? What if Lionel and Alvin got there and they'd already killed Daddy? How would she be able to live with herself? She'd kill herself, that's what she'd do. She'd just kill herself.

"Tiara, you've got to have faith. It's all going to be okay."

"Ya think?"

"Yeah. The police probably got there and got your father out of the apartment before those two goons got there," Rashad said reassuringly. "Or, you know what? Maybe they didn't and they got over there, and your father kicked both of their behinds. I wouldn't put it past him, drunk or not. Yeah, I wouldn't put it past him, you know. Your old man is something else."

"Yeah, he is, isn't he?" Tiara nodded.

"Yep. A wonderful man. A really wonderful role model, too. I'm trying to talk him into giving counseling sessions at the center. Have him teach these young brothers about responsibility. There aren't many men I've seen out here who would step to the plate and raise their family without a woman," Rashad sighed. "I can't tell you how much I admire him."

"Yep," Tiara nodded again. "Me, too." Her chest began to heave with whispery sobs as she wondered whether she'd get a chance to tell him so. Rashad was right, all she'd ever thought about was herself. How could she have walked out on her father after all he'd done for her? All her life he'd done everything he could to give her what she wanted, and how did she repay him? By leaving him for someone she thought could give her more. She never loved Lionel. There was never anything she'd found in Lionel worth loving, except his money. There was nothing else to him.

"Tiara, we're almost there. Just another couple of minutes, okay? Let me know if you see any police cars. We'll flag them down, okay?"

"Yeah," she nodded and sat up straight to get a better view out of the window.

"Tiara. I owe you a big apology. I shouldn't have said everything I said to you back there," Rashad said slowly as he turned the car off the 116th Street exit.

"Why? It was all true," Tiara said wearily.

"Yeah, well, but my timing was really messed up."

Tiara said nothing.

"I want you to know that I do think there's more to you. I just think you've really got to do some soul searching. Get your priorities together, and get your head together. And I really like you. More than you probably know. And I'm hoping . . ." Rashad sighed. "I do have messed-up timing, don't I? We'll talk about all this later."

"Look!" Tiara pointed out of the window at three police cars and an ambulance parked on the sidewalk outside her building, lights flashing. Her heart jumped into her throat. They were too late!

"Shit," Rashad said as he pulled up on the pavement behind them. Before he could put the car in park, Tiara had jumped out and darted

224

toward the building, pushing through the crowd gathered around the doorway.

"God damn, girl! What happened to you?" Shakira was standing just inside the building door, her hands shoved deep in her jacket pockets. Tiara ignored her, instead running toward her apartment door.

"Let me in!" She pounded on the door. "Daddy! Daddy!" She shouted at the top of her lungs as tears streamed down her face. "Are you in there? Please let me in."

"Tiara, it's okay. Your father's fine." Alice was suddenly there tugging at her arm. "He's over at Shakira's house."

"He is?" Tiara whirled around to face the girl. "Is he okay?"

"He's fine. When I got here I found him passed out on the living room floor. I thought maybe Lionel had gotten there already and beat him up, but he was just . . ." Alice hesitated. "Well, he was just drunk. I saw Shakira outside, and I asked her to get her dad, and him and some of his friends carried your father over to her building."

"Oh, thank God." Tiara leaned against the hallway wall and slid down to the floor. "I thought he was dead."

"Why would you think something like that?" Tiara looked up to find Shakira had joined Alice. "Shit, you're the one who looks about dead. Who the fuck did that to your face?"

Before she could answer, Rashad walked up. Gently pushing Alice and Shakira aside, he knelt down beside Tiara. "I just talked to the police. They're here because a pit bull attacked a man on the third floor."

"It wasn't nothing. Miss Joanie sicced her dog on her ex-husband again," Shakira shrugged.

"Come on." Rashad stood up and extended his hand to Tiara. "Let me help you up."

Tiara shook her head, letting out a deep sigh as she stretched her legs out in front of her. "No, that's okay. You guys just go ahead. I'm just going to sit here for a while."

"Are you sure?" Alice asked worriedly.

"Girl, you need to get your ass in the house before someone sees you looking all fucked up like that," Shakira added.

Tiara let out a sad chuckle as she once again shook her head. "I kind of think everyone's seen me fucked up before. Maybe not physically, but real fucked up in the head. But y'all go ahead. 'Cause I got a lot to think about."

19

"Aunt Charlie, is Daddy up yet?" Tiara asked as she quietly closed the apartment door behind her and walked into the kitchen.

"Yeah, he woke up about a half hour ago. He's in the bathroom now shaving, or trying to. Jo-Jo's in there with him, talking her little narrow behind off, I bet. I'm cooking breakfast now. Want some?" Charlene said as she simultaneously cracked two eggs on the edge of a mixing bowl. "Where've you been, anyway? I went to wake you and Jo-Jo up and you were gone."

"I wasn't able to sleep all night, so when it got light outside I decided to take a walk," Tiara shrugged, then pulled out one of the kitchen chairs and sat down.

Charlene nodded. "It took me forever to get to sleep, too. Partly because that couch is so damn uncomfortable, and partly because of all the drama last night." She opened the refrigerator and pulled out a package of breakfast links. "You want some French toast and sausage?"

"Naw, I'm not hungry."

Charlene turned and fixed a worried look on her niece. "Are you sure, Tiara? When's the last time you had something to eat? There's no use in your starving yourself because of all this. God knows you're skinny enough already."

"Naw, I'm okay, really." Tiara shook her head.

"For real?"

"For real for real." Tiara gave a weary smile as she removed the dark sunglasses that had hidden her two blackened eyes. She propped her face up on her elbows on the table. "Does Daddy know everything that happened last night?"

"Yeah, pretty much so. You know Jo-Jo told him everything she knew, and then he called Rashad and got the gaps filled in." Charlene walked over and sat down next to her, also propping her elbows on the table. "I wish you had let me and James take you to the emergency room last night. I think that cut under your eye might need some stitches."

"What did he say?" Tiara licked her swollen lips anxiously.

"You know your dad. He was furious. Wanted to go find Lionel and kill him. That boy better be glad the police got him and locked him up last night, because I wouldn't have been able to stop Reggie otherwise. And he's really going to blow his stack when he sees you looking like this."

"I know, I know." Tiara nodded her head. "Oh, Aunt Charlie, I really messed up, big time." She hung her head and sighed. "I've been thinking about all this, and my life, all night. I've been such a little bitch, not listening to anybody, or caring about anybody but me."

"Tiara, don't be so hard on yourself. You're just a kid," Charlene said gently.

Tiara shook her head violently. "No. No. I'm not going to use that as an excuse. I've just been stupid and selfish, and I wouldn't blame Daddy if he threw me out on my behind. I wouldn't . . ." She suddenly felt two strong arms circle her shoulders from behind.

"Stop it. I'm not going to throw you out, Girl," her father was saying in a broken voice. "Don't you know I love you? Don't you know you and your sister are my whole world?"

Tiara turned in her chair to face her father. "Daddy I . . ."

"Oh my God. Oh my dear God. That bastard did this to you?" Reggie reared to his full height, and then to Tiara's horror he sank to his knees and started sobbing in her lap. "Oh my poor baby. I'm sorry. I'm so sorry."

"No, Daddy, please." Tiara pushed her chair back and tried to pull her father up from the floor, though she was also crying. "I'm the one that's sorry. It's my fault. You don't have any reason to be sorry. You didn't do anything wrong. I'm the one that wouldn't listen to you. I'm the one that made all the wrong choices. I'm the one that left."

"And I'm the one that should have dragged your butt back. But instead I sat up in this house feeling sorry for myself." Reggie shook his head and stood up, then reached for a napkin from the table and wiped his eyes and nose. "I'm sorry, Baby, I don't mean for you to see me like this, crying like a little punk."

"Oh, Daddy . . ."

"Tiara, I've been a lousy father . . ." Reggie's chest heaved as he tried to control himself.

"Daddy, that's not true. You've been the best father in the world," Tiara cried. "It's me that's been rotten."

"If you're rotten it's because I've spoiled you rotten." Reggie closed his head and bowed his head. "And I did spoil you. I purposely spoiled you and your sister. I tried to give you everything you wanted, not realizing what the consequences would be."

"Well, you got that right," Charlene said, but both Reggie and Tiara ignored her.

"I wanted to be a good Daddy, but in doing so I was a lousy father."

"Oh, Reggie, you were doing the best you could." Charlene walked over and placed her hand on her brother's shoulder.

"Well, then my best wasn't good enough," he told her before turning back to Tiara. "You hurt me to my heart when you walked out that door a couple of days ago, Tiara, but when I really started thinking about it, I raised you to do just what you did. Go with the glitter. I never taught you to worry about it if it was really gold. I tried to give you everything you wanted, and never even attempted to make you realize that everything in this world has a cost."

"Oh Daddy, you're making yourself out to be a villain. Please don't do that." Tiara walked over and lay her head on Reggie's chest. "You're acting like it was you that was all wrong, when it was me that messed up."

"No, Baby, actually I'm not," Reggie said as he rubbed his daughter's back. "You were dead wrong. I'm just trying to let you know that I realize I had more than a nickel in that dime." He grabbed Tiara in a bear hug, burying his head in her hair as he once again started to sob. "And I just want you to know that I'm so sorry, and I'm going to do better."

"Daddy?"

Reggie and Tiara turned to see Jo-Jo standing by the kitchen door.

"Daddy," Jo-Jo continued, "you're scaring me."

"Come here, Sport." Reggie reached out his arm, and Jo-Jo rushed to him.

"My precious little babies," Reggie said as he tightly hugged the two of them. "I love you both so much."

"We love you, too, Daddy," Tiara said through her tears.

"Yeah, me too," Jo-Jo said.

Tiara nudged her sister. "I said, 'we.' That included you."

"I know," Jo-Jo nudged her back. "I just wanted to say that I love him. I don't need you to talk for me."

"Shut up, Jo-Jo," Tiara growled.

"Make me."

Reggie threw his head back and started laughing.

"Haven't you girls ever heard the phrase, leave a tender moment alone?" Charlene snapped. She grabbed a dish cloth and started furiously wiping the kitchen counter. "Here your father's pouring his heart out and you're up in arms arguing like little kids."

Tiara broke away from her father and walked over to her aunt, then put one hand on her hip and looked her up and down before sucking her teeth.

"You're just mad because no one said they love you," she said.

Charlene threw the dish cloth down and started jabbing her finger close to Tiara's face. "You look here, young lady . . ." Charlene couldn't finish because Tiara grabbed her in a sudden hug that almost knocked her down.

"We love you, Aunt Charlie. We love you so much!" Tiara started showering her with kisses.

"And I love you, too!" Jo-Jo piped, while still holding on to her father. "And some of those kisses are from me."

"Okay, okay, that's enough," Charlene chuckled as she tried to push Tiara away.

"But I just wanted to show you how much we love you," Tiara giggled as she tried to move closer to her aunt.

"And I love you little nutcases, too," Charlene said. "Now hurry up and take your showers so we can have breakfast."

Tiara turned to leave the kitchen, but then paused and walked back to her father. "Daddy, thank you for forgiving me," she said quietly. "You do, don't you?"

Reggie nodded. "And thanks for forgiving me, Tiara. You do, don't you?"

Tiara nodded and gave him a quick hug before walking out, Jo-Jo trailing behind her.

"And since I'm cooking breakfast, don't be expecting me to come back and cook dinner," Charlene shouted after them. "I don't care if it is Thursday night."

"Yes, Aunt Charlie," the girls said in unison.

"You know she's going to, though, right?" Jo-Jo nudged Tiara.

"No doubt," Tiara nodded.

"Hey," Jo-Jo said when they were in the bedroom with the door closed. "I talked to our mother yesterday."

"What?" Tiara whirled to face her sister. "When? How?"

"I found her number on a napkin on your night table after you called me."

Tiara scowled. "That number was in my jacket pocket, Missy."

Jo-Jo shrugged her shoulders. "So okay, I was looking for some change. Anyway, I called her. But I only got to talk to her for like two minutes."

"Why?"

Jo-Jo plopped down on her bed and reached for a magazine, and then started flipping the pages. "She was busy. I told her who I was, and she was all like 'oh, that's nice, my little Josephine,' and then I asked if I could come see her and she said she was leaving town today. So I told her I could come see her right then, but she said she was getting ready to go out to some concert. So I said 'cool,' and that was that."

"You're kidding." Tiara sat down on the bed next to Jo-Jo. "Are you okay?"

"Yeah," Jo-Jo shrugged. "Why shouldn't I be?"

Tiara studied her sister closely. The hurt in Jo-Jo's voice was evident, but her eyes were dry, her demeanor calm.

"I mean, Tiara, you know," Jo-Jo continued. "I got you and Daddy and Aunt Charlie, why should I care about someone who can't even cancel a concert to see her own daughter."

Tiara nodded, and then sighed. "I guess what they say is right. Opening your legs twice doesn't make someone a mother."

"Huh?" Jo-Jo looked up from the magazine. "What does that

mean?" A look of realization suddenly crossed her face. "Oooh, Tiara, you are so nasty!"

Tiara gave Jo-Jo's shoulder a little push. "You're so stupid," she said as she got up from the bed.

"No, I'm not." Jo-Jo threw the magazine at her.

"Yes you are." Tiara rolled up the magazine and swatted Jo-Jo over the head.

"Daddy!" Jo-Jo yelled. "Tiara's hitting me again."

"Jo-Jo, shut up." Tiara grabbed her nightgown and headed out of the bedroom to take her shower.

"Make me."

God, it's good to be home.

20

ommunity Legal Services, may I help you?" Tiara yawned. How, she wondered, could so many people have so many problems so early on a Saturday morning?

"I'm sorry, Mr. Jennings is not in. May I take a message?" The pen she was reaching for rolled onto the floor, and when Tiara reached down to retrieve it, she fell off the tilted swiveled chair. *Shit, when are they going to fix this damn thing?* She got up, kicked the chair out of the way, and scribbled the message on a pink note pad.

"Okay, I'll have Mr. Jennings call you as soon as he gets in. . . . Yes, I understand that your son is at Rikers Island and hasn't seen a lawyer . . . yes, I understand that your son's never been in jail before . . . yes, I understand that you're scared, Mrs. Anthony, and I promise I'll give Mr. Jennings your message as soon as he walks through the door. . . . He should be in around eleven . . . yes, ma'am, in about an hour . . . yes, ma'am, you can feel free to call back then if you'd like. . . . Thank you for calling, Mrs. Anthony. You have a nice day."

Well, shit, if she's going to call back why did she even bother to leave this long-ass message? Tiara finished writing the note and put it with a growing stack on the corner of her desk.

When she decided to volunteer for a law office she thought she'd be working for one of the attorneys, helping to prepare briefs or doing research. After all, she was a pre-law student. But here she was doing receptionist duty in a rinky-dink storefront. Community service sucked. Well, it did make her feel good in a way. Rashad had been right about that. There was nothing better than seeing a parent weeping in relief because her child had been freed from jail, or having an old woman cry from joy when her landlord was legally barred from evicting her out of a rent-controlled building so he could turn the place into condominiums. It made her feel that she was helping the world at large, even if all she did was answer telephones while the lawyers got all the glory.

She looked up at sound of a jingling bell, indicating that someone was opening the front door. She smiled at the sight of Rashad and her father.

"Hi, Daddy." She came from behind the desk, almost tripping over the overturned chair. She righted it and kissed her father on the cheek, then turned to Rashad and embraced him warmly.

"Hey, sis." Rashad patted her back before she broke away. "How you liking it here?"

"It's all right, thanks. You guys on the way to the rec center?"

"Yeah, we just stopped by to bring you some coffee and doughnuts since you had to leave so early this morning."

"Yeah, I've had to open up three weeks in a row now," Tiara grumbled as she opened the bag her father handed her. "Oh, good, jelly doughnuts. I'm starving."

"Don't sit on—" Tiara started laughing as her father sat down on the wobbly chair and fell unceremoniously to the floor. "Sorry, Daddy. It's broken."

"Now you tell me," Reggie chuckled as he stood up and brushed himself off. "Anyway, there's another reason we stopped by."

"What's that?" Tiara scooted a chair from another desk and sat down and took a sip from the hot coffee.

"Well," Reggie said as he sat on the side of the desk, "I got an interesting telephone call this morning."

"From whom?"

"From a Daniel Evans."

"What?" Tiara almost spit out her coffee out in surprise. "Lionel's father?"

"Yep. He started with this song and dance about Lionel being a good kid who just keeps getting caught up in the wrong crowd, and how it didn't make sense that a young man's future be tarnished by a few stupid mistakes."

"A few stupid mistakes, huh?" Tiara grunted. "That man almost beat me to death. And the only reason he didn't get to you was because Alvin wouldn't go into the building when he saw all those police cars outside."

"Well, the bottom line is he's willing to pay you twenty-five thousand dollars if you drop the assault charges against him, and five thousand dollars to me if I convince you that you should," Reggie said.

"You're kidding? That's a total of thirty thousand bucks." Tiara gasped. "That's a lot of money."

"Yep." Reggie crossed his arms and looked at his daughter.

"It sure would help with the brownstone fund," Tiara said slowly.

"Oh, yeah, he also mentioned that one of his cronies runs an urban development corporation out here, and could make sure we could pick up a brownstone for a song. You must have told Lionel that we were looking to buy a brownstone?"

"I might have mentioned it, I don't remember." Tiara shook her head.

Wow, Daddy could get his brownstone, and I can have my own room. And I can buy a banging car with my money, and maybe even have some left over to buy some new clothes. Maybe even a fur coat. Man, I would really be cool then. Tiara started drumming her fingers on the desk.

Riiiing.

Damn, she thought, she was forgetting about the stupid telephones.

"Good morning, Community Legal Services . . . No, I'm sorry, Mrs. Anthony, Mr. Jennings hasn't come in yet. . . . Yes, I know I said he'd be back in an hour, but that was only fifteen minutes ago. . . . Yes, ma'am, I'll make sure he calls you as soon as he gets in. . . . Just try and relax, okay? . . . There's no reason to thank me, I haven't done anything. . . . Okay, you take care."

She hung up and sighed. She looked at Rashad, who had seated himself at a desk a few feet away and was flipping through a magazine. When he looked up and saw her watching him, he smiled.

"Looks like you're actually developing some people skills, Tiara," he said in a teasing tone. "You're turning into quite a woman."

"Anyway," her father interrupted. "I'm not finished, there's more."

"More?" Tiara shook her head.

"Yep. He's in New York right now, and wants to talk over dinner. He wants us to meet him at seven at the Waldorf-Astoria. Said he'd even send a car over to get us."

"A car?" Tiara said excitedly. "Like a limousine?"

"I don't know, he just said a car." Reggie chortled. "Car, limousine, what difference does it make?"

Tiara shrugged. "Yeah, well, it's just that I've never ridden in a limousine before. Or eaten at the Waldorf-Astoria. And I've never been offered twenty-five thousand dollars before. I'm just trying to take it all in."

"Well," Reggie said slowly. "While you try to take all that in, you should try to take this in, too. I've already turned down his offer to me. I did say I'd tell you, though. Whatever decision you make, you have my support. But this is solely your decision, because after all," he smiled, "you are a grown woman."

He kissed Tiara on the top of the head and walked over and patted Rashad on the shoulder. "Let's get out of here, man. We can't keep those kids waiting all day."

"Daddy," Tiara rushed to the door after them. "Did Mr. Evans leave his telephone number?"

"Oh yeah, I forgot." Reggie dipped into his jacket pocket and came up with a crumpled piece of paper. "Sorry, here you go."

"Hold on while I call him, okay?" She tugged on his arm.

"Well, I'm going to go on ahead, then." The scowl on Rashad's face was unmistakable as he took long strides toward the door. "I'll see you when you get there, man. See you later, Tiara."

"Can't you just wait a second? Dang. It's obvious that you think you know what I'm going to do." Tiara stamped her foot. "Well, for your information I'm going to call him and tell him that he can take his money and shove it."

"You are?" Reggie started chuckling. "My girl! I didn't think you had it in you."

"I mean, just because Mr. Evans has money he thinks he and his family can do anything they want to anybody and then just buy their way out of trouble." Tiara was facing her father, but she glanced out of the corner of her eye to make sure Rashad was paying attention. "I'm just not going to let them get over like that. Not on me."

Rashad stared at Tiara, his hand still on the doorknob. "Are you sure that's what you want to do?"

"I'm positive. Now, see, you were thinking I was going to take the money and run, didn't you?"

Rashad shrugged sheepishly. He gave Tiara a light tap on the shoulder. Then he touched her lightly on her chin, grinned, and grabbed her into an embrace. "Girl, you surprise me sometimes, you know?"

"Yeah, I know." Tiara smiled happily.

"But for real now, are you not doing this because you think I might judge you or something? I mean, if I weren't here and your father gave you that message, would you have come to the same decision?"

Tiara placed her hand on her hip and rolled her eyes at Rashad. "Please, I might be trying to change, but there ain't that much change in the world. If I decide I want something do you really believe I would really consider what you might think? Not likely?" She snapped her fingers and turned to her father. "Some people really think a lot of themselves, don't they?"

"Oh no, she didn't say that!" Rashad started laughing, and Tiara and Reggie joined in.

"Baby, I'm really proud of you." Reggie walked over and hugged his daughter.

"Thank you, Daddy."

"I'm proud of her, too," Rashad added. "But we really gotta get up outta here."

"Okay. I won't be getting in until late this afternoon, Daddy. Me and Alice have to go downtown to pick her up an outfit for her audition on Monday." She turned to Rashad. "And you'd better give my girl the lead in your film, buddy." She smiled.

"Hey, if she earns it, she's got it." Rashad threw up his hands. "You know me, I don't play favorites."

"Well, she'll be starring in your film, then," Tiara said, as she went back and carefully sat in the broken chair behind the desk. "The girl's got it like that, you know."

"Yeah, she does," Rashad said softly.

"But listen." Reggie had gone out the door. "What do you think about us going out tonight? Go to dinner or something and just talk."

"Anything in particular you'd like to talk about?" Tiara smiled.

"Just, you know, stuff." Rashad gave a sheepish grin.

"Okay. Sounds good." Tiara waited until Rashad had left before she let her smile turn into a full-fledged grin. She sashayed over to the middle of the office floor and did a quick dance step before sitting down at her desk. "Yeah," she said as she started shuffling papers. "'Cause I got it like that."